Sweet Home Carolina

Also by T. Lynn Ocean

Fool Me Once

Sweet Home Carolina

T. Lynn Ocean

THOMAS DUNNE BOOKS
ST. MARTIN'S PRESS ❦ NEW YORK

THOMAS DUNNE BOOKS.
An imprint of St. Martin's Press.

SWEET HOME CAROLINA. Copyright © 2006 by T. Lynn Ocean. All rights reserved.
Printed in the United States of America. No part of this book may be used or re-
produced in any manner whatsoever without written permission except in the
case of brief quotations embodied in critical articles or reviews. For information,
address St. Martin's Press, 175 Fifth Avenue, New York, N.Y. 10010.

www.stmartins.com

Library of Congress Cataloging-in-Publication Data

Ocean, T. Lynn.
    Sweet home Carolina : a novel / T. Lynn Ocean.—1st ed.
        p.   cm.
    ISBN 0-312-34334-5
    EAN 978-0-312-34334-7
    1. Advertising executives—Fiction.   2. Women public relations personnel—
Fiction.   3. City promotion—Fiction.   4. City and town life—South
Carolina—Fiction.   5. South Carolina—Fiction.   I. Title.

PS3615.C43S84 2006
813'.6—dc22   2006040162

First Edition: May 2006

10 9 8 7 6 5 4 3 2 1

Simple Things

It's the simple things . . .

a touch, a glance, a smile
fond memories to file

the brilliance of a purple flower
heat from a steamy shower
spicy bites to devour

a handwritten note,
cheerful, with a funny quote

a wind-caught sail
a shell so frail
an old pirate tale

a shaded park bench waiting,
inviting, for the taking

a low-slung moon
a jazzy tune
a white sand dune

a sunny day to spend
laughing with a friend.

It's the simple things
each day brings
that pull heartstrings.

—T. Lynn Ocean

Acknowledgments

To those who happily answered research questions: boat captain Bobby Strickland of Murrells Inlet, South Carolina; National Weather Service Warning Coordination Meteorologist Tom Matheson of Wilmington, North Carolina; attorney Carolyn Hills of Myrtle Beach, South Carolina; private investigator Jack Geren of Port Royal, South Carolina; antiques appraiser and author Emyl Jenkins; historian and author Bo Bryan; coastal cruising specialist Claiborne Young; Myrtle Beach City Manager Tom Leath; educators Edwin Brown and Roy Moye of Coastal Carolina University in South Carolina; and Chris May of the Cape Fear Council of Governments in Wilmington.

To my knowledgeable agent, Stacey Glick, and the savvy people at St. Martin's Press and Holtzbrinck.

To all the fiction-loving folks who read *Fool Me Once* and sent e-mails to say they were eagerly awaiting my next novel.

And to all the fabulous booksellers who make the publishing word go 'round by putting books in the hands of readers.

Many thanks!

Sweet Home Carolina

1

They lined the round mahogany bar at Frankie's Sports Pub like a display of exciting new releases in a bookstore. Men, and lots of them. Drinking and eating and talking back to the flickering television screens in front of them.

A titillating variety of males, appetizing as trays of decadent chocolates in a gourmet candy store. The type of flavorful truffles that were meant to be savored on the palette until the very end. And in my dating circles, there always was a sweet and quick ending. Long-term relationships were to be avoided, like day-old sushi and last season's fashions.

Sitting at a nearby table and waiting for Sheila to return from the bathroom, I covertly studied the masculine lineup. Just when my imagination shifted into overdrive, my boss walked up to the bar and abruptly interrupted my daydream.

Aaron Ackworth founded Shine Advertising and Public Relations some forty years ago, and tonight's party was his way of thanking the team for our latest client acquisition. The Frankie's account, all fifty-six locations, was enough of a victory to mandate a celebration for the entire office. Aaron had personally recruited me from another agency, and I felt a strong sense of loyalty to the man who was a legend in the industry. A strong leader, he treated his employees fairly, and, almost as a protective father might watch over his children, he looked out for us. Clutching a bottle of Corona beer, Aaron melted back into the crowd. I returned my attention to the men encircling the bar and wondered what each of them might be like in bed. Slow, sensual, and teasing. Roughly passionate. Or something enjoyably between.

I studied the pair at the far end of the bar. Animated as they watched the game, they cheered for opposite teams. Both wore quality suits and sported salon haircuts, but one was GQ cover material, while the other was more suited to *Outdoor Life*. Blended into one, they would make the perfect man.

"Marry me, Jaxie," someone whispered into my ear, the tickle of his breath jolting me from my reverie. Mark, a coworker and former fling, grinned down at me. This was probably the sixth or seventh time he'd proposed. The shock effect wore off weeks ago, after I learned that he proposed to everyone who broke up with him.

"You know I don't believe in matrimony, Mark. But thanks for asking."

He slid into Sheila's vacant chair. "Helluva bash, huh? I love this job. Where else can two people work their asses off to strike gold with a new account and the entire office gets credit?"

Mark always thought he did more work on a project than anyone else did and that he alone was responsible for 95 percent of Shine's client roster. His charm was the reason I broke my no-dating-coworkers rule, and his ego was the reason I reinstated it. But the breakup remained cordial. We are advertising and PR people. We love what we do. We're clever. Thick-skinned. Always on the lookout for the next trend. And, above all else, we do what it takes to close the deal. Business is business and dating is business.

"For the record"—I raised an eyebrow at him—"we *all* worked our asses off to land Frankie's."

Before he could argue, Sheila returned to reclaim her chair. Mark kissed us both on the cheek and sauntered off in pursuit of more available prey.

"He ask you to marry him again?" my best friend said. Like me, she was a senior account executive for Shine.

I nodded. "Yep."

She popped a pretzel into her mouth. "Gotta love his persistence."

"Yeah, right," I said, giving her a look. "About as much as you gotta love the city smog."

Sheila's dark golden eyes narrowed as she leaned close to talk over the noise. "Jax, you love everything about Atlanta. Smog included."

I smiled. She was right. I wouldn't trade my home for anything. Big-city living energized me. It was the massive buildings and constant movement, and the anonymity of living with four million neighbors. It was shopping at Nordstrom, barhopping in Buckhead, and ordering Chinese delivery at one o'clock in the morning. The theater and art, the live jazz, and the unique taste of boiled peanuts purchased from a street vendor.

From the homeless junkie begging for spare change to the extravagant five-star hotel, where scented toilet paper was folded for easy retrieval, a big city represented the entire gamut of humankind from one extreme to the other. And living in the midst of it induced the survivalist instinct. Just like Abraham Maslow's hierarchy of needs, the first order of business upon arriving in Atlanta was food, water, and shelter. Then came safety. Park in well-lit areas, pay attention to your surroundings, and lock your dead bolts.

I was well versed in the third level of the pyramid: love, acceptance, and affection. My social life was jam-packed, and I did okay in the esteem department, too. I was nowhere near the top of the pyramid, self-actualization, but I was having too much fun to worry about analyzing the meaning of life. My mother once had it all figured out and thought that life meant marriage and children and hard work. That theory left her abandoned and broke, with stretch marks and a baby girl to raise. I had no desire to follow in her footsteps.

"You're right," I admitted to Sheila. "I wouldn't trade living here for anything."

Justin Connor, the vice president of market research, appeared at our table. "Hello, ladies. Enjoying the party?" He looked the way he always did, wearing a dark suit and a white oxford button-down shirt. The only thing that changed from day to day was the color of his tie. If he wanted to get really wild, he'd wear one with subtle stripes.

"Absolutely," Sheila said, raising her glass to him. "Any time someone else is picking up the tab, I enjoy the party."

He smiled and put a hand on my shoulder. "Care to dance, Jaxie? The band started playing upstairs."

"No thanks. I, uh, didn't wear my dancing shoes." Although I would have enjoyed a dance, Justin was the last man I'd choose for a spin around the floor.

"Okay," he said, dropping his hand. "But you two should get up there before all the food is gone. The teriyaki chicken is delicious."

We nodded.

"Well, then. See you later."

"Sure," I said and, as soon as he moved on, rolled my eyes and stuck a finger in my mouth like I wanted to puke.

Sheila shot a frown my way. "The man just wanted to dance. Cut him some slack."

"You dance with him, then."

"He didn't ask me," she countered.

"He's socially challenged."

"What are you talking about? Half the women in our office would jump at the chance to dance with him."

"Hello?" I said. "Can you say *boring?*"

She shrugged. "You don't like him because he's not eye candy."

I shrugged back. "Can't tell if he's candy or not, through those ugly glasses and all the bean-counter suits."

"Well, maybe"—she smiled slyly—"you should remove the

specs and the clothes to find out. That man is hot for you, woman!"

"Give me a break."

"Well, besides his not being your usual spray-tanned, muscle-bound pretty boy, I think the real reason you avoid Justin is because you're afraid you might actually like him. A settle-down-with kind of like."

"That's ridiculous. I have no intention of settling down with any man. I mean, look where it got my mother. Even my grand-mother got dumped, or so I'm told, and that was way before divorce was an acceptable part of society. The women in my family aren't blessed with good man-choosing genes."

"Maybe not, but at least you could spend some time to get to know Justin. The only guys you hook up with are the ones you know you'll dump soon. After you've had your fun and want to move on to something new. Which typically takes"—she studied the ceiling to think—"about three weeks."

"So it would be better to do it your way?" I said. "Date a guy long enough to get to know him, but go out with two or three other ones at the same time?"

"I'm not actually *with* them all at the same time," she countered.

I raised my glass in a toast. "Good point."

We finished the bowl of pretzels and debated whether to go upstairs for some real food.

"I still think you should get to know our marketing VP a little better," Sheila said. "You might be pleasantly surprised."

I was about to remind her that I didn't date coworkers, boring or otherwise, when her eyes moved to a spot over my shoulder. I turned to see Aaron approaching.

He stopped at our table. "Jaxie, do you have a minute?"

"Sure."

We moved outside, onto a covered balcony with a view of Buckhead's busy streets, and when the door shut behind us, the decibel level dropped to a muffled hum. We walked to the railing and admired a mesmerizing spread of lights.

He pulled a cigar out of his breast pocket. "Mind if I light up?"

"No sir."

I studied the flow of headlights and taillights, the city's pulsing arteries and veins, while my boss tended to his Cohiba Cuban. Using a cutter, he clipped off one end and, with a monogrammed torch lighter, puffed a few times to get it going.

"At the board meeting this morning," he said through a mouthful of smoke, "the partners approved my nomination for our annual pro bono project."

I nodded, wondering where the conversation was headed and why he had singled me out. Our firm was one of the few in the country that did a pro bono marketing and public relations campaign each year. The effort produced a great tax write-off and invaluable publicity for Shine. Previous pro bono projects ranged from a national organ-donation awareness campaign to a series of radio and television spots encouraging people to vote.

"We are going to save a small town," he continued, exhaling a cloud of rich smoke into the night. I stifled a cough when some of it hit my nose. "Rumton has been slowly deteriorating for years and years, and now it's in real trouble. Farming has dried up. The downtown district is deserted. Kids have grown up and gotten the hell out of Dodge. The population is dwindling and, basically, the town is broke. The remaining few hundred residents can barely afford to keep their roads maintained and their school operational. If nothing is done, there won't be anything left to call a town."

"Rumton? Where is that?"

"On the South Carolina coast," he said, studying my face. "And we are going to figure out a way to revitalize it."

"Um, that's great. It sounds like a worthwhile project," I said, feeling a nervous twitch flare up in my left eyelid. "But what does any of this have to do with me?"

A chunk of ash fell from the end of his cigar and landed between our feet. Almost immediately, a gust of wind nudged it off the edge of the balcony, and it disappeared into the darkness.

"You are going to head up the project, Jaxie."

"Me? Head up the project?" I was too busy to lead a pro bono project. "You mean from our office, right? We'll send out a few interns, and I'll be their guidance contact?"

He chuckled before rolling the cigar between his fingers and taking another pull. "Well, yes, you'll get your two interns. But they'll be working from the office as your support staff. You're going to Rumton. For a month, or maybe more. You'll be there however long it takes to scope things out and devise a plan."

Concrete moved beneath my feet and the air thinned. I was stunned. I gripped the railing for support. He was sending me to a backwoods town in the middle of nowhere for a *month* or more? The muscle in my eyelid spasmodically danced for a full three seconds.

"Me?"

"I grew up there, Jaxie. It used to be a thriving town full of friendly folks. Lots of farmland. Beautiful oak trees and scenic watering holes. And Rumton has beautiful views of the marsh, even if it is landlocked."

"Aaron, I, uh . . . I don't really, uh, do small towns."

He studied me, and the reflection of the glowing cigar tip twinkled in his irises. "Have you ever spent any time in a small town?"

"I went camping once, when my mother made me join the Girl Scouts. A park near Stone Mountain, for a week. I came home with chiggers and poison ivy."

He laughed, as though ruining my life was no big deal. "It will be good for you to get out of Atlanta for a spell. Of course, the firm pays all your travel expenses, including mileage, and you even get a per diem for meals. Think of the money you'll save."

I didn't want the extra money if it meant weeks of torture. In fact, I'd pay *not* to go. I wondered if he could see the movement in my eyelid.

"You're one of our best, Jaxie. Saving this town means a lot to me, and I wouldn't trust it to anyone else," he said.

"What about Mark?"

"Mark is working the Procter and Gamble project. Disposable dog-grooming cloths and paw wipes."

"What about Lizzy?"

"You know she's pregnant," he said. "With twins. As I recall, you chipped in for the double-wide stroller."

"I'm sure Rumton has some great doctors," I mumbled.

He frowned around the cigar. "Rumton has one doctor. She's retired, so people have to drive to another town when they get sick."

"Sheila?" I tried vainly, with only a hint of guilt at suggesting my best friend.

"Sheila was the lead on last year's pro bono. And besides, she's already knee-deep in the spec campaign for Pepsi's new low-sugar cola." He removed the cigar from his mouth and held my eyes with his. "It's your turn, Jaxie. I want you to leave as soon as possible. Next week, to be exact. My aunt Millie still lives in Rumton; she'll be happy to show you around. In fact, you can stay with her. She'll be thrilled to have some company. I've already spoken to the town mayor, and you have his full support."

I studied the woven straps of my Casadei slides and wiggled my toes inside them, wondering if one could get a pedicure in Rumton. Probably not. A town with a few hundred people wouldn't have a nail salon, much less a massaging spa pedicure chair like the one I relaxed in every two weeks.

Why me? I made a name for myself in the advertising world

with sharp wit and sophistication, and now I was expected to extol the joys of the simple life? But my fate was sealed. The best I could hope for was to slap together a plan and be home in two weeks.

"I'd hate to impose on your aunt, Aaron. I should probably just stay in a hotel."

"Rumton doesn't have a hotel," he said.

"A bed-and-breakfast?"

He shook his head. No. "You'll like Millie. I'll give her a call in the morning."

"Sure, okay," I said. "Thank you." *For a big, fat nothing.*

"Besides, you'll get a better feel for the area if you stay in Rumton and get to know the people. Stir the pot, so to speak, and try to find a hook we can use to appeal to investors and developers." He chuckled, as though it were all crystal clear. "You know that the market value of property is simply what somebody is willing to spend on it. Put that brilliant creative streak of yours into action and figure out how to make Rumton property more desirable."

Feeling as if I was being punished for no good reason, I wondered if I should update my résumé and look for a new job. The idea, though satisfying in a vengeful way, dissolved immediately. It would be ridiculous to give up such a great job because of my distaste for one assignment.

He eyed me over the top of his wire-rimmed eyeglasses. "There's a lot riding on this, Jaxie. Not just for me personally but for small towns across America. Rumton is not the only town in trouble. We want to show people that a dying town in rural America can be saved with a little ingenuity."

He stuck the cigar in his mouth and gripped my shoulders in an attempt to summon enthusiasm. "This could be *huge*. I'm talking coverage in *Advertising Age* and *Newsweek* and *The Wall Street Journal*. Maybe even a documentary to air on one of the cable networks!"

Dread blurred my vision as Buckhead's colorful buildings went out of focus. I sucked in the pungent cigar smoke, accepting my fate, and tried to think of some positives. Long seconds passed; nothing came to mind.

Releasing my shoulders and giving me an encouraging pat on the back, Aaron told me how much confidence he had in me. Then he was gone, leaving a lingering cloud of cigar smoke. I wanted to run after him, grab his arm, and plead with him not to send me away. But Aaron was a straightforward and decisive multimillionaire, a powerful executive accustomed to getting his way. One did not run after the man and grab the sleeve of his custom-tailored Italian suit unless one wanted to be fired.

Rubbing my eye to stop the annoying twitch—but carefully so as not to dislodge a contact lens—I followed him back into Frankie's. The good thing about being single with no kids or pets was that I remained mobile. When I wanted to take off on vacation, I simply notified my landlord and bribed the doorman to water my plants. But the bad thing about being single with no kids or pets was that my boss knew I was mobile, too. It wasn't fair.

Since Sheila had designated herself driver for the evening, I designated myself drinker and retrieved a double Absolut vodka on the rocks, not bothering with the fruit. My glass of cabernet wine was no longer going to do the trick.

Drink in hand, I dropped into a chair and told Sheila my fate.

Unsympathetic, she laughed loudly. "I'm just glad it's you and not me!"

I shot her the finger.

2

Rumton was a dive. The type of place I wouldn't stop for fuel as I passed it during a road trip, even if the needle bumped empty. The type of place so devoid of traffic, it had only one four-way stop and no stoplights. Although the town was off a main highway that paralleled the coast, nothing appeared for long miles on either side of it. No nightclubs. No health clubs. No shopping malls. No entertainment venues. *No movement.*

To make things worse, Rumton residents couldn't get to the beach, even though their little piece of desolate paradise sat a mere two miles from the ocean. An expanse of wetlands separated the town from a sparkling strip of sandy beach beyond, and there was no way to get from one to the other. Anyone wanting to play on the strip of beach neighboring Rumton had to get there by boat—from the ocean. Not only that, but they had to navigate the boat from another town.

As I drove east, a narrow paved road turned into a bumpy dirt road that dead-ended into splotches of woods mixed with wetlands. Although the view of grassy marsh was pleasant, I couldn't see the Atlantic, even though I knew it was just beyond the horizon. While it was scenic, it was also a breeding ground for bugs. I'd barely stepped out of my Range Rover when a cloud of vicious mosquitoes descended on me. I immediately abandoned my plan to explore farther on foot, but nevertheless, I drove away with six or seven bites that quickly grew into quarter-sized itchy welts.

I felt limp and worn-out, as though I'd been driving for seven days instead of seven hours. Nerves had prevented me from getting a decent night's sleep, I'd skipped breakfast, and I'd eaten only a few bites of the fast-food cheeseburger bought somewhere near Columbia. Filled with apprehension, mosquito-bitten, tired, and hungry, I cased the entire town. Even driving slowly, it took only fifteen minutes. It resembled any quiet small town that someone might drive through on their way to somewhere else, had they inadvertently taken a wrong turn. Mostly, Rumton consisted of large fields, which may have been farmland at one time, and sporadic crumpling wooden buildings, which may have been huts or barns in a prior decade. Patches of tired-looking houses on a network of several roads made up the residential section. And a three-block section of buildings, connected by four-way stop signs, made up the downtown area. Some people might call it quaint, but all I could see were the abandoned boarded-up buildings and blaring *inactivity*. I knew I'd have to get a much more thorough look around, but a complaining stomach made me pull into the only place that looked as if it might serve food. A sun-bleached wooden sign hung over the front door. It read: CHAT 'N CHEW.

Hungry but not wanting to leave the security of my car, I sat in the dirt parking lot and decided to call my boss's aunt. The stupid phone blinked NO SERVICE. I held it up higher, craning my neck to see if any signal-strength bars appeared, and waved it around over my head. Nothing. Of course, Rumton wouldn't have wireless phone coverage. What had I been thinking? They probably didn't have cable television or high-speed Internet access, either. Thank goodness I'd signed up for satellite Internet service last month; I wouldn't be totally cut off from the outside world.

Driven by rage over my uncooperative phone and the growing

hunger pain in my stomach, I took a deep breath and boldly entered Chat 'N Chew.

A twangy song emanated from the bill of a five-foot-tall pelican. The bird, a radio hanging from its pouch, was one of several carved wood sculptures scattered among square tables. A soda fountain, complete with swivel barstools, stretched along the back of the building.

The restaurant was deserted, except for two old men drinking coffee and playing a game of dominoes. One was completely bald and looked seventy-five or eighty, whereas his friend had a full head of thick white hair and may have been ten years younger. They nodded in my direction and the younger of the two tipped an imaginary hat.

"Bull had to run home, but she'll be back in a bit," one of them said. "Coffee's there behind the counter, next to the iced tea. Get me a refill when you pour yourself some, would you, lass?"

The waitress was a woman named Bull? Who'd left the place wide open in the middle of the day? And had the man really called me "lass"?

A black and tan basset hound ambled up to sniff my legs before lazily stretching out over one of my feet. Trying to get comfortable, it farted loudly and almost immediately started snoring. A string of drool trickled slowly onto my shoe. The man eyed me, awaiting his refill.

Careful not to disturb the sleeping dog, I removed my foot, retrieved the coffeepot, and refilled his cup.

"Do people make their own food here, too?" I joked, carefully pouring another cup for myself. I set it on the table and decided not to bother looking for cream. Wishing I hadn't worn my melon-colored Versace pantsuit, I wiped crumbs out of the chair before sitting down.

"Go ahead and help yourself. She's got a pot of chicken soup back there and some corn muffins," one of them said. "Butter ran out, though."

"Don't need no butter if you're eatin' corn muffins with soup!" the other challenged.

"If Bull's going to go to the trouble to make corn muffins," the first argued, "she ought to make sure she's got butter to go with them. Real butter. Not that spreadable stuff that tastes like goat shit."

"How do you know what goat shit tastes like?"

The man with the hair caught me staring in disbelief. I think my mouth might have been open. He asked where I was from.

"Atlanta," I said, casually, trying to fit in. I made sure to shut my mouth after I'd finished speaking.

A thick wrinkle between his bushy eyebrows grew deeper.

"Georgia," I added.

"I know where Atlanta is," he grumbled. "Was just wondering why in the heck anybody would want to hang their hat there."

"It's where I work."

Perplexed, he shrugged his shoulders and went back to the corn muffin debate. I drank my black coffee. Eventually, a round woman with an amazing amount of peroxide-blond hair piled on top of her head barreled through the front door.

"Haven't seen you 'round here before," she said in greeting. "I'm Bull. I own the place. Can I getcha something, hon?"

"Did you say Belle?"

"Nope, you heard it right, hon. Bull. Real name's Dixie, but ever since I took down Bucky Junior with a body tackle twenty years ago, people have been calling me Bull," she explained. "It grows on ya."

"Why did you, uh, tackle Bucky Junior?" I asked.

"We was throwin' a real nice party for his mama's birthday, and he stormed in like a maniac, all liquored up. He was convinced that my boy, Albert, was sweet on his girl. So he started tearin' up the place, demanding for Albert to come out and face him." Remembering, she clucked a few times. "Problem was, Albert was down at the Bellamy fishin' hole with—you guessed it—Bucky's girlfriend. But still, I didn't appreciate him tearin' up my place. Not one teeny bit. Especially during his own mama's party. So I took him down. What can I get ya to eat?"

Dumbfounded, I asked to see a menu.

"She wants a menu," one of the men said. They chuckled and turned around to get a better look at me.

"No menus, here, hon," Bull said. "You got a hankerin' for anything specific?"

Yes, I thought. *A wood-fired rib eye and chocolate chunk crème brûlée from Buckhead Diner.* My stomach growled loudly. "Um, anything will be fine. Maybe a sandwich?"

"Comin' up. You allergic to anything, hon?"

Just small hick towns. I shook my head.

She grabbed a cup of coffee and joined me at the table. "That's good. So many people nowadays can't eat this or can't eat that. Take Riley over there, for instance." She waved a hand in the direction of the men. "He just went and got himself one of them fancy allergy workups at the Medical University of South Carolina in Charleston? They told him he can't eat wheat anymore. You know how many things got wheat in them?"

"A lot?"

"Breads, muffins, cereals. Heck. 'Bout everything you can bake has wheat flour in it."

I raised my eyebrows with feigned interest.

"And soy sauce, if you can believe that." She added three spoonfuls of sugar to her coffee and took a gulp. "Not that I'd ever use soy sauce. But who would've guessed it has wheat in it?"

"Not me." My left eyelid twitched and my stomach growled simultaneously. "Listen, uh, Bull, I'd love to talk. In fact, I have some questions that you might be able to help me with. But could you go ahead and turn in my sandwich order?"

Bull hooted and slapped the table. "This one wants me to turn her order in," she said to her only other customers. The men laughed, too, as though I'd said something funny. Even the basset hound picked its big head up to look at me.

"Guess you better get back there and turn it in, then, Bull," the man with hair said. "Maybe your left hand can turn it in to your right hand!"

Bull stood and walked to the kitchen, shaking her head. "Turn yer order in," she muttered. "That's a good one."

Embarrassed, I could feel my cheeks warm. How was I to know Rumton's Chat 'N Chew was a one-woman operation? At least I'd been able to provide the trio with some entertainment.

"Excuse me," I said to the men, feeling more out of place by the second. "I need to call Millie Ackworth, but my mobile phone doesn't work here. Is there a pay phone nearby?"

"Mad Millie? She a friend of yours?"

"She's my boss's aunt, and I'll be staying at her house for a few days," I said. "Why do you call her Mad Millie?"

"What's your name, lass?"

"Jaxie. Jaxie Parker."

"I'm Pop and this here's Riley," the one with the hair said. "We call old lady Ackworth Mad Millie because of the cats."

"Oh, she's not mad, like kooky mad." Riley's fingers made a swirling motion by his head. "Not much so, anyhow."

"The woman just likes her cats," Pop added. "Must have ten or fifteen of the critters."

"Inside?" I asked, feeling the color drain from my face. I was horribly allergic to cats. I would get itchy skin and sneeze if I was near someone who had been near a cat. One cat. And this woman had ten or fifteen?

"Right-o," Pop answered. "She's got playhouses and scratching posts and all those gizmos, according to Riley. Don't know why. A cat can play in a tree for free."

"But Mad Millie don't let hers outside," Riley added. "Says they're *indoor* cats."

"Only reason they're indoor cats is because she won't let them out," Pop said with a shrug, much like the one he'd given me upon finding out I lived in Atlanta. Neither made sense to him. "Got to be a little crazy to keep an animal cooped up. One of the reasons I don't much care for the woman."

"Pop and Mad Millie ain't spoke to each other in years and years," Riley informed me. "Now, me, I could care less 'bout Millie havin' so many cats."

"Only reason you talk to her is for her pie," Pop said.

Riley shook his head, disagreeing. "Not *just* for free pie. She makes good jam, too."

Bull appeared with a giant deli meat sandwich on rye bread and asked if I wanted something to drink besides coffee. I shook my head, staring at the food, wondering if the nearest hotel would be north or south of Rumton.

"What's wrong, hon? You don't like ham?"

"The sandwich is fine, thanks," I said miserably.

"Jaxie here is s'posed to be staying at Mad Millie's place," Riley explained. "But she must not like cats."

I sniffled just thinking about sharing a house with ten felines. "I'm allergic to them."

"Huh," Bull said, plopping into the seat across from me. She took a potato chip from my plate, ate it, and took another. "Guess you'd best find somewhere else to stay. Whatcha doin' in Rumton, anyhow?"

The two men listened for my answer, too, and I decided there were probably no secrets in this town. A visitor from Atlanta was big news. I'd probably be the talk of the town for the next week.

I explained that my boss grew up in Rumton, told them about

the firm I worked for, and revealed the purpose of my visit. They all knew Aaron well, and Bull said something about his family being good people.

"Going to save the town, huh?" Pop chuckled. "What exactly do we need saving from?"

I answered, throwing in a few statistics for good measure, and hoped they couldn't see the tic in my eyelid.

"Huh," Bull said again, raising a penciled-in eyebrow. The moment passed and her attention went back to my food. "Aren't you going to eat? I thought you were hungry."

"Yeah, that's why Bull rushed to turn yer order in!" Riley teased.

Not wanting to make a bad first impression, if that was still possible, I bit into half the sandwich. I made some appreciative noises, even though the cat issue had caused my appetite to vanish.

Bull eyed the other half of my sandwich, and I told her to help herself. She did, with gusto.

"Pop's got a room you might could stay in," she said through a hearty bite.

The old man looked me over, as though sizing up a stray dog to determine whether or not it was a biter.

"It's okay, really," I said to everyone. "I'll just get a hotel. I'm sure I could find something near Charleston. Or go in the other direction, toward Georgetown."

Bull harrumphed and helped herself to a handful of my chips. "How you gonna save Rumton if you're beddin' down somewhere else?"

She had a good point.

I took another bite. "Maybe Millie has a room the cats don't go in." Despite the circumstances, my appetite had returned and the ham sandwich was delicious. She'd spread cream cheese on the thick bread and added pieces of tomato, sliced paper-thin. I suddenly wished I hadn't given up half my meal.

"Oh, go on and offer her a room," Bull told Pop. "That big ol' house of yours is wasted with just you livin' there. How many bedrooms you got, anyhow? Five or six?"

"Seven," he said, giving me the once-over. "How long will it take you to save our town, lass?"

"I'm hoping I won't be here more than a couple of weeks. But my boss has allocated a month or up to six weeks, just in case."

"Huh," Bull said, polishing off her half of my sandwich. "Amazing that a tiny thing like you from big ol' snazzy Atlanta can up and save our little town in a few short weeks. I mean, we all been livin' here our whole lives."

I couldn't tell if she was being sarcastic or just making an observation. "It's basically the same as coming up with an advertising or public relations campaign for a business," I explained, feeling silly, wondering if my boss was nuts for thinking I could do this. "But in this case, the goal is to promote your town—so it's called a revitalization plan. We need to come up with some ideas to bring in new business and new residents, like maybe a manufacturing plant that will create jobs. Or promote Rumton as a tourist destination. Find a hook or an angle to capture people's interest in the area. Then it's just a matter of getting the word out. And, of course, the more interest there is in an area, the more valuable the property will become."

"Huh," the three of them said.

"Aaron said that Rumton needs some basic things, like a medical office. A new fire truck for the volunteer squad. An ambulance. Updated equipment and computers for your school. And a way to bring in new residents, to grow the area." I ate some chips before Bull managed to finish them off. "To make these things happen, the town needs to see an appreciation in property values and needs something to generate revenue. Which takes us back to the PR side of things. What would bring people and business to Rumton? That's the bottom-line question."

I drank my coffee and hoped I looked as confident as I sounded. As if it would be easy. Just another campaign. No big deal.

"Aye, I have a room you can bunker down in for a spell," Pop finally said. "Got a private head."

"I don't have much cash, since I planned on staying with my boss's aunt. And I was going to put everything else on a credit card, then expense it."

"Your company payin' for everything?" Riley asked.

I nodded.

"Pop's rooms go fer a hundred dollars a day," he said.

Bull laughed. "Leave it to Riley to exploit a situation! You need a swindler in your revitalization plan, you know where to find one."

"It ain't comin' outta her pocket," he said. "A big company is payin' it. Heck's fire, that income'll be the start of our revitala-zaah-shun plan."

"A big company owned by Aaron Ackworth," Pop reminded Riley. "His folks were good people. E'eryone hated to see them move when they caught the Florida bug."

Riley shrugged, conceding the point. "I s'pose yer right. Aaron called last week ta make sure his girl would have the town's support. Guess we ought to give it to her."

Realizing they already knew who I was and why I was there, I felt silly. Why had they let me ramble on trying to explain it all? What else did these seemingly simpleminded people know?

Bull refused to take any money for the sandwich, saying she would see lots more of me, and Pop offered the use of a room in his house for free, as long as I'd cook an occasional meal for him. I didn't tell him I couldn't cook. I was just happy to have a bed without cats. I'd fake the cooking part.

Before I followed Pop to his house, I used Chat 'N Chew's phone to call Mad Millie. I was very much looking forward to meeting her, I said, but I wouldn't be staying at her house, since Pop had offered a room in his house.

"What?" she said. "You're staying with Pompous Pop? That man is an oddball, living in such a big house all by himself, all snootylike. Why, he doesn't even have a cat!"

3

I awoke to see a furry masked animal staring at me. Four or five inches from my face, it studied me with a cocked head. My first instinct was to scream and knock it off my bed, but I figured I was still asleep and dreaming. As I blinked hard and tried to remember where I was, the animal disappeared. It was definitely a dream.

Delicious cooking smells of sausage and biscuits brought me upright. Surveying the unfamiliar surroundings, I realized where I was and, breathing deep, decided that Pop didn't need help with the cooking, after all. I even detected the aroma of coffee brewing. I dug through my luggage, pulled on some shorts and a T-shirt, and followed my nose to the kitchen. At the stove, Pop skillfully removed sausage patties from a skillet.

"Morning, lass," he said. "You city people always sleep so late?"

I smiled. It was not yet seven o'clock. "Only on weekends."

"There's a pitcher of orange juice in the refrigerator," he said.

Not feeling as odd as I thought I would about waking up in a complete stranger's home in the middle of nowhere, I poured myself a glassful and sat at the table.

"I don't think I've slept that soundly in a long time," I admitted, gulping the juice. Fresh squeezed, it had just the right amount of pulp.

"The absence of noise," he said, "makes for a peaceful night's sleep. That, and the salt air. Ocean's a bit away, I'll agree, but the breeze makes its way here."

Pop put two plates of food on the table, and my stomach growled in response. Not only had he cooked sausage and biscuits, but he had also made scrambled eggs and fried potatoes. I rarely ate a big breakfast but suddenly had a ravenous appetite.

I started to dig in when loud, squeaky purring noises caught my attention. On the table, sitting up on its haunches, a fat raccoon snatched a potato wedge from my plate and munched away.

"It wasn't a dream!"

"Her name is Bandit," Pop said, "and she'll steal from you in a heartbeat. Food off your plate, a shiny penny from the dresser, any bauble that catches her eye. She once pulled a watch from my arm while I napped on the sofa."

I told Pop that Bandit was on my bed earlier and asked how she got in. I felt sure I'd closed the bedroom door. Laughing, he admitted that Bandit had the run of his house. She could open doors, cabinets, and drawers, and even turn on lights.

"Is she housebroken?" Maybe Pop was more insane than Mad Millie, letting a wild animal live inside. Cats were meant to live with people. As far as I knew, raccoons weren't.

"Aye," he said. "She's cleaner than a cat, as smart as my dog, and she does her business outside. She lets herself in and out as it suits her."

"Aren't you afraid of rabies or something?"

"She goes to the vet in Georgetown, same as my dog. 'Course, Roy likes to give me a hard time. Always asks to see my permit, which I always tell him I don't have."

I drank some orange juice, savoring the freshness. "Permit?"

"Not supposed to keep a wild animal without a permit. But like I tell Roy, I don't *keep* Bandit. She just hangs 'round."

"Huh," I said, sounding just like the locals I'd met so far.

Pop gave Bandit a nibble of sausage. She dunked it in his glass of water and ate it.

"She washes some things before she eats them. A raccoon will do that, so watch your drinks 'round her. Last night I gave her one of Flush's biscuits and she dunked it in my whiskey."

"Who's Flush?"

"That's my dog. I won him in a poker game, with naught but a pair of threes."

"If your winning hand was just a pair, why did you name the dog Flush?" I asked.

Pop winked. "Because the boys *thought* I had a flush. That's why all four of them folded good hands. Perceptions are oft' more powerful than reality."

He had a point. Perception was *everything*, at least when it came to advertising.

As we ate, I asked Pop about his house, a rambling place that looked as though it had been enlarged several times. The original building, he explained, was one room and a kitchen, built in the early 1700s. A summer home for an indigo, cotton, and tobacco grower, it originally belonged to Pop's ancestor. Back then, he told me, inland plantation owners sometimes built a small place on the ocean to escape the sweltering summer heat and take advantage of a cool ocean breeze. A slave would keep it up for them, and the plantation owner would visit periodically, especially during summer months. The two homes might be only thirty miles apart, he said, but in that time period, it took an entire day to travel by horse and carriage.

The Rumton summer house had been handed down from generation to generation, and the resulting home was a product of numerous renovations and additions. Pop's grandfather bequeathed it to him and his sister. She couldn't wait to leave town, though, and gave up her half of the house. But the area and its laid-back lifestyle suited Pop just fine, he told me. He was a sailor at heart and would never stray far from the Atlantic Ocean. As a boy, he'd practically lived on a boat. But the boating trips got to be fewer and fewer by the time he'd become a teenager, he said. Rumton's inlet closed up.

He got up to serve more eggs. I looked at my near-empty plate; stunned, I couldn't believe I'd eaten so much. I'd have to remember to buy some groceries, especially since he wasn't even charging me rent.

"So then, there used to be an inlet deep enough to get a boat through the marsh and out to the ocean? That would explain how the town of Rumton first got started, since many older towns originated around water, like a river."

"Right. In the past, Rumton was a water town. Seventy, eighty years back, we were a popular shrimping community. But o'er time, our inlet slowly filled in. Got to the point where a boat couldn't get through, even at high tide. By the time my grandpappy taught me to sail, he had to keep his boat in the next town. We'd pile everything in his old Ford truck and take off for the day. Sometimes two." He paused, reminiscing, drank some juice. "A fine man, he was. Died before I was barely a man. Fourteen or fifteen, maybe."

"Did your parents sail, too?"

"Don't know. All we had growing up was my grandpappy."

I wondered why Pop never moved out of Rumton. It was easy to envision him as a misplaced boat captain. He fit the role of a man well suited for the high seas. "How does an inlet just close up? I don't understand."

He offered Bandit another nibble of sausage. "Motion of the sea always moves the sand, lass. The coastline is in a state of constant change."

I'd never thought about it that way. "So old inlets can just close up and new ones pop open?"

He nodded. "The ocean is like a beautiful strong woman. She can be loving and nurturing . . . or wickedly evil." He gave me a wink. "But she's always captivating."

Smiling at the comparison, I chewed some eggs. "What about the Intracoastal Waterway? It borders the north end of Rumton, right? And from the waterway, you can get to the ocean at various points. I studied a maritime chart last week."

"True, a stretch of Rumton borders the waterway. But it's marshy, with a lot of wetlands, just like the land between us and the ocean. The town owns the property by the waterway, but we can't do much with it. We were going to put in a boat ramp, but there isn't even an area suitable for a road."

"So Rumton sits right next to the Atlantic Ocean to the east, *and* the Intracoastal Waterway to the north, but you can't get to either one from here?"

"Right, unless you drive to the next town."

"Do you have a boat?"

"I sold the sailboat because she got to be too much for me, but still keep a motorboat docked outside of town. She's a Cape Dory." He stopped eating and got a faraway expression. "But of late, I don't take her out much. I don't like the road traffic to get there."

If he had trouble with the small amount of traffic between Rumton and the next town, he'd have a coronary driving in Atlanta. I changed the subject.

"So what else can you tell me about Rumton?"

He drank some juice, sighed. "It's 'bout the same now as always. Except less people. Few youngsters. Used to be a big farming community, but that's gone by the wayside. And, o' course, the shrimpers went out o' business a long time ago. Folk couldn't earn a good living, so they left. And nobody new has moved to town for years and years."

Bandit zeroed in on my last potato wedge, but I stabbed it with my fork before she could get to it. "Is Pop your real name?"

"You're chockful of questions."

"Well, I'm curious. I need to learn as much as I can, as quickly as I can. So why do people call you Pop?"

He gave Bandit a nibble of biscuit. She ate it without washing it first and clapped her little paws together in thanks. "I taught shop classes in the schoolhouse. We ne'er had any of our own, but all the youngsters hung 'round our house after their schooling. They came for Suzie's cookies and my stories. Somewhere along the way, they took to calling me Pop."

I scooped up the last bite of eggs and chewed. "Suzie was your wife?"

"A beauty, she was. Cancer took her. Now, quit yabberin' and finish your breakfast."

We looked at my plate and burst out laughing. Except for a few biscuit crumbs, it was already empty.

"You city people always eat so much?" he teased, eyes twinkling. I noticed that one of them was dark brown and the other was light gemstone green. The effect was startling.

"Only on weekends," I said.

After breakfast, I got online and sent my daily update to Aaron. So far I didn't have much to report, except that allergies had forced me away from his aunt Millie's and in with Pop and a kleptomaniac raccoon.

I e-mailed the interns with their first Rumton assignments. I needed some topography reports, from the present and back as far as early 1700. I wanted whatever they could dig up on the farming plantations that thrived in the area in the same century, even though I wasn't sure exactly how the information would help.

And I wanted a set of detailed navigation charts that covered the waterways of the entire South Carolina coast.

Before I set out to do some more exploring and interview some of the townspeople, I dialed Sheila's extension.

"How's the backwoods expedition going?" she asked. "You tapping your toes to the tune of 'Dueling Banjos' yet?"

I grinned into the phone. "I'm barefoot and mosquito-bitten, staying in a three-hundred-year-old house that's owned by an old man who calls me 'lass.' And Chat 'N Chew, the only restaurant in town, doesn't have menus or dry martinis. Any other questions?"

4

Other than a few pesky mosquitoes, the day was wonderful. It was the end of August, and although the temperature remained summer-hot, a steady breeze kept me comfortable as I explored Rumton's streets on foot.

The air carried a unique mixture of salt, sand, and marsh, and the smell reminded me of vacationing in the Florida Keys. Had there been a shady cabana, I might even have imagined I was on vacation. But Rumton was in a time warp and was the last place on earth I'd choose to stay, despite the fact that Pop was being so nice to me.

Only evidence of a once-thriving downtown area remained: boarded-up storefronts and abandoned warehouses, an out-of-business bank, unruly shrubbery, and sun-faded wooden benches spread along uneven sidewalks. I counted nine churches, which seemed unusual, even for the South. A colorful water tower rose from the center of a small park and, in an explosion of red, white, and blue, told me to have a happy Fourth of July. As I stood staring at the outdated message, a passerby explained that high-schoolers and those "young at heart" decorated the tower before each holiday. It was a tradition that all the townspeople gathered to watch. But since they'd run out of white paint, the tower would most likely retain its Independence Day message until Halloween, when it would become a giant orange jack-o'-lantern.

An even bigger oddity was the single-screen movie theater that doubled as a police department, one-truck fire and EMS department, town hall, and meeting place for the Rumton Roses ladies' auxiliary group.

Feeling as if I'd fallen asleep and awakened in a bad episode of *The Andy Griffith Show*, I entered the theater. The police chief's assistant, Amy, occupied the ticket window and was kind enough to leave her glass-walled cubicle to introduce me to everyone else in the building. Volunteer firefighters, mostly in their seventies, hung out at the concession counter, playing Scrabble and watching TV. A town maintenance worker napped on a sofa. And the man in charge of enforcing law in Rumton sat at a desk in the middle of the lobby, right next to a quad of pinball machines.

Beside the restrooms, a wall-mounted chalkboard listed the week's events. Just one movie was scheduled, and it ran only once each Friday night. A comedy, the current flick had been out on DVD for a year.

"You look a right bit thirsty, Jaxie," a firefighter drawled when I'd finished my tour. "Do you have a hankerin' for a Pepsi or a Mountain Dew? Either way, your dollar goes to the department."

Nervousness about being an out-of-place city-dweller made my left eyelid vibrate. I didn't even know what the word "hankering" meant, although I got the gist of his question. "Uh, Pepsi would be great," I said, and asked about the big rubber boot sitting on the counter. It was for tips, he told me, which were really donations. I handed him a five. He put it in the boot without asking if I needed change.

"So then, you guys sell popcorn and candy on movie nights?"

"Sure, every Friday." He passed over a drink and a paper-wrapped straw. "Truth tell, we're open for business anytime, since this is our volunteer headquarters and a firefighter or two is always here, least during the day. Lots of time, when they're out for a walk, folk just stop by for a cold drink. That, and they want to catch up on the latest gossip. Personally, I don't spill anything I heard coming outta the chief's office until they drop some money in the boot, and coins don't count for the latest-breaking news. We're saving for a new portable AED. That's an automatic electronic defibrillator."

I stuck another five in the rubber till. After all, there were a lot of old people in Rumton and an AED could come in handy. Imagining it to be a gin and tonic, I downed the Pepsi and dropped the cup into a trash can on my way out of the theater. Perched in the ticket window, Amy waved good-bye and told me, through the intercom system, to have a nice afternoon.

In a residential section just five blocks later, outdated houses displayed an eclectic assortment of lawn decorations, such as an old bathroom pedestal sink reincarnated as a planter. In no hurry to get anywhere, dogs roamed freely, tongues hanging out and tails wagging. People rested on their front porches doing absolutely nothing, unless rocking in a rocking chair qualified as a hobby. And something I'd never seen in Atlanta: As though participating in a perpetual, multifamily garage sale, Rumton residents put up signs in front of their houses to let passersby know what they were willing to part with. Handwritten signs tacked to trees and fence posts advertised bluetick hound puppies, a dinette set, and a Martin guitar (that needed strings). One family sought patrons who wanted to trade homegrown zucchini squash or collard greens for assorted wigs.

Half an hour into my walk, I stumbled upon two wooden sentries that stood guard at the front walkway of a house; I immediately recognized the carving style. Following the sound of whistling, I found a man in a carport behind the house, carving a duck's head into the handle of a walking cane. Sun-weathered black skin covered a tall lanky frame, and the small knife in his hand seemed to move with a will of its own.

"Hello?" I said.

Not startled to see a stranger standing in his driveway, he nodded without skipping a beat.

"You made the pelican in Chat 'N Chew, right? It's really good."

He smiled and waved a hand in the direction of an upside-down wooden barrel, offering me a seat.

"I'm Jaxie," I told him, sitting down, "from Atlanta."

He ran a large hand over the cane, checking its smoothness. "Elwood."

Sensing a visitor, a woman appeared with a tray of lemonade to welcome me. "You must be the one from Atlanta, here to save our town," she said warmly. Her smile was genuine and put me at ease. "I'm Gladys, Elwood's devoted wife, or Miss Gladys to all the patients I've seen in my practice over the years."

"You were the doctor, then? My boss, Aaron, mentioned that Rumton has only one doctor, now retired."

"Got to the point where I just couldn't do it full-time anymore. We tried to recruit a new family physician, but it seems like all the young kids coming out of medical school want to go to the big cities." She shrugged. "But I still help out in an emergency and write a prescription if I need to. Keep my license active, to be legal. We're still looking for a doctor, though."

I thought about that and wondered what would entice a medical professional to live in Rumton. It wouldn't be for the excitement, and they certainly wouldn't get rich. "Maybe it would help if the town could offer free housing as an incentive or maybe provide the facility at no charge." After all, lots of med school graduates had some serious student loans to pay off.

She nodded. "I've been thinking the same thing! There must be a creative way to get a good doctor here. Really, it's a perfect setting for someone just starting out. And a good place to raise kids. That's what I keep telling my granddaughter, who's studying medicine and about to graduate. She could do her internship under me."

"That would be ideal!"

Gladys frowned. "I think so, too. But, understandably, she wants to live in a place where other young people live. Here, she wouldn't have much of a social life."

I could identify with the girl's reluctance. "Well, maybe we can change that. With a successful revitalization plan, Rumton will appeal to people of all age groups."

Gladys asked me about my job in Atlanta, and before I realized it, we'd been talking and laughing for an hour. All the while, Elwood whistled softly to a beat in his head and contentedly whittled away tiny pieces of wood, creating a grass design in the body of the walking cane. I asked about his sculptures and learned that he'd been carving since he retired at age sixty-five. He was now eighty-two, which added up to a lot of years' worth of inventory. Taking a closer look at the oversized carport, I saw that it was crammed with carvings. Pieces stacked behind other pieces, filling the shelves and lining the floor, all delightfully animated. Had his work been displayed in one of Atlanta's trendy art galleries, the larger sculptures would easily bring a few thousand dollars apiece. I asked why he kept making so many new things when he wasn't trying to sell them, but Elwood just shrugged.

"I like to carve."

"But you don't want to sell?" All the artists I knew built up a supply of their paintings or sculpture only when they planned to show and sell their work.

"Oh, if someone were to ask," Gladys said, "he might be inclined to sell them something. A few years back, Bull convinced him to put some carvings in her restaurant, to keep her company when nobody else was around. Told him she'd sell them to tourists, if any ever stumbled in."

Elwood nodded his agreement. "Nothing here I can't live without."

"She did sell a whooping crane last year," Gladys told me. "A couple from North Carolina was headed to Hilton Head when their van broke down. They stopped at Chat 'N Chew for dinner, and the woman just gravitated to Elwood's crane statues. So Bull dickered on Elwood's behalf and got fifty dollars for the bird. Next morning, the wife came back and left with the other one."

"He sold two pieces, then."

She laughed and looked at her husband with an expression of genuine adoration. "Not exactly. The second time the woman came in, she was in tears. Since they'd spent the night and didn't check in at Hilton Head, the hotel gave their room away. It was the honeymoon suite, where they'd spent their first married night together. Turns out they were celebrating their ten-year anniversary. A romantic getaway, without their children. So Bull felt sorry for the woman and gave her the matching crane, as an anniversary present. No charge. She knew Elwood wouldn't mind."

Elwood shrugged and stopped to run a piece of sandpaper lightly over the cane. "You've given away medical care plenty a times, woman. Before and after you retired."

The doctors I knew were full of self-importance, and I couldn't imagine a single one of them welcoming a perfect stranger with a tray of lemonade or giving away free medical services. For that matter, a new patient couldn't even schedule an appointment without first disclosing what type of insurance they had or, if they were uninsured, how they intended to pay for the visit.

"Yep, she pretty much refuses to take any money at all, now that her practice is officially closed," Elwood continued, his dark eyes moving up to look at his wife with blatant devotion, before quickly dropping back to the piece of wood in his hands.

Gladys patted his arm. "No reason to be greedy. We don't want for anything."

If I were them, I'd sure want for something. A moving van.

But they were clearly happy. And quite possibly more committed to each other than any married couple I knew.

After leaving Elwood and Gladys and their kingdom of wood characters, I walked in the direction of my car, introducing myself to more locals as I went.

There was a seventy-nine-year-old pharmacist, who, as her front yard sign attested, was also a beekeeper. The drugstore, known as the Always Open Apothecary, occupied the bottom floor of her home, and Gertrude lived above it. Despite the name, she only opened for business when someone climbed the stairs and banged on her front door. Or happened to catch her resting outside in the hammock, as I had.

"Doorbell's out of sorts, but you feel free to knock on my door anytime you need somethin', sugar," Gertrude told me, squinting into the sun from her horizontal position. "Gotta knock right loud, though, in case my hearing-aid battery has gone out. You gotta replace the dad-blasted things every couple a days."

I met lots of colorful people who may have just been humoring me with their friendly nods when I explained why I was visiting.

And I met the town's only judge, a magistrate and former Ringling Brothers' circus clown. Since Rumton's town hall burned down in the eighties and was never rebuilt, he heard misdemeanors and traffic violations every Wednesday at high noon in the movie theater. But only when there were cases to hear, he explained, which happened every two or three weeks.

"A lot of the defendants are travelin' folks who detoured through Rumton for a look-see. 'Course, we also have jurisdiction over a small area of the highway, so they could just be passing us by. The chief will pull 'em over for speeding, just so as he can make sure his siren still works. Some of 'em actually show up for court."

"The movie theater doubles as your courtroom?" I envisioned the judge, perched on the narrow elevated stage, outlined by the white movie screen. People probably munched popcorn while they waited to approach the makeshift bench, all in the name of helping the volunteer fire department's fund-raising efforts.

He shrugged. "Seats are more comfortable than the folding chairs in the old town hall building."

I had definitely landed in Mayberry. When I told her about this, Sheila would think I made it all up. Incredulous at my surreal surroundings, I could feel the muscle in my eyelid tighten, threatening to start twitching at any moment.

"Where are you from?" the judge asked as I was leaving.

"Atlanta."

"No, I mean originally."

"Atlanta," I repeated.

Confusion spread across his face. "Well, where are your people from?"

I'd never known my grandparents and hadn't thought much about where "my people" were from. Genealogy didn't interest me.

"I was born and raised in Atlanta. My mother grew up in Marietta, but that's the same general area," I answered. "I never knew my father. And my grandparents died before I was born." I didn't tell him that I wasn't even sure where they were from.

"Huh," he said, not bothering to ask what I did for a living, which was a topic I *could* have talked about.

As I walked the last block to my car, it occurred to me that the locals were more interested in learning where I was from than what I did. In Atlanta, people couldn't care less where I grew up or who my parents were. Everyone was defined by the position they held, the view from their office, and the paycheck they brought home.

Wondering about my ancestors, I pointed a keyless entry fob at my Range Rover, and a woman walking her dog stopped to stare. When the locks popped open, she shook her head with in-credulity. Apparently, people in Rumton didn't bother to secure their vehicles.

I decided to pick up some groceries for dinner and ended up at a combination grocery store, hardware store, post office, and gas station. Outside stood one regular unleaded gasoline pump, one diesel pump, a mail drop, and a portable marquee that read: COLD BEER & WORMS. Inside, as promised, I found cold beer and worms, the cans of brew iced down in a keg-sized wooden barrel and the worms happily burrowing in a container of dirt.

"Howdy, howdy," the man behind the counter said through a wad of chewing tobacco stuffed in one cheek. He was reading a gossip magazine, and bold headlines across the cover declared that Oprah was pregnant with triplets. "I'm Billy. My friends call me Buckshot."

"Buckshot?"

He pointed to a small dark spot on his forehead, just above an eyebrow. "Been here since I was a kid. Got hit by a stray pellet when I was out quail hunting with the fellows. But you can call me Billy. You must be that gal from Atlanta."

It was as though my forehead was marked in red ink: Atlanta Girl. People knew me upon sight, even after I'd dressed to blend with the locals in khaki shorts, sandals, and a white cotton top I'd found hanging in my closet at Pop's house.

"Well, nice to meet you, Billy. I'm Jaxie, and yes, that's me. The one from Atlanta. I just need to pick up a few groceries and some shampoo." I'd forgotten to pack mine. "Where would I find shampoo and conditioner?"

He spit a stream of tobacco juice into a soda can. "Right yon-der, third aisle, next to the shells."

I'd seen polished seashells in tourist-town beachwear shops, but I never would have guessed Rumtonians bought shells. "You carry shells?"

"Sure, sure," he said, putting down the rag mag and giving me the once-over. "I got twelve gauge and twenty gauge. You bird hunt?"

I shook my head. Wishing I were at my favorite Atlanta grocery store and sipping an iced latte, I filled a carry basket with the makings for a pork chop dinner. When I got to the shampoo aisle, I found two choices. Dandruff-control or regular. I would have to make a trip out of town soon to buy my regular hair products from a salon, not to mention to get a biweekly touch-up on my roots. A massage would be good, too. I *needed* a massage. And a facial. Stress lines were probably wreaking havoc with my skin.

While Billy rang up my purchases, punching in the price of each item by hand, I picked up a *Rumton Review.* The town's version of a newspaper, it was a weekly newsletter that Billy produced on his computer in the back room. He explained that stories were routed to him via fax machine or gossip, and a local teenager took a picture for him once in a while. But what caught my attention was the back page of classified advertisements, which gave me an idea. I needed information about the history of Rumton and figured Pop wouldn't mind if I used his phone number for people to contact me. I'd already used his phone more in two days than it had been used in two months—or so he said. Without writing anything down, Billy listened to what I wanted my ad to say.

"Can do. That'll cost you a ten-spot. Oh, and don't be surprised if it's more'n a week till the next *Review* hits the newsstands. I always aim to get it out on time, but sometimes things get busy around here. Get busy around here."

I'd have to ask Pop if getting shot had caused Billy to repeat things.

Rubbing the spot on his forehead, he nodded. "Yep, can get real busy around here."

I thought about my Sunday morning tradition: stretching out on my balcony with the three-inch thick *Atlanta Journal-Constitution*, a chocolate-dipped biscotto, and a giant cup of coffee. I'd pore over the arts and leisure section, read book and movie reviews, check out travel stories, and flip through a stack of sale flyers. Feeling a bout of homesickness, I decided that I needed to get my assignment done and get the heck out of Rumton. Sooner rather than later.

"No problem, uh, Billy," I said. "By the way, where are the *Rumton Review* newsstands?"

"Aw, they're not stands, really. It's just a figure of speech. I print up a hundred or so copies and put a stack on the counter at Bull's place, one at the theater, and another stack at Duckies."

"What's Duckies?"

"That's Walter's place. A pub. Horseshoes every Thursday and karaoke every Saturday."

So Rumton had entertainment, after all. People threw rings of metal at poles sticking out of the ground on Thursday, watched an outdated movie on Friday, and listened to one another sing badly on Saturday.

"Thank you, thank you," Billy said when I left.

Returning to Pop's house, I was greeted by a large dog I surmised was Flush. Tail wagging at full speed, he shoved his nose into my bag of groceries. Right behind Flush, Bandit snatched the car keys from my hand and ducked behind a tree.

"Hey, you little thief! Bring those back here!"

Chasing her inside, I found Riley and Pop playing a game of cards at the kitchen table. Skipping pleasantries, I dropped the food on the counter. "Which way did she go?"

Pop shuffled the deck and dealt two hands. "You won't find

her, lass, if she's of a mind to hide. But no worries." He grinned at me. "I know where she keeps her stash."

"Good, then you can get my car keys back while I cook your dinner. We're having pork chops, mashed potatoes, broccoli, and rolls."

"It won't take you long to recover the keys. Aye, there's an old spittoon by the living room fireplace. Take a gander in there. They'll be on top."

A faraway look suddenly came over Pop's face, and I realized he was staring at me. Or, rather, the cotton top I wore.

"What's wrong?"

He smiled, but his face held sadness. "Nothing's wrong. Just made me think of Suzie, you wearing that top. I thought I gave all her clothes to the church."

I looked down at the shirt. It was a simple white scoop neck, with orange stitching around the collar and sleeves. Seeing the expression on Pop's face, I felt awful. "I'm so sorry. It was hanging in the closet, and, well I guess I should have asked before I put it on. I didn't know."

"It's okay, lass. No worries. It looks pretty. You ought to keep it."

Riley laid down some cards. "Suzie's been gone for more'n thirty years, and he still pines for that woman."

"Have you ever wanted to get remarried, Pop?"

"Heck, no!" Riley answered for him. "There was some ripe pickins 'round here, too, twenty-five, thirty years ago."

I found my keys, and Pop formally introduced me to Flush while I familiarized myself with the kitchen and started dinner. I'd heard that meat should be marinated before cooking it and decided to give Sheila's method a try. She marinated everything in a formula of Coke and bourbon for at least an hour, and I knew firsthand that her meals were delicious. I dumped the pork chops into a bowl and added the cola and booze. So far, so good.

"It smells mighty good in there," Riley said, even though I

hadn't actually started cooking anything. It was his way of inviting himself to eat. "You got enough to fill another belly?"

"Sure," I said and added another pork chop to my marinade. And since Flush had shown up, I added another and finally threw the last one into the bowl, thinking that one of the men might want a second helping, if Bandit didn't get to it first. I might as well go ahead and cook the entire package.

Next, I washed potatoes, jabbed them with a fork, and stuck them in the microwave. Thank God Pop had a microwave. If I was expected to cook on occasion, I needed all the help I could get. I had no idea how long it took to boil potatoes and figured the microwave would be quicker, anyhow.

I wasn't sure about microwaving the broccoli, though, and decided it would taste better steamed. Dropping it in a pot, I added a little water and turned on the heat. Next, I arranged the frozen rolls in a pie tin and stuck them in the oven to cook. Three hundred and fifty degrees for twenty minutes, the package said. No problem.

Looking at my watch, I realized I'd done it all in about ten minutes! The whole cooking thing wouldn't be so bad after all. Feeling victorious, I rewarded myself with a glass of chardonnay. It wasn't the Beringer I usually drank, but it was all the general store had in stock, and it wasn't too bad.

"Well, we're waitin', Jaxie," Riley said, patting a seat at the table. "Come an' tell us all about it."

I joined them. "All about what?"

"Yer first official day traipsin' around Rumton!"

"Well, I haven't learned much about the infrastructure yet, but I met a lot of people that are really, uh . . . quite fascinating." Bizarre was more like it.

" 'Round here?" he said. "Fascinatin' people?"

Flush nuzzled my hand, wanting to be petted, and I obliged him. "Sure. A circus clown judge who hears cases in a movie theater, a pharmacist who opens for business only when someone wakes her up, and a man who carves beautiful sculptures but doesn't bother to sell them."

Pop looked confused. "What's so unusual 'bout all that? In Atlanta, you got a judge with three wives in three different cities, a pharmacist headed to the brig for selling pain pills to young'ns, and an artist painting canvases with endangered reptile feces. I read that newspaper of yours. Last Sunday's, I believe it was."

I didn't subscribe to the daily paper because I didn't have time to read it. But I never missed a Sunday edition and had brought last week's paper with me. Pop must have thoroughly read all the local news stories that I always skipped over.

"We're just plain ol' ordinary folk 'round here," Pop continued. "You want to cross paths with fascinating people, seems to me Atlanta's got a good supply."

It was clear we came from opposite sides of the world. "Atlanta has a lot more people, that's for sure. I think I met every single person in this town today. Except the mayor. I really need to introduce myself to Mayor Handstill and discuss his thoughts on revitalization."

Riley stuck out his hand. "Pleezed to meet ya."

"You're the mayor?"

"Got it by default when Cappy kicked the bucket. Nobody ran against me."

"You didn't run," Pop reminded him. "You were a write-in."

Riley shook his head. "Still don't know who in the hell wrote me in."

Before I could answer, Bandit made unhappy chirping sounds and danced around our feet. I smelled something burning and jumped up to find smoke spiraling from the stove top. Not only was the broccoli blackened, but it stuck to the bottom of the pot. I dropped it in the sink and turned the faucet on, which created a giant cloud of hissing steam. Bandit made little sounds of delight, laughing at me. Pop and Riley observed from the table without comment.

"I was just going to steam it, but the water must've been a tad low," I explained, wondering if I could shave off the parts not stuck and serve them as chopped broccoli. "Vegetables are better for you when they're steamed."

Pop nodded and drew a card. Riley shrugged. "Well, at least there's still the mashed potatoes and rolls," he said.

Not wanting to scorch the potatoes, too, I pulled them out of the microwave, burning my fingertips in the process. They felt hard instead of soft and mushy, so they might have been undercooked. But I figured the mashing part would soften them up. Rummaging through the cabinets, I found an antique-looking hand mixer that, judging from the amount of dust on it, hadn't been used in years. Irritating my already burned fingers, I sliced the potatoes into quarters and dropped them in a bowl. When I turned on the mixer, its little motor let out a high-pitched squeal and the beaters jammed.

"Ain't ya gonna put some milk and butter in there?" Riley said. My backseat chef for the evening, he kept one eye on his hand of cards and the other on me.

"Of course, I am," I said, and did so. The second time I turned on the mixer, something exploded and an eruption of hot, milk-drenched potato chunks pelted me in the face. Seizing the opportunity, Bandit jumped onto my shoulder to pluck pieces from my hair. Just as happy with my mishap, Flush lapped at the floor.

"Well, at least there's still the rolls to go with the pork chops," Riley said with a shrug.

"Oh, damn!" I'd forgotten about the pork chops, and they weren't going to cook themselves.

"Gin." Pop laid down a hand of cards, unconcerned about the mess I had made in his kitchen.

I tried to remember how my pork chop was cooked the last time I'd ordered one in a restaurant. It was covered with shrimp and some type of cream sauce, but I recalled seeing the telltale crisscross markings made by a grill. "Pop, do you have a grill?"

"Aye, beneath the big oak tree at the side of the deck."

I found it easily enough and turned on the propane tank, as I'd seen people do at cookouts. But after pushing the red starter button a bunch of times, still no flames appeared. Like everything else around Pop's place, the grill was old. Back inside, Pop had just won another hand of gin rummy. I asked if there was a trick to lighting the grill.

"Nah," Riley answered for him. "Just turn on yer gas and toss a matchstick in there."

Trying not to accidentally brush against the soot-blackened grill, I went through a half pack of matches before a lit one finally went through the cracks of the grate and remained lit when it hit the bottom of the grill. The resulting fireball that shot out made me scream, and Pops, Riley, Flush, and Bandit appeared all at once. Stunned, I patted myself down to make sure nothing was in flames. Grilling always looked so easy when other people did it.

"Singed the tips of your hair, you did," Pop observed. He moved in for a closer look at my face, green eye sparkling. "Eyelashes, too. You okay, lass?"

"I'm perfectly fine," I insisted as I caught a whiff of burning hair and cringed at the thought of what my stylist would say when he saw the damage. "I just wanted to get it good and hot, to uh, sear the meat and seal in the natural juices." Although I'd seen that tip on Emeril's cooking show while channel surfing, Riley didn't buy it.

"Yer supposed to turn on yer gas and light it right then," he said, shaking his bald head. "Not ten minutes later."

Ignoring him, I placed the Coke- and bourbon-soaked meat on the grill, shut the lid, and went back inside to finish the potatoes. Miserably, the result resembled potato soup with small hard chunks in it. I shoved the bowl back into the microwave and punched in ten minutes. They couldn't get any worse.

A glass of wine later, I pulled the rolls out of the oven only to find hard golf-ball-sized chunks of heavy dough.

"Double damn!"

"Did you let the dough rise before it went into the oven?" Pop said, fetching a beer from the refrigerator.

"Rise? What are you talking about?"

"Those frozen rolls you bought, lass. They have to thaw out and the dough ought to rise."

"You should have got the kind that don't have to rise," Riley commented. "They even make some you can microwave. But you musta bought the kind you have to let rise."

"How could I have let them rise?" I almost yelled, wondering why he hadn't said something before. "I just got here! And who knew dough is supposed to rise, anyway? What's that all about?"

Pop shrugged and took a swig from his bottle of beer.

Riley shuffled the cards. "Well, at least there's still the pork chops."

"Oh, damn, damn, damn!" I ran outside to find meat that was charcoal black on one side and bloody raw on the other.

"Cusses like a sailor, that one," I heard Riley say through the open door.

Pop chuckled. "And cooks like a deckhand."

5

"Go away!"

Ignoring me, Bandit remained perched on the dresser. Propped up in bed with my laptop, I pored over my e-mail inbox. It was nearing lunchtime, and I'd slept through breakfast.

"You're making me nervous, wondering what you're going to take next. And if you even think about swiping my new couture watch, your furry ass is grass. Got it?"

She scurried off the dresser and brazenly got in bed to get a better look at my computer. She put both little furry hands on the edge of the wireless card that connected me with the outside world via satellite Internet, and tugged.

"I've got one word for you, Bandit." She stopped pulling on the device and cocked her head.

"Taxidermist," I said slowly. As if understanding my threat, she backed up and sat on her haunches to watch from a few feet away.

My e-mail was the usual stack of inquiries and electronic newsletters. There was a message from Sheila, asking if there were any good-looking guys in Rumton. I sent a one sentence reply: *I wish*. The next e-mail was from Mark, asking if I was ready to marry him yet. I sent another one sentence reply: *No*. I preferred my men in short-term doses, like a month or two at the most. I couldn't comprehend spending the rest of my life with anyone.

From Justin, the subject line on another message said simply, *Hello*. I almost deleted it without reading it first but quickly changed my mind. After all, he was in charge of research. He could have some information for me.

> Just wanted to say hello. I've been thinking about you and wondering how you're getting along. It's apparent you're on the ball, based on the data you're having the interns gather. If you need anything, give me a call. I haven't been to Rumton in a while and thought about paying a visit this weekend. Might see you then.

Oh, great. Mr. Zero Personality might pay a visit. And why had he been to Rumton before anyway? I was curious but decided not to lead him on, even virtually. He probably wasn't serious about visiting anyhow, and I certainly didn't want to encourage the trip. On several occasions, he'd asked me to dinner or invited me to a charity event or a Braves baseball game, but I'd always declined. I didn't want to open any doors now.

Another message from Aaron reminded me to try one of his Aunt Millie's peanut butter cookies. The postscript instructed me to overnight him a box next time she baked a fresh batch. She always made three dozen at a time, he wrote, and they were the best I'd ever taste. Although I'd been in Rumton a week, I'd been so busy doing research that I hadn't yet met Mad Millie. The thought of cat hair swirling through the air made my nose itch, but I needed to at least knock on her door and introduce myself. And eat a cookie or two. Maybe I could avoid the cats altogether if I invited her to Pop's house for dinner and asked if she'd bring the famous cookies for dessert. Surely my next attempt at dinner would be edible. Better yet, maybe Pop would cook.

As I was finishing checking messages by replying to a friend—I was mad because I would miss her birthday party at the Cotton Club and punching the keyboard much harder than necessary to put words on the screen—Pop knocked on the open bedroom door and handed me the telephone.

Aaron's booming voice rumbled through the line. "Enjoying the quiet life, Jaxie?"

"Yes, sir." Of course, I wasn't enjoying it. But then, he already knew that.

"Great. How about you give me a progress report? Any ideas brewing?"

"Well, it's been only a week, so mainly I've been working to learn what I can about Rumton." I took a deep breath and tried to summarize a dismal picture into a few sentences. "The infrastructure isn't the best . . . Water and sewer systems are less than favorable and all electric lines are aboveground. There is no wireless phone service or cable television in place. Police and EMS services need to be modernized, and the single schoolhouse for all grades, even though there are very few school-age kids, will deter families with children from relocating here. Of course, I'm not telling you anything you don't already know, but the lack of medical professionals, shopping venues, and arts programs creates a real problem."

"True, that's everything I already know."

I was at a loss for anything positive to say. "Rumton's proximity to the ocean is the best thing the town has going for it, but even that doesn't help since it remains maddeningly landlocked."

"So what do you suggest we do?"

"I think we need to hire an environmental consultant. A scientist who can do a survey to determine several things. Mainly, I want to find out if there is a feasible way to gain direct access to the water." I pulled up some notes on the computer. "Pop, the man I'm staying wi—"

"I know Pop," Aaron cut me off. "Heck, I used to hang out at his house as a kid. We all did, after school."

It was easy to forget that my boss grew up in this godforsaken place. Nobody would ever guess it to look at him now.

"Well, Pop says that in the past, there was an inlet. Shrimpers used it to get their boats out to sea, but it slowly filled in over time until it became completely unnavigable."

"Go on."

"Considering its remote location, not to mention that there is practically no labor pool and less-than-desirable amenities, we won't be able to get the big business sector interested in Rumton."

"I agree. Unless it was a company who needed a lot of cheap land for a specific purpose and didn't want to deal with municipal red tape. But that would be the type of industry we don't want in Rumton, anyway."

"Right. So I'm thinking the best chance at revitalization lies in either residential development marketed to retirees who want a get-away-from-it-all lifestyle, or tourism. Maybe some of both." Bandit suddenly reappeared, making me jump. I glared at her before continuing, but she didn't take the hint to get off the bed. "Surrounding coastal towns draw hordes of retirees and tourists, but they use the water to do it. You know, boating and fishing and the promise of a relaxing coastal lifestyle. The appeal of seeing the sun rise over the water and all that."

His silence indicated that he agreed.

"The good news is that Rumton has great weather. We just need to figure out if there's a way to capitalize on the ocean and the nearby Intracoastal Waterway."

"How much will an environmental survey cost?" Even on a pro bono project, it always boiled down to the raw numbers.

"I'll find out and get back to you. I'm not sure how involved it will be, but the main thing to determine is where the old inlet was and find out if it could be reopened with dredging or some-thing. And, of course, if the land is suitable for development."

"Interesting possibility."

"Or maybe, financing could be obtained to build a bridge that jumped all the marshy wetlands and dumped out on the beach, so you could get there by car."

"Another interesting possibility," he said. "Okay. Get me some environmental survey estimates. Produce a rundown sheet of what information you want to obtain and send it out for bids. And take a drive to the next town to buy a fax machine for Pop's house. Be sure to keep the receipt and expense it," he said. "And Jaxie?"

"Yes, sir?"

"Good work. Keep it up."

I found Pop in the kitchen making a pot of something that smelled incredible. Since my dinner fiasco, he'd done most of the cooking, although I had managed to pitch in with a few meals of lunchmeat sandwiches and potato chips. It was pretty hard to screw that up.

"So do you know any environmental consultants?" I asked, with a laugh.

"Aye."

"You do?"

"My nephew, Avery. He hangs his hat in Charlotte but skirts about the country working jobs. It's mainly the land developers that keep money in his pocket."

"What does he do? And whom does he work for?"

"He's a marine scientist, among other things, and worked for a big research company. But a couple years back, he got fed up with the politics and went to work as an independent contractor, making top dollar. Doesn't dance 'round the issues to keep politicians happy, like he had to before."

The fact that Pop had family in the business was great, but, unfortunately, "top dollar" were two words Aaron wouldn't want to hear.

"Well, I have to find a consultant to do a survey of Rumton. And a feasibility study. But Shine Advertising and PR won't want to pay a lot of money, not for a pro bono effort."

Pop's green eye sparkled. "Let's ring him up and see what 'appens."

He dialed the number from memory and spoke into the handset for a few minutes before handing it over to me.

"Uh, hello?" I said, caught off guard.

"So you're Jaxie," Avery said in a velvety deep tone that instantly made me wonder if he had the looks to back it up. "And you're going to save the town."

I heard a faint chuckle, or perhaps I just imagined it. I began to wish I'd never told Pop, Riley, and Bull that my assignment was to "save the town." Like a bad jingle from a television commercial, the phrase had stuck, and it sounded ridiculous every time I heard it repeated.

"Well, yes," I said, a bit embarrassed. "That's why my firm sent me here, anyway."

"Tell me what you need, and I'll see if I can free up some time to get down there and help you out."

"Great. But I have to warn you—this is a pro bono project for an advertising and PR firm. My boss, Aaron Ackworth, grew up here, but since Rumton isn't a paying client, we probably can't pay your normal rate. I have to send the job out for bids."

"I'm familiar with your firm. And there's no need to look for bids."

"You are? And why not?"

"Because my price is free. Now, tell me what it is you're after."

"Free?" Nobody gave away anything for free, especially when he was in business for himself. "Why free?"

"Pop is like a father to me and I'd do anything for him. And he seems to have taken a liking to you."

"He has?"

"And besides," Avery continued, "some volunteer work might be just the thing for me right now. I could use the tax write-off."

I inhaled deeply. "Okay, here goes. I'd like to find out where the old inlet is located, the one the shrimpers used eighty years ago, and if there's any way to get water flowing through it again. Deep enough water to accommodate a forty- or fifty-foot boat." I knew that recreational boaters with money, the kind of retirees who might think it attractive to move to a quaint small town, would want a marina with slips to accommodate their upscale toys. "I also need a feasibility study on whether or not the land in Rumton is developable. You know, condos with a view. An up-scale residential retirement community with a golf course or two. That sort of thing. And, lastly, I need to know if there are any natural resources that could bring in revenue."

This time I definitely heard a chuckle. "Is that all?"

"Pretty much."

We chatted for some time, and the rich tone of his voice intrigued me. I hoped he wasn't a geek. Or married. Or ugly.

"So, tell me, Jaxie, what do you get out of working this assignment?" Avery said, after informing me he'd be in Rumton before the week was out.

"Besides my regular paycheck, you mean? I get to get the heck out of here when I'm done."

Still wondering what Avery looked like, I brought my laptop to the kitchen table and shot off some more assignments to the interns. I wanted a report on available federal or private grant money tagged for anything along the lines of coastal development, floodwater control, improving rural schools, small town business development, or arts programs. I understood that grant money wouldn't save the town, but it was a start.

Pop set two Pepsis on the table and asked if I wanted a glass of ice. "No thanks. I'll just drink it from the bottle. At least that way Bandit can't dunk stuff in it."

An instant message popped up on the computer screen. It was one of the interns, who had just read my e-mail.

Grants on flood control? Rumton has flooding problems? It read.

No, but it could, I fired back, typing furiously. *I don't care if it's a foundation that promotes mass transportation by pogo sticks! I want to know of every single grant over $10K the town could feasibly apply for.*

Carrying two bowls of something that resembled lumpy cream soup, Pop joined me at the table. Almost immediately, Flush and Bandit materialized to beg. Or, in Bandit's case, to steal.

I pushed the laptop aside to make room in front of me. "What's this? It smells great."

"Chicken and dumplings. Eat up."

I took a closer look, frowning. "What's a dumpling?" Sheila warned me that country people would eat anything: calves' brains, pigs' feet, rattlesnake meat. Anything that walked or crawled and could be caught and cooked, she'd said.

"Just boiled dough, made from flour. Give it a try."

I took a tentative bite and chewed. It tasted as good as it smelled. My appetite revved up and I dug in. "It's like chicken noodle soup, but better."

Pop sat down to eat. "How'd you e'er grow up without eating chicken and dumplings?"

My mother didn't cook, I explained. Growing up, I ate most meals at the nearby twenty-four-hour diner.

"What about your father? He cook?"

"I never had a father."

Another instant message popped onto the screen, and I angled the laptop so I could read it. It was Sheila, telling me to go easy on the interns. One of them was questioning her decision to pursue a career in the seemingly glamorous world of advertising. I put down my spoon to reply. *Tell her that someday she'll be able to terrorize a few interns of her own.*

"Do you have to work while you eat lunch, too?"

"Oh, sorry," I said. "I'm being rude. I don't usually eat at a table."

He stopped grinding a peppermill to give me a dubious sideways look.

"I mean I *have* a dining room table," I continued. "But since it's just me, I usually eat at the kitchen counter or on the sofa. Mostly, I eat out."

"Huh," he said, shooing Bandit off his lap. I shut the laptop and apologized again.

"It's bad for your digestion to eat and work at the same time. Might ought to take a break and enjoy your dumplings."

Keeping Bandit at bay with one hand and eating with the other, I did just that. When we finished lunch, Pop cleared the dishes while I offered to feed Flush. Feeding people wasn't so easy, but feeding a dog, I could do. Pop's recipe was easy: two cups of dry food with a splash of olive oil.

I found Flush's bowls against a wall on the kitchen floor and dumped the kibbles in one of them. The dog shoved his snout in and munched away. While he ate, I rinsed out the other bowl to fill it with fresh water. Upon closer inspection, I noticed that the cream-colored opaque glass had a pattern of intricate tiny flowers and a large flowing dragon. A metal band capped the rim. About the size of a punch bowl, except with a wide foot on it, Flush's water bowl would have looked very nice as a home accessory. The food bowl was similar but smaller. Together, the two would have looked great on my coffee table.

"These sure are odd dog bowls," I commented. "They look like something I'd use in my apartment for decoration."

"Like them that much," Pop said, "you can have them."

They were really quite striking, in a minimalist sort of way, and I almost wanted to take Pop up on the offer. His generosity was genuine, and I knew that he'd gladly part with the bowls simply because I thought they were pretty. "Where did you get them?"

"Been 'round e'er since I can remember, so they were my grandpappy's. Found them in a box when I was searching for the coffee percolator. Ne'er did find the percolator, but figured the bowls would work well for the dog. He can't tip them o'er."

I decided against packing them in my luggage, even though I really wanted the pair because they were unique. "Thanks for the offer, but I can't take Flush's bowls." Mismatched and chipped, Pop's dishes were out of fashion and in need of replacement. But the dog ate out of decorator bowls. I smiled, thinking that both seemed equally content. Their pleasure was in the food they ate, not what they ate it from.

Pop finished cleaning the kitchen and talked me into taking the rest of the day off. Chalking it up to research, I agreed to accompany him to his favorite crabbing spot.

After loading his Chevy truck with lawn chairs, coolers of ice, drinks, crabbing supplies, and Flush, we bounced over dirt roads for three or four miles before ending up on something that looked more like a hiking path than a road. A mixture of pines, oaks, and wild brush enveloped the truck, scraping the sides. The bumpy trail reminded me that I had to pee, and it suddenly struck me that we were miles from anyplace with a toilet. Being so isolated with an old man I barely knew was a strange feeling. On the other hand, something about Pop was comforting and familiar, as though I'd known him forever.

We slowed, and recognizing the spot, Flush jumped from the truck before it came to a complete stop. Nose to the ground and tail wagging like crazy, he bounded off to explore. Suddenly the woods cleared and the view was so incredible that I forgot about my complaining bladder. We parked at the edge of an expansive flat marsh, interwoven with winding channels of perfectly calm water that mirrored their surroundings. Patches of tall wispy grass stretched toward a cloudless blue sky. A cluster of white birds with long beaks and even longer legs stood in a clearing.

Climbing from the truck, I could see a sliver of ocean beyond the marsh, perhaps a mile away. Like shimmering pale glass, it stretched along the horizon as far as I could see in either direction, and it was difficult to tell where the water ended and the sky began.

As I took in the magnificent view, Pop unloaded the truck. "Cold beer, m'dear?"

I accepted a can and we both took a swig as we settled into the chairs he'd put out. "Pop, it's awesome. What an amazing view."

"Aye."

"Why didn't you tell me about this place before? When I went exploring, I ended up where the main road stopped. In a swamp, or wetlands, or whatever you call them. But I had no idea Rumton butted up to something like this. It's incredible."

The corners of his mouth flickered upward in a brief smile. "A small town oft' holds secrets and surprises. There is a bit more to Rumton than you might think."

"That's for sure," I said, breathing in the briny scent and trying to commit the tranquil scene to memory. "But you can't get a boat anywhere through here?"

He shook his head. "The channels are too narrow and too shallow, even at high tide. At low tide, they're naught but puddles o'er a layer of silt."

"So there's no way to get from here to the ocean? It's like, right there!"

"Aye." Pop pulled something yellowish and slimy from a cooler. "I reckon you could pull on a pair of hip waders and make the hike at low tide. Be pretty tough going, though. You'd sink with every step. Have to keep an eye out for gators and snakes, too."

I almost dashed for the truck. "Alligators and snakes?"

"Got to live somewhere. Just like us." He tied a piece of string around the slimy bait, tossed it into the shallow water in front of us, and did the same with a second piece before handing me the string attached to it.

"What is that you're putting in the water?"

"Chicken necks."

My stomach rolled, making me forget about the alligators and snakes. "Oh, gross!"

He shrugged. "Crabs don't think so."

Panting, Flush returned and plopped down between our chairs while Pop taught me how to catch a crab. He explained how commercial fishermen anchored crab pots and marked them with brightly colored buoys. But we needed only enough crabs to throw on the stove for dinner, and the string method worked just fine for that. All we had to do was wait for the crabs to come tug on the bait and then scoop them out of the water. Easy enough.

We held our strings and drank our beers while I questioned Pop about growing up in Rumton. "What was it like?"

A smile spread across his face. "I couldn't imagine any better place to be a boy. Me and my friends, we could get lost for an entire day exploring these woods, tracking down the location of a particularly loud frog or climbing an old oak tree. We each had our favorite tree with thick curved branches that were low enough to the ground so as you could hop right on." He pointed to just such a tree, behind where we sat. "Like that beauty there. It's more than two hundred years old, I'll bet."

I wasn't sure if I'd ever seen a tree that old before and twisted in my chair to admire it. Stately and proud, the tree's limbs stretched gracefully in several directions and I could easily imagine boys scampering up them, perhaps playing hide and seek.

"I also loved spending time with my grandpappy. E'ery day was an adventure, especially on his boat." Pop sighed, remembering. "Some of my best times were on the water, even if we were anchored and playing cards or backgammon."

I wondered what my childhood would have been like had I grown up in a small town with a father or grandfather. I felt a peculiar sense of loss, as though I'd been cheated out of something that kids are supposed to experience.

He caught my expression and asked about my childhood. After a few minutes of trying to figure out how to explain it, I told him the truth. That, while my adolescence wasn't particularly bad, nothing fabulous stood out in my memory. "Things were pretty basic for me growing up, I guess. As normal as they could be with a single mom who struggled to pay the bills. That is, until she learned how to use men to better our lives."

Pop looked at me, seeking an explanation.

Unaccustomed to talking so openly about my life, I shrugged and plowed on. "She was a beautiful woman and decided that she could just as easily date rich men as poor men. That's how we got to eat at nice restaurants and go on vacations. She did the best she could to make a good life for me. But I never went tromping in the woods or fishing or crabbing or did any activity that was just me and her. Mainly, I just did school stuff. Summers, I'd play with my friends at their houses or on the playground. Swim at the YMCA. And when I got old enough, go see movies or hang out at the mall."

He laughed. "Me, I'd rather be anywhere than stuck inside a shopping mall."

I grinned at him. "Me, I drool at the thought of spending an entire Saturday afternoon scouring the stores for bargains. It just doesn't get any better than a shoe sale at Scott Cepada's or a fifty-percent-off rack at Macy's."

"Maybe, but there's only so much a person can use."

He was right, but I didn't concede the point entirely. "Okay, I'll give you that. I probably needlessly buy things, just because they're on sale. But every once in a while, you find a treasure that you just can't live without, even if you don't really *need* it!"

The green eye sparkled. "Aye. Like my boat."

As we sat and enjoyed the afternoon, the complete absence of people and traffic startled me. Unfamiliar sounds caressed my ear canals: the rustle of tree leaves rubbing together behind us, the piercing cries of seagulls in front of us, and what may have been the distant sound of the rolling ocean. I brought up the subject of Pop's wife and asked why they never had any kids.

"Suzie ne'er got pregnant, much as we both wished it. Just wasn't meant to be."

"Well, I think you would have made a wonderful father," I said, when something tugged on my string. I jumped and dropped my beer. With a splash, the can rolled into the water and my line went slack.

Pop chuckled. "Scared by a little blue crab, are you?"

"Of course not! I just wasn't ready, and now I've frightened it off." My first time ever to catch a crab and I blew it.

"No worries. It'll come back. When you feel the tug again, pull in your string real slow." He gave me a long-handled net. "As soon as you see the crab, scoop it out of the water with this. Got to be quick with the net, before it lets go."

I waited and watched, but my line remained slack. Pop handed me another beer. I watched the line some more. "I forgot to tell you that I put an ad in the *Rumton Review* to see if anyone has information on Rumton's history. I put your number in there for people to call me. I hope that's okay."

He nodded. "E'erybody knows e'erybody else's number 'round here, anyhow. What are you searching for?"

"I'm not sure, exactly. I suppose anything that might give me some clues on what Rumton used to be like. What people did for a living. How the town first got started."

"That will help?" he said.

"I don't know. Maybe I'll learn something that will give me a fantastic idea."

An almost imperceptible shudder moved across the slack string. I jumped to attention. "It's back!"

"Pull it in easy. Get the net in position."

Making sure not to lose the crab that munched on my chicken neck, I pulled it to the surface and, with a quick sweeping motion, snagged it. "Got it!"

Pop removed my crab from the net, explained how to hold it so I wouldn't get pinched, and passed it to me. "Put it in the blue cooler there, lass, and let's see if we can net a few more."

I'd barely gotten the cooler lid open when the crab went wild in my hand. I screamed and threw it toward the cooler but missed. It scuttled sideways back into the water.

"It tried to pinch me!" I said in explanation. Flush sat up to bark at the disappearing crustacean. Pop laughed a deep full-body belly laugh.

Determined to catch another crab, I swung my chicken neck back into position. It flew off the end of the string.

"How about I cook us a few steaks on the grill tonight?" Pop half said and half laughed. "You *can* put together a salad, eh?"

I pretended to be offended. "Yes, I know how to make a salad." *Sort of.*

"Tide's headed out anyway. Can't catch much during low tide. Blue crabs are swimmers."

Still chuckling, Pop pulled out an ancient-looking camera and snapped a few pictures of me and Flush. Poking fun at myself, I posed with the empty net. Then it was my turn with the camera, and I took a few shots of Pop relaxing, feet propped on the cooler. Before putting the camera away, I pointed the lens toward the marsh and captured a couple of magnificent shots of the landscape.

We gave up on picture taking and crabbing and, in no hurry to get anywhere, drank our beers and watched a dropping sun throw prisms of orange and pink across winding fingers of water.

I wasn't sure how much time had passed, but when I stood to put our empty cans back in the cooler, my bladder screamed and I remembered that I had to pee. Just thinking of the bumpy dirt roads was painful.

"I don't suppose there's a store or someplace around here with a bathroom, is there?" I asked, knowing there wasn't.

"Just go o'er there in the trees. Nobody 'round here to see you."

"In the trees?" The last time I'd gone in the woods was during my one and only time camping, as a girl. And then, it was inside a Porta-Potti.

"What if . . . something bites me or something?"

"Flush will go with you to keep the critters at bay. I'll pack up."

Squatting in the woods, peeing in the middle of nowhere with a dog as my lookout and shooing mosquitoes away from my exposed bottom, I wondered how things were going at Shine Advertising and PR.

6

I awoke to something tugging on my earlobe. Reaching up, I felt fur, and interrupted a burglary in progress. The raccoon had attempted to steal an earring.

"Get away from me, you two-bit, four-legged thug!"

The night before, I'd uncharacteristically fallen asleep while reading a book on how small towns could reinvent themselves and neglected to wash my face or take out my diamond studs. Bandit managed to loosen one of them enough to make the back come off. Cursing her, I found it tangled in my hair.

I typically never went to bed before midnight and always awoke before six on workdays. But since I'd been in Rumton, I found myself falling asleep earlier and sleeping longer. And yesterday, I'd even taken a nap—something I'd thought was reserved for the geriatric crowd.

The aroma of brewing coffee urged me out of bed, and I realized Pop had a male visitor. Focusing on the sounds of their conversation, I decided the second voice was the same velvety one I'd heard on the phone a few days earlier. Not wanting Avery to see my puffy morning face, I put myself below a cool shower to wake up.

Half an hour later I made my way to the kitchen and almost gasped when the visitor looked at me. The man sitting at the table with Pop was gorgeous.

"Morning, lass," Pop said. "This is my nephew."

Avery stood to shake my hand. A tight T-shirt stretched around a sculpted upper body, showing actual ripples—ripples! And when he smiled at me, it was a celebrity's smile. I could have sworn I saw a starburst of light spin off his teeth, as in the chewing gum commercials on television. "Good morning."

"Good morning to you, too," I managed. Life in Rumton suddenly looked brighter. I poured myself some coffee and refilled Pop's cup. "It's wonderful that you were able to get here so quick."

He aimed the star-quality smile at me again, and an adrenaline rush spread through my body. "I brought all my equipment with me, so I can get started today. But only after one of Pop's notorious breakfasts. You can't get cooking like his anywhere else."

Pop winked at me. "Reckon I better get started on it then."

I sat next to Avery and tried not to drool. "So tell me all about your business. It must be fascinating." It was one of my standard conversation starters.

I paid rapt attention while he told me about the different levels of environmental surveys and explained how each contract job differed from the last, since no two places on earth were exactly alike. I could have listened to him talk for days and decided that he was much more interesting than the last guy I'd dated, who was a GM and Chrysler dealer.

"That's pretty much the nickel version of what I do," he said, reaching down to scratch Flush's head. His ring finger was completely, delightfully naked. "I'm an investigator, really. But nature is my subject instead of people."

Simmering onions and peppers made my mouth water. A block of cheese sat on the counter next to some cubed ham, and it looked as if Pop was cooking omelettes.

"So you're a detective of sorts," I said, throwing my best smile at him. Flirty but not obvious. "It must be hard on your family, though, since you travel so much."

"I don't mind the travel," he said, leaning back in his chair. "And I don't have a wife or kids to worry about."

No ring and no baggage. Yes, my life in Rumton had absolutely taken a turn for the better! Before I could do something stupid, like impulsively run my hands over Avery's ripples, Pop intervened to see who wanted juice with the coffee.

We both did.

"Well, I can't wait to see what you uncover," I told Avery, thinking that it would be fun to watch him uncover his entire body. "It's great of you to help out like this."

"No problem. But I have to give you a heads-up on something. You mentioned the old inlet—just so you know, odds are slim to none that we can do anything to open it up. Environmental rules have really gotten strict in recent years due to all the coastal development, a lot of which has really damaged the environment. You have to follow county ordinances, plus there are state regulations from various agencies, and the Army Corps of Engineers on top of that. It's gotten really tough to do anything that involves disrupting marsh or wetlands."

"That's disheartening."

He shrugged. "It was necessary, although now some people think the regulations are too restrictive. But, in any event, we'll get your survey done."

"I'm serving from the stove, so grab you a plate and come fill it up!"

Effortlessly, Pop whipped up omelettes, sautéed mushrooms, hash browns, and a fresh fruit salad sprinkled with mint leaves and walnuts. When we loaded our plates and sat down, he brought a basket of toasted English muffins and a pitcher of juice to the table.

"Pop, you're the best," I moaned appreciatively through a bite. "You could open a restaurant. Or be a famous TV chef!"

"Jaxie is accustomed to eating out," Pop explained to Avery. "She can't cook."

"I can too cook!" I fibbed.

Pop raised a bushy eyebrow at me.

"Sort of," I added.

"Aye, she can make a mean deli sandwich," Pop said. "Even puts a slice of pickle on the plate."

Avery laughed. "Sounds like Mike. He can't cook worth a damn, even after I made him take a class. His claim to fame is grilled hamburgers and microwaved baked beans."

"Mike?"

"My partner."

"Your business partner?" I persisted.

"My life partner."

"Oh," I said, trying to keep the disappointment off my face. Usually, my gaydar was operative, but I was so starved for male attention that I'd completely missed the mark with Avery. "I mean, I'm cool with that. It's just that . . ."

Pop laughed. "You were flirting with him, but that's okay. All the ladies do."

"I haven't been out with anyone since I got here," I told Avery, "and noticed how incredible-looking you were . . ."

"Still am," he deadpanned, slicking back his hair as if looking in an imaginary mirror.

The awkward moment passed as everyone laughed, and we got to the business of eating. I stole another look at Avery, trying not to be bummed out. God was punishing me for something, I decided. I felt sure of it. First, I get sent to Rumton, and then the only man who's not AARP material turns out gay. *Sheeesh.*

Flush ambled to the back door and woofed. A second later,

someone knocked but entered without waiting for an answer. Avery jumped up to give the visitor a handshake and a hug. "Justin! Pop didn't tell me you were coming. Good to see you, bro."

Shine's vice president of market research got another handshake-hug from Pop.

"Justin. What are you doing here?" I said, stunned. He'd threatened to visit, but I didn't think he was serious. And how did he know Avery?

"Came to see my uncle." Although the ugly glasses remained a fixture on his face, the standard suit had been replaced by a red cotton shirt, khaki shorts, and leather loafers with no socks. It was the first time I'd ever seen his legs. Or arms, for that matter. Even during the summers, he wore only long-sleeved button-downs to the office.

"Your uncle?"

"Avery and Justin are brothers, lass," Pop said.

Clearing dishes from the table, I did a double take from one man to the other and almost dropped a plate. "Brothers?"

Pop nodded.

"Huh," I muttered, filling the sink with soapy water and wondering how a bore like Justin could have emerged from the same womb as a charismatic hunk like Avery. "Why didn't Aaron tell me you were from here? For that matter, why didn't he send you instead of me?"

Justin poured himself some coffee and added cream. "I'm not *from* here, Jaxie. Our mother moved away at sixteen, years before we were born. But as kids, we came to visit Pop as often as we could talk her into it."

Pop had mentioned that his sister left town, giving up her half of the house he inherited. But he neglected to tell me that one of her kids was my coworker! I stared at Pop with narrowed eyes, irritated with him for withholding information. But, cooking an omelette for Justin, he ignored me.

"And as far as Aaron sending me instead of you," Justin continued through a mouthful of fruit salad, "I'm research, remember? You're creative. Not to mention that I have a department to run."

I finished the dishes and joined the men.

"Pass me a muffin, would you, Jaxie?" Justin said.

Knowing the basket was empty, I passed it to him anyway. Perched in a chair, her head barely visible over the tabletop and her cheek pouches full, Bandit happily munched away on the last muffin. Feeling the weight of the basket, Justin frowned.

I grinned. "Looks like she beat you to it."

"Sneaky little vixen," he mumbled to the animal. "I ought to come over there and fight you for it."

As the three of them chatted and shared one another's news, I decided that, away from the office, Justin almost looked like an interesting person. Tanned skin suggested he spent time outdoors, so he must have had a life outside of work. His clothes were plain but shabbily stylish. And he had a pleasantly toned body with biceps that were probably the result of lifting weights or working out on Nautilus machines.

"Being unusually quiet, over there," Pop said. "Cat got your tongue, lass?"

I shook my head. "No, I was just thinking that I should go ahead and get on the road."

"To where?" Justin asked.

"I'm taking the day off and heading to Atlanta for a long weekend. Do some shopping, check on my place, get my mail." *Get back to the real world for a few days so I don't go stir-crazy.*

"Thought your mail is being forwarded," Pop said. "A big envelope full of it comes e'ery few days."

Everyone looked at me.

"Uh, I mean my, uh, *work* mail." My left eyelid twitched, just as it did every time I lied or got stressed out. "I'm sure there is a pile of stuff in my office that I need to sift through."

Justin reached for his duffel bag. "I brought your mail, along with a survival kit from Sheila. She said you were probably missing your Starbucks bottled frappuccino. And she sent a manicure in a can, whatever that is."

"Oh. Thank you." I attempted a smile. "But she didn't need to do that. I mean, I planned to head back this weekend anyway. Just to, uh, check on things."

"Well, do what you need to do," Justin said, polishing off a glass of milk. "But Aaron asked me to come help you out for a few days. And this weekend was the best time for me to get away."

"Besides," Avery said, "shouldn't you be around while I'm doing your survey? I might want to run some findings by you."

He was right. How would it look if I left the same weekend that Avery graciously volunteered? And what would Aaron think if I disappeared after he'd sent in backup? My eyelid did aerobics as my weekend plans deteriorated.

"You're right," I relented. "There's nothing in Atlanta that can't wait."

"Good," Avery said, handing me a two-way radio. "I'm going to head out and get started, then. Keep your radio on, so we can chat. It's already set to the right channel. If you hear me call, just push the button to talk. Release it to listen."

"Ten four," I said, stifling a sigh. I had to keep my eye on the prize. The sooner Avery did his work, the sooner I could finish my assignment and go home. "But I need to get a fax machine so I can send and receive stuff from the office. Is it okay if I'm out of touch for a few hours this morning? I'll have to drive to a town with an office supplies store to get one."

"Sure. Just leave your radio with Pop until you get back."

"Why don't I go with you?" Pop said to Avery.

"Even better."

I waited for Justin to say that he'd join Avery, too, but suspected otherwise.

"While they're out romping in the marsh, why don't I help you shop for your fax machine?" Justin said. "I'll even drive."

My eyelid twitched so violently that I had to shut it for a moment. I prayed Justin didn't perceive the motion as a wink. "Uh, sure. That would be fine."

A surprising amount of traffic flowed in both directions as we headed north on Highway 17. I asked Justin where all the people had come from. It was a surprisingly well-traveled road.

"DOT statistics indicate that the volume of traffic on this stretch of highway remains steady year-round," Justin said from behind the wheel, making good on his offer to chauffeur me. "You've got travelers coming from feeder cities to visit tourist destinations like Charleston and Savannah. And people going the other direction to visit popular North Carolina spots like Southport and Wilmington. In the summer, it's families with kids. In the spring and fall, it's retirees and golfers. Plus, a fair amount of northerners head south to winter each year, so they're driving this route. And then, there's always the usual general business traffic and truckers."

He was a walking, breathing spreadsheet. I almost rolled my eyes before I realized something important.

"So all these people whiz right by Rumton every day?"

"Of course. But there's no reason for them to stop. Most probably don't even realize the town is there."

He was right. Other than a weatherbeaten faded sign, nothing indicated that a town lived between the highway and the ocean. It stated simply: RUMTON. YA'LL HIDEOUT.

"What does the slogan mean, anyway? Ya'll hideout?"

Justin thought for a few seconds. "Good question. Maybe it's an invitation for people to hideout here, as in stay awhile and relax. We'll have to ask Pop when we get back."

"Holy cow! The famous research guru is stumped," I teased from the passenger seat.

He smiled. "A good challenge is half the fun of doing research."

"What's the other half?"

"The prize. Solving the puzzle. Getting what I want."

Although historic Georgetown would have been much closer, we decided to pass it and keep driving until we reached Myrtle Beach. The area had a reputation for drawing millions of visitors every year to its various tourist attractions, and I wanted to see if I could pick up any good ideas for Rumton.

Highway 17 stretched all the way from the mountains of Winchester, Virginia to Florida's Gulf Coast at Ponte Vedra, Justin explained as we drove. Portions of the road were in use prior to the Revolutionary War, he said, and probably followed ancient Indian foot trails that ran north-south along the coast. Laughing, I told him the amount of trivia and general knowledge he possessed astounded me.

"Mostly useless stuff," he said, glancing at me with a grin, "but fun to know. I mean, hey. It's impressing you." Half an hour and more trivia later, we hit a string of quaint beach towns.

"Very pricey real estate along here," Justin commented. "But these folks can waltz right up to the ocean or dock a boat in their backyard."

When we got closer to Myrtle Beach, miles of big box stores, strip malls, beachwear shops, restaurants, and miniature golf courses outlined our approach. We found an electronics store and accomplished our mission. Walking back to the car, we decided it would be a nice gesture to leave the combination fax, copier, and telephone answering machine with Pop after my assignment ended. It was a pretty high-tech gadget for his place, but if nothing else, Bandit would have some fun trying to steal the shiny buttons off it.

"And speaking of your assignment, I get the impression you aren't thrilled," he said as we got back in the car.

"Gee, what gave you that idea?"

He looked at me before starting the ignition. "Seriously, Jaxie. What's so awful about it?"

"Look, I just don't do small towns, you know? Rumton is so uneventful. I like Atlanta."

"I like Atlanta, too," he said. "But I'd be just as happy living in an *uneventful* town if I could earn the same salary I make now," he said.

"I wouldn't."

"Maybe big-city life has desensitized you. Pop once told me that it's the simple things that pull heartstrings. You know, stop to smell the roses and all that?"

"Since when does being a research analyst qualify you to be a shrink?" I said, miffed.

"I'm not trying to get in your head. I just think a change of pace is good once in a while. It's healthy to get away from your normal environment and see things from a different perspective."

I was stuck with him for the drive back and didn't want to make it worse than it had to be. "Whatever."

"Don't get mad. I came to help you, remember?"

"Correction," I shot back. "You were *sent* to help me."

"I don't need an excuse to visit Rumton, Jaxie. And I don't need an excuse to help you. I've always been there for you."

I squirmed in the passenger seat, not knowing what to make of that. Probably, he just meant that he was there as a company resource for every employee. "Well, anyway, I miss Sheila and all my friends. And I miss going to my favorite restaurants and just having something to do after work. I would really love a night out on the town."

He turned to study me and grinned mischievously. "Tell you what. Tonight I will take you out for a night on the town. Avery and Pop may even want to join us."

"You've got to be kidding. There is no *town* to go out for a night *on*."

"Might be surprised."

"Doubtful."

Justin pulled into traffic. "Is there anything you like about Rumton?"

"Well, sure. Pop is awesome. And the area where we went crabbing was incredible. What a view! But Rumton just doesn't excite me."

We wove our way to Ocean Boulevard. Both high-rise hotels and mom-and-pops dotted the street. Justin found a parking lot and talked me into a beach walk before heading back to Rumton.

"This is what Myrtle Beach is all about," he said, after we crossed sand dunes on a wooden walkway. "The beach, the ocean. It's a magnet. Without this, there would be no malls or golf courses or theaters."

I kicked off my sandals and headed straight to the water to get my toes wet. Waves lapped at my feet before dissipating to foam as I stood and took it all in. Toddlers played in the surf, people walked and jogged in the strip of hard sand at the water's edge, and clusters of tourists were perched in chairs beneath bright umbrellas, reading and drinking and talking.

Loafers in hand, Justin joined me at the water's edge and waved a hand at the Atlantic. "Without the beach, nothing else would have developed. Did you know that one hundred years ago, you could have bought an oceanfront lot, right here, for a hundred dollars? And if you agreed to build a house on the land, the state gave it to you. Free."

I had to laugh. "You're a walking encyclopedia. How do you know this stuff?"

"It's a curse. I can't help it. Once I read something, it sticks. And I read a lot. I'm a sucker for lists. Surveys. Rankings. Ratings." He shrugged. "Just love trivia."

"Well, a hundred bucks for an oceanfront lot is pretty amazing. I wonder what they sell for today."

He grinned. "There aren't many left, but now you can't touch an oceanfront lot for less than a million dollars. Just for the dirt. Or rather, sand. And that's a relatively small one—just big enough for a beach house."

As we walked, I studied his feet. Like the rest of his body parts revealed to me in the past day, they were nice and strong-looking. Clean, tanned skin, and just a smidgeon of curly blond hair on top.

"Hungry?" he asked.

I was. From the beach, we walked up to Bumz, a burger and sandwich joint with a large outside deck that faced the ocean. Sitting outside under an umbrella, we ordered grouper sandwiches with French fries and iced teas.

Offshore, a parasailing boat glided by, and I heard faint laughter from the two people strapped to the parachute. When our food came, we ate leisurely, observing the mix of tourists and locals around us. Afterward, we walked along Ocean Boulevard's sidewalk, stopped at a few attractions and even rode a Ferris wheel at the Pavilion Amusement Park. We forgot about helping Avery and blew the entire afternoon sightseeing. On the way back to the car, we found a grocery, and I bought a few things for Pop's house.

"This has been fun!" I said, when we were on the road driving back. "There's something going on at every turn."

"Rumton's appeal lies in the exact opposite," he said. "I bet people would go there to enjoy its quaintness."

"You mean its quirkiness," I said.

"Call it what you like, but every town has a personality and character. The key is to find a niche and figure out a way to market it."

"I thought you were research," I said. "Not creative."

"This weekend, I'm both."

7

Flush sunned in the driveway when we got back. Instead of running to greet us as dogs are supposed to do, he rolled over on his back to get his belly scratched. While Justin busied himself getting the fax machine out of the trunk, I obliged the animal. His tongue fell sloppily out of the side of his mouth, and his eyes rolled back in canine ecstasy.

Justin shook his head over the bulky box. "Sometimes I wish I were a dog."

An image of Justin sprawled in the driveway with his tongue hanging out made me laugh. And made me wonder if he was flirting with me. I couldn't wait to tell Sheila that I'd spent the entire day with our vice president of market research. Mr. Dullsville. Who admittedly had much more personality than I'd figured.

Inside, Pop and Avery drank beers and studied a printout. An old butcher block in the middle of the floor held some sort of analytical equipment. Buzzing with a low-pitched tone, one mechanism seized Bandit's full attention, and she sat staring as though hypnotized.

"Must have been one fancy fax machine," Avery said, his eyes moving back and forth between the two of us. "Sure took you a long time to find it."

I rolled my eyes at the insinuation.

Justin put down the big box. "I decided to show Jaxie around Myrtle Beach. A study in tourism."

"See anything interesting, lass?" Pop asked.

"The beach is inviting, and there are a ton of restaurants. And theaters and shopping. But the city is one giant tourist attraction. Everything has some sort of a theme, and the place almost overloads your senses. I can see why kids beg to go there for vacation. I was hoping to pick up some good ideas for our revitalization effort. But I can't even begin to imagine Rumton looking anything like Myrtle Beach, even if it did border the beach."

"Me neither. Wouldn't want it to."

All the locals were happy with their slow-paced lifestyle. If I did manage to come up with a plan to stimulate their economy, the second battle would be to get everyone on board in support of it.

Justin handed me a beer and opened one for himself. "I know you prefer wine or dry martinis, but your only choice right now is beer or whiskey."

He knew what I liked to drink? Seeing Justin out of the office got weirder by the minute. "Uh, thanks," I said, and took a gulp of the beer.

"You're welcome," he said, plopping down next to his brother. They eyed each other, communicating without words in the way only best friends or siblings can. Watching his nephews, Pop grinned.

"So how'd it go today?" I asked.

"Yeah," Justin said, with raised eyebrows. "How did it go? I recognize that shit-eating grin of yours! What did you find?"

Justin wore something besides suits, drank beer, and actually cursed once in a while? I think I raised my eyebrows, too. I was curious to find out what other surprises were in store. Maybe a night out on the town with him wouldn't be so bad, after all.

A wide grin spread across Avery's face. "Remember the low-lying spot we always used to go play in as kids? We called it Devil's Tail because it was skinny and curvy and ended in a fork?"

"Yeah. And we always got in trouble because we'd come back

caked in mud," Justin said. "And then Pop would tell Mom that boys will be boys, or something to that effect."

"Right. At which point, Mom would reply that, when we were at home, we didn't return filthy and scraped up after going out to play."

Pop laughed. "And then I'd tell my sister that's why she ought to bring you more often. Because this town is a wonderful place to get muddy and bloody!"

"Well, I went to Devil's Tail to look around and take some core sediment samples. I thought that's where the original inlet might have been. And I wanted to see if it had totally dried out, or if the opposite had happened and water is flowing again. I haven't poked around there in years and years."

Realizing Avery's lab equipment was off-limits, Bandit climbed up my leg and hopped to the table to look for food. I pushed her long snout away from my beer. "And?"

"It's shifted a mile or so from where it was when we were kids, but there is some definite water flow that appears to be coming from Skirr Creek, which snakes out of the waterway. Water in Devil's Tail is shallow, even at high tide, but it's there."

Not finding any food on the tabletop, the raccoon scurried up Pop's chest and settled on his shoulder, as though interested in our conversation. "And?" I urged again.

Avery's grin grew bigger. "And then we took Pop's boat out to explore from the ocean, where we found a swash that I think can be traced back to Devil's Tail."

I wasn't catching Avery's enthusiasm. "But wait a minute. You said we'd never be allowed to dredge, even if we found the old in-let. So I don't understand how all this will help."

Justin leaned forward and looked into his brother's eyes. "There's more. C'mon. Spill it."

"I found something else."

"What?" I demanded.

"A piece of a skeleton."

My stomach turned. "Oh, gross."

"From a boat," Avery added. "Just a few ribs of rotted wood. But definitely pieces of an old ship."

I was relieved it wasn't human bones, but I still didn't understand why he was so excited. "So?"

"I may have found an undiscovered shipwreck."

"Unbelievable!" Justin said. "How old? Where? How deep?"

Avery chuckled and gave his brother a "calm down" motion with his hand. "I'll be able to tell you more tomorrow, but since pieces of wood were preserved, it's either a recently sunk boat, or it was buried deep under sand for a long time and just recently became exposed." He slid a large cloth-wrapped item across the tabletop. "But I found this, still attached to a piece of the wood. It's the ship's bell. And it looks really old. Check out the engraving. That was her name."

Eyes gleaming as though it were a solid gold bar, Justin unwrapped the bell and leaned forward to read it. "The *Aldora*. Amazing. Have you told anyone else?"

Riley came through the back door with Flush at his heels. "Told anyone else what?"

Justin quickly rewrapped the tarnished bell.

"It's all right." Pop waved a hand at his best friend. "Like any good politician, Riley can keep a secret if you bribe him into it."

Avery repeated the day's events. When he finished, Rumton's mayor rubbed his bald head and said, "Huh."

"I don't mean to undermine your find, but I'm still confused as to how it can help the revitalization effort. What's the big deal about finding an old buried boat?" I asked.

I knew I'd asked an ignorant question when Avery shot me an incredulous look.

"The ocean floors are peppered with shipwrecks, Jaxie," Justin explained, shifting into encyclopedia mode. "There are hundreds in the eastern seaboard alone. They were torpedoed during acts of war, sunk in storms, or just mysteriously disappeared."

"Divers like to call North Carolina the graveyard of the Atlantic," Avery said. "And the waters off South Carolina hold their share of failed voyages, too."

Justin nodded. "Marine charts pinpoint the location for lots of them, especially ones that scuba divers can explore. But there are plenty more undiscovered. Most of those are totally submerged beneath sand, usually in deep water. They have a tremendous historical value. And some have booty buried with them."

"Booty?"

"Loot. Gemstones, gold, and other valuables."

Pop nodded. "Aye. Take Odyssey Marine Exploration, for example. It's a publicly held company out of Florida that locates shipwrecks. They excavate ones that, as rumor has it, went down with booty aboard. Spent years looking for the SS *Republic* that sank in the 1800s."

"Eighteen sixty-five," Justin confirmed. "It was a paddle wheel steamer traveling from New York to New Orleans. Got caught in a hurricane."

"So they found it?" I said.

Nodding, Justin slid the heavy bell my way. "And recovered gold and silver coins. Seventy-five million dollars' worth."

"Amazing." I ran my hands over the bell and wondered about the ship it had been attached to. The bell was tarnished and dented, but the engraved name was unmistakable. The *Aldora*. Was it named after a woman, and if so, who was she? "So how does this company find shipwrecks?"

Of course, Justin knew the answer. "They utilize historians, who do research to narrow the search area. Then they perform scientific research to find targets, usually in very deep water."

"Side-scan sonar and magnetometer technology, among other things," Avery said. "Once they find an anomaly that looks promising, they send down a ROV—a remotely operated vehicle—to take a look around."

"So you think our shipwreck could have gold coins?"

Justin's eyes gleamed beneath the black-rimmed glasses. "Probably not. But to locate a new shipwreck, whether or not there might be valuables associated with it, is exciting. It's a piece of history!"

"We'll have to see what we can find on the *Aldora*," Avery explained. "It could be a supply ship. A wealthy plantation owner's pleasure boat. Even a pirate's ship!"

Pop told me that remains of the *Queen Anne's Revenge*, one of the pirate Blackbeard's ships, was discovered in recent years just a few miles off the North Carolina coast.

"But the reality is that most shipwrecks worth excavating are in very deep water," Justin said, bringing my enthusiasm level down a notch or two. "They're the ones that are preserved and often undisturbed. Our bell could belong to an old boat that just happened to wash up on Rumton's shoreline. It might not have been carrying any valuable cargo."

"Or it might," Pop said.

"And it's going to be fun to find out!" Avery tipped his head back to drain the last sip of beer and showed off a magnificently sculpted jaw. One that looked a lot like Justin's. In fact, the two of them shared the same bone structure.

"Huh," Riley said again.

"So, who owns it?" I wanted to know. "Do we go by the finders keepers rule?"

"All depends on what our research turns up," Avery answered, "and if somebody besides us can stake claim to it. If it's something we wanted to pursue, we'd have to be awarded title and ownership."

Wanting to get her paws on the bell, Bandit jumped from Pop's shoulder to mine and pulled out some hair when she landed. "Ouch!"

She chirped out an indignant response and moved on to find a more sympathetic human. I rubbed the stinging spot on my scalp. "Okay, so you'll dig this thing up. And maybe you'll even find some gold or something. But that still doesn't help my revitalization assignment, does it?"

"First of all, we won't just dig it up," Avery told me. "If there is anything left of a ship down there, we would preserve what we can. The first thing we've got to do is determine who it belonged to, what it may have been carrying, and why it ended up on Rumton's doorstep. If there is any loot, we'll deal with that when we get to it."

Justin nodded. "Whatever happens, we need to keep this under wraps until we learn more and know what we're dealing with."

"Absolutely," Avery said and made a point to look at Riley. "For now, nobody talks to anyone about this, okay?"

Everyone nodded in agreement.

While the men conspired to come up with a course of action on the shipwreck, I decided to take care of dinner. I found my car keys and went to retrieve homemade takeout from Chat 'N Chew. They breathed a collective sigh of relief when they learned that I wasn't actually going to *cook*. Flush tagged along, and I didn't even worry about the dog hair that I'd have to vacuum out at the car wash when I got back to Atlanta. Maybe life in Rumton had destressed me. Maybe we'd find a treasure that would revitalize the town, and I could head home. Maybe I'd even be rewarded with some gold bling for my troubles!

As usual, Chat 'N Chew looked empty. A few locals sat at a table playing dominoes, and a woman leaned against the counter talking to Bull. The black and tan basset hound I'd seen earlier was back, sprawled just inside the doorway, folds of skin spread loosely around its massive body. Flush leaped over it, and hurried from person to person, seeking a handout. One of the dominoes players shelled a peanut and passed the nuts over. Flush munched contentedly before backtracking to sniff the hound in greeting. It never woke up.

I took a closer look to see that it wasn't dead. "Hey, Bull. Whose dog is this?"

"Hiya, hon. She's a community dog. We all take care of her."

The dog farted in its sleep. It definitely wasn't dead. "What's her name?"

"Don't think she has one. I just call her Dog."

"Huh," I said. "I need some takeout. Whatcha got cooking today?"

"Meatloaf or chicken salad," Bull said. "How many plates you want this time?"

I knew Riley would still be there when I got back. "Five," I told Bull. "Meatloaf. With whatever vegetable you've got. And rolls or cornbread, if you have any. And maybe some pie. Just throw in a whole pie."

She asked if I wanted extra for Bandit and Flush. I shook my head. "The dog's already been fed. And I'm mad at the stupid raccoon. She pulled a clump of my hair out today."

Bull hooted. "Probably wasn't on purpose, Jaxie. I'll throw in an apple muffin for her."

Bull's friend suddenly spun around and hugged me tight. "So you're Jaxie! What a beautiful girl you are!"

I sneezed. Twice. "Millie?"

"That's me, in the flesh! Was wondering when I'd run into ya. Aaron told me you'd be by the house soon. Practically begged me to make a batch of cookies." Her whole body moved when she chuckled. Short and plump, she reminded me of an actress playing Mrs. Claus in a Christmas movie.

I dug two Sudafed pills out of my purse and swallowed them without water, sneezed again, and rubbed my left eyelid to ward off the twitch that I knew would be forthcoming. "Yes, your cookies are famous. He wants me to mail him a box."

"I've got plenty," she said brightly. "The secret ingredient that makes them so good is a splash of spiced rum in the dough. My mama's recipe. Why don't you come sit a spell after you eat your dinner, and I'll fix you up a Tupperware container of them?"

I'm not sure which came first—another sneeze or the eyelid spasm. My eyes watered from the mere thought of cat dander. "Tell you what. Why don't you join us for dinner at Pop's place, and you can bring your cookies with you. Justin is here, so he can take them back to Aaron."

She cocked her head for several seconds to think about it. "Why not? Don't care much about breaking bread with Pompous Pop, but meatloaf sounds good. And I haven't run across Justin in quite some time."

"Great." I smiled, willing the antihistamine sitting in my stomach to dissolve quickly.

"Make it six plates, Bull!" Mad Millie yelled into the kitchen for me.

Before leaving Chat 'N Chew, I used Bull's phone to call the guys and warn them I'd be returning with a guest in tow. Justin answered, and when he relayed the message, Avery's laughing drowned out Pop's grumbling in the background.

Toting six cardboard containers of food, a pie, and one apple muffin, I loaded Flush back into the Range Rover.

Millie cocked her head sideways. "Whose dog?"

"That's Flush," I said, climbing into the driver's seat. "Pop's dog."

"Pompous Pop has a dog?"

I nodded. "Has a raccoon, too."

"Well, I'll be. Maybe he's not as weird as I thought," she muttered, heading to her own car. "Must be something decent about a man who has animals."

I headed home. Mad Millie made a detour to fetch a batch of cookies but promised she'd be right behind me.

8

Justin made good on his promise of a night on the town, and after dinner everyone piled into my SUV, except Riley who called it an early night and said he was going home. Avery drove and Pop rode shotgun. Justin and I settled into the backseat, with Mad Millie sandwiched between us. I thought about popping a few more antihistamines, just to be safe, but didn't want to pass out during my night out. We cut through the residential area, and it dawned on me that I'd become accustomed to people waving at one another. But I hadn't yet adapted to their way of driving. Avery had to brake when a pickup truck pulled in front of us, then immediately made a left turn.

"Doesn't anybody in this town use turn signals?" I asked.

"No need to," Avery said. "Everybody around here knows where everybody else lives."

"And which church they go to, and who's headed out of town for a doctor appointment, and who's in the Tuesday night poker group at Gertrude's," Pop added.

"Gertrude the pharmacist plays poker?"

Pop nodded. "Woman cleans up, when she can stay awake. Gotta be careful cutting a deck of cards with that woman, especially if she's had a good nap before the game."

We bounced into a dirt parking lot and eased up to an old brick building that was so ensconced by kudzu vines, I hadn't noticed it during my exploration drives. Crusted with layers of paint, a sign tacked above the door advertised PEAS FOR SALE. Hanging on chains in front of that, another sign read: PINK PETUNIA—EXOTIC DANCERS.

"We're going to an adult club?" I said, incredulous.

Justin pointed to a third and newer sign affixed to a post near the front door. It read: DUCKIES.

I got out for a better look. "Billy at the general store told me about Duckies. It's Walter's place?"

Pop chuckled. "Walter is an entrepreneur."

"Well," Justin said, holding the door for everyone. "He has opened some creative businesses. Everything from a drive-through hot dog stand—"

"An inherently flawed plan," Mad Millie cut in, clucking her disapproval. "People 'round here don't want to drive through somewheres to get a hot dog."

"To a comedy club, which lasted two months," Justin continued. "Eleven, twelve years ago Walter read a story in the *Wall Street Journal* about the flourishing adult entertainment industry and decided that Rumton was ripe for a club."

Avery grinned. "Thus, the Pink Petunia."

We found a table and settled in. The place looked like an old lodge. Fishing paraphernalia and animal heads covered wood plank walls, and strings of multicolored Christmas bulbs decorated the window frames. Above our heads, fishing nets draped across the ceiling, connecting rafter to rafter. Stacked in the corners, some painted bright colors, large wooden barrels held fishing poles and hiking sticks. An L-shaped bar decorated one side of the room, and a small stage stood at the other, where a man busied himself testing a karaoke machine.

Millie pointed at him. "That there's Walter."

Absorbing the decor, I decided the place had ambience. A unique ambience. "So tell me the rest of the Pink Petunia story."

Pop chuckled. "Drive-through hot dog stand lasted one week. Pink Petunia made it one night. Couple of hours, actually. Holds the record for Walter's shortest-lived business venture."

Avery nodded. "Walter will tell you he knew that finding dancers would be a challenge, and there might not be enough of a population to support an adult club. But ever the optimist, he plowed ahead. Even managed to hire a dancer."

Justin smiled and it suddenly hit me: He looked like Avery. A lot. Or, perhaps Avery looked like Justin. I didn't know who was older. But I did know which of the two was straight, and I entertained the idea of getting to know him a little better. Even if he was a coworker and I'd be breaking my rule. Extreme circumstances called for extreme measures. And living in Rumton was about as extreme as it could get.

"As opening night drew near," Justin said, "old man Walter assured his pals that he did indeed have an exotic dancer. But he kept her identity a secret."

Walter strolled over and introductions were made. He sat with us a few minutes, found out what we wanted to drink, and ambled off. He spoke slowly and moved even more slowly.

"So the Rumton men assumed Walter had found an experienced out-of-town girl," Avery said. "You can imagine their shock when, on opening night, he pulled the curtain aside and there stood little Ellie. Everybody in town had babysat her at one time or another."

Pop grinned. "The crowd got on Walter for talking Ellie into dancing and scolded Ellie for listening to Walter."

"Riley yanked down the curtain, wrapped it 'round the young'n and told her to go put some clothes on. Walter refunded e'eryone their ten-spot cover charge and closed the Pink Petunia that night," Pop said, finishing the story.

"But the sign remains," I mused. "Does he still sell peas?"

"Sure do," Walter said, serving five orange juices on ice. He put a bottle of rum in the middle of the table and told everyone to pour his own.

"Didn't we ask for beers and a vodka martini?" I said.

"Sure did. But I'm out of both. Serving rum an' juice tonight. Got pineapple, too, if you'd rather."

I shrugged. "Orange is great with me." I was getting used to small-town eccentricities. In Rumton it didn't do to be choosy.

We mixed our liquid ingredients and toasted to good health. The rum and juice was tart and surprisingly good. People filtered in, and before long, Duckies was packed. Walter took drink orders from each new arrival and returned with a corresponding number of juices, and the bottle of rum was passed from table to table. Everyone knew everyone else and the atmosphere reminded me of a fifty- or sixty-year high school reunion. At some point Walter cranked up the karaoke machine, and two women belted out a pretty good rendition of country singer Gretchen Wilson.

Justin and Avery dared each other to sing next but got into a quiet debate about something before they made it to the stage. Straining to hear their conversation, Mad Millie perked up. "Sunken boat? Where's a sunken boat?"

Everyone stopped speaking at once and looked at her.

"What?" she said.

"Well, boys," Pop said. "Looks like you'll have to tell her the secret."

Millie leaned in and put a hand on Pop's arm. "I love secrets!" Pop didn't pull away, and Millie's hand lingered much longer than necessary for simple emphasis.

Her eyes grew big when Avery gave her a condensed version of the ship's bell discovery. They remained that way until she blinked them back to their normal size.

"It could be an exciting find, or it could be nothing," he told her and drank some rum and juice. "For all we know, the thing has been submerged for hundreds of years and has just recently worked its way to the surface. We need to do some research. See if the *Aldora* can be found in any journals. It may even turn up in Rumton's history."

I changed the subject before Millie could grill Avery. "Speaking of local history, does anybody know what the saying on Rumton's sign means? 'Ya'll hideout.' It's an odd slogan."

"Hmmm," Pop said. "Maybe 'twas a good place for folk to hide."

I grinned. "Still is."

"Well, we're not hiding out tonight." Avery guided his brother to the stage. "We're singing for all to hear and all to cheer!"

In rich smooth voices, they sang Chairman of the Board's "Carolina Girls," complete with the corresponding dance moves. Millie whispered something into Pop's ear that generated a belly laugh, Walter came by to refill our juices and return the community rum bottle, and I watched Shine Advertising and PR's vice president of market research entertain a crowd of jovial Rumtonians. As I added a splash of booze to my glass, two things occurred to me. One, I was having fun. And, two, Justin was pretty damn fine-looking. *Why hadn't I noticed it before?*

Amidst much clapping and whistling, the brothers returned to our table and plopped down, laughing.

I fawned over them and batted my lashes like a starstruck groupie. "It's really you! Wait till I tell my friends about seeing Justin and Avery perform live! Can I get your autographs? You can sign here," I teased, pulling the hem of my cotton top up just enough to expose the skin of my lower back.

A pair of hands took my hips, and before I knew what was happening, Justin produced a pen and quickly wrote something in the small of my back.

I spun around. "I can't believe you actually did that!"

He shrugged and took off his glasses to wipe his forehead with a napkin. "Hey, opportunity knocks, I answer." He looked at me with one brown eye and one sparkling green eye.

"Oh, my God! You've got it, too!"

Watching us, Pop chuckled.

"Got what, too?" Justin said.

"The green eye! Just like Pop!" I couldn't stop staring. I couldn't believe I'd never noticed it before. I'd always avoided looking directly into Justin's eyes at the office because I didn't want to strike up a conversation with him.

"Runs in our family, amongst the men, lass," Pop said. "Grandpappy had the green eye, too."

"But I got ripped off," Avery said, fluttering lashes over two golden brown eyes. "The gene passed me by."

My eyes were riveted to Justin's, until he put the thick glasses back on, breaking the spell. "Your green eye is amazing. But that doesn't let you off the hook for writing on me! What did you write, anyhow?"

The corners of his mouth inched up in a teasing smile. "For me to know . . ."

Before the night ended, much more rum was consumed, Pop danced with Mad Millie, Justin and Avery took a few more turns at the mike, and I laughed so hard my stomach muscles hurt.

On the way home, Avery dropped Millie at her house so she wouldn't have to drive from Pop's, and I found myself alone in the backseat with Justin. Feeling happy, I impulsively gave his hand a squeeze. "Thanks for my night on the town. I didn't think it possible in Rumton, but you delivered what you promised! I had a great time tonight."

"You're welcome." He returned the squeeze and made a quick pass along the inside of my bare forearm with his palm before stretching his arm across the top of the seat, behind my neck. I didn't know if the caress was intentional or simply happened because of our tight quarters, but a shiver shot through my body at his touch. "It was my pleasure."

Pop and Avery chatted away in the front seat, but my attention was focused on Justin's warm hand, now hanging loosely over the top of the car seat, just inches from my shoulder. His body swayed in conjunction with mine to the movement in the road. And his knee brushed mine, just barely, each time we hit a bump.

By the time we got home, my body felt like one giant, electrified bundle of nerves. Justin was becoming more and more intriguing by the minute. "Take a walk with me?" I asked.

"Okay."

As soon as Justin and I were a few blocks from the house, bathed in bluish moonlight, he took my hand and stopped beneath a giant oak tree to say something. "Jaxie, I've really enjoyed spending—"

I kissed him on the lips, lightly. Just a hint of contact but enough to interrupt his sentence. Being far removed from our normal environment in Atlanta made me want to discover more about the man I'd previously thought of as a dull vice president. Thinking about his incredible green eye and wondering what other secrets his body held made me nuts. And being relaxed by the rum made me reckless. I figured he was trying to say something about us working together and having to remain professional, but I didn't want to hear it. I kissed him again lightly, but this time let my mouth linger for a few seconds before breaking away.

"—time with you," he continued. "It's been—" He pulled me against him and kissed me deeply without finishing the thought. I backed away to take off his glasses and, after getting a glimpse of the green eye, moved back in. His arms wrapped around me and his hands went beneath the hemline of my shirt to make direct contact with my lower back.

"Tell me what you wrote down there," I demanded through another kiss.

"Nothing," he answered through a deep laugh. "Never took the cap off the pen. But had it been open, the message on your back would say, 'I'll sing for you anytime.'"

"Mmmm," I murmured, thinking that I might like a private serenade. I thoroughly explored his mouth and got a lingering taste of sweet orange juice. Our bodies fit together nicely, and our sensual embrace on the sidewalk became that much more tantalizing when I realized he was aroused.

I did a slow rub against the stranger I'd known for years. "Your room or mine?" I whispered, meaning it.

"Dammit." He moaned and backed away to put a few inches of distance between us. "We can't do this."

I closed the gap to nuzzle his throat. "Why not?"

He took my hand and started walking again. "Jaxie, I've been crazy about you for a long time. Ever since you came to work at the agency."

"Really?"

"Yes, really."

"So then, what's the problem?"

"You'd never give me the time of day before now. And while the thought of being with you is . . . driving me crazy, I have mixed feelings. I feel like, now that I'm the only game in town, you're going to give me a whirl."

Frowning, I pulled my hand from his. Maybe Sheila had been right when she said Justin was hot for me. But I'd never seen it. "Look, Justin, I think you're great. Tonight has been a blast. And I'm sorry I haven't gotten to know you better before. I had no idea you felt that way about me."

"I've fantasized about going to parties with you on my arm." He looked at me, shook his head slowly. "I go on dinner dates with nice, beautiful women and end up wishing I was sitting across the table from you, instead of them." He blew out a long sigh. "And I don't know why in the hell I'm telling you this."

I stopped walking, my happy alcoholic buzz quickly fading and a bundle of mixed emotions dancing in my stomach before settling into frustration. "Justin, you've never been anything but polite, almost distant, at work."

Looking down, he shuffled in place before capturing my eyes with his. "I never wanted to come across as pushy, but I have asked you out a number of times, Jaxie."

"You never told me how you felt."

"Would it have made a difference?"

I thought about it. "No, I guess not."

He shrugged. "But I kept hoping you'd come around. See that I'm a decent guy."

I didn't want to talk anymore and didn't want to end a perfect evening on a sour note. I pressed against him and wrapped my arms around his neck. "I just did."

He gently removed my arms and shook his head. "I'd like to think you want to get to know me because you're genuinely interested in me. Not because I'm the only man around."

I pulled back. "What are you talking about? So what if it took us both being in Rumton to get to know each other a little better. What difference does it make?"

"As much as I'd love to rip your clothes off and fall into bed with you, it's probably not a good idea. I don't want to be just another of your . . . meaningless dates."

Blood moved in my face and my cheeks got hot. "What do you mean by that?"

"Your feelings on long-term relationships are well known

around the office. I've heard you and Sheila joke about your latest string of boyfriends. What's the motto? If you dig him—date him, do him, and ditch him?'"

"Oh, hell," I mumbled to myself, feeling like a total schmuck. *Had Sheila and I been that blatant with our talk at the office?*

"I couldn't bear to be ditched by you," he said softly. "It would tear me up."

9

Accompanied by two four-legged critters, Justin and I drank coffee beneath a gazebo in Pop's backyard. Clean crisp air complemented an agreeable temperature. Early-morning puffy clouds slowly changed shape as they drifted across a vividly blue backdrop. I tried to remember the last time I'd taken time to watch the sky. Justin reached across me to retrieve some cream, angling his body awkwardly so as not to accidentally touch me.

"You could have just asked for it," I said. "I would happily have given it to you."

"The cream?" he said, smirking at the double meaning.

"Ha, ha."

We sat in silence, him sipping java and me gazing at the clouds, until he finally sighed. "Let's forget our conversation last night ever happened, okay?" he said. "It was just the booze talking."

"Fine." I hadn't slept well. If anybody is going to turn down a physical advance, it should be me. And besides, who was he to eavesdrop on my conversations with Sheila or judge how I conducted my social life?

"I don't want it to be uncomfortable every time we see each other," he went on. "We have to work together. Let's be professional."

"I agree," I said, still watching the sky. An **O**-shaped cloud playfully stretched until it resembled a full pair of lips, and the feel of his mouth tantalized my memory. *Sweet Jesus.* I looked at

Flush so that I couldn't see the wispy sky-lips or the real ones on Justin's face. Or seek out the green eye through the thick lenses. *He's not your type,* I told myself, *and besides that, he's a jerk.*

"And speaking of work, it's time to get back to the office. I've got to hit the road."

I wanted a good-bye kiss, but he obviously had other things on his mind. I shrugged. "Drive safe."

He stood. "Okay, then. Call me if you need anything, and I'll see you back in Atlanta."

I gave him a nod. A short *professional* nod. "Sure."

We went inside, where he said good-bye to Pop and Avery.

I shoved a bag at him. "These are cookies for Aaron from Millie. And one of Elwood's carvings I bought for Sheila. Would you please take them?"

"Be happy to," he said politely.

I tried to keep my voice pleasant, but the words came out stiff. "Thank you."

Avery's eyes ping-ponged between us with raised eyebrows. Before he could ask questions, Justin gave his brother a hug and disappeared.

I finished my coffee and told Avery I was at his disposal for the day. Helping him would keep me occupied at least and keep my mind off Justin. As long as I didn't look at the sculpted jawline. Or star-quality smile. Or Avery's well-toned build. All of which were interchangeable with Justin's.

"Wanna tell me what's going on?" Avery said, when Pop went into the kitchen to feed the animals.

"Other than your brother is an asshole? No."

He didn't press the issue. "I've got a tidbit for you, then."

"Go."

"The town slogan? It's not 'Ya'll Hideout,'" Avery said.

"But I read it myself. That's what the sign says."

"Originally, it was 'Yawl Hide'. *Y-a-w-l* like a small sailboat.

Somewhere along the way, the word *yawl* got changed to *ya'll*. And the word *hide* changed to *hideout*. I asked around and one of the old-timers gave me the story. Actually has an old black-and-white photo of a kid standing next to the sign. And get this. The original sign had crisscrossed swords at the bottom."

"Hmmm. A yawl and swords. You think a pirate used to hide here?"

Avery shrugged his shoulders. "Pirates were known to run the coastline of North and South Carolina for a period of years back in the early 1700s. But I doubt a single pirate hid here. The more likely scenario is that pirate gangs came and went. And because the locals couldn't adequately defend themselves, they would have cooperated with the pirates. Sold them supplies like fresh water and food and tobacco. Or bartered."

"But I thought pirates commandeered big ships."

"Well, sure they did. But the big ship would carry a smaller sailboat with it. A yawl. They'd anchor the ship offshore and use the yawl to come ashore."

I had trouble envisioning swashbuckling pirates tearing up sleepy, quiet Rumton.

"Tough to say what Rumton might have been three hundred years ago. It could have been a crazy, swinging, lawless place!"

"How do we know Rumton was even here way back then?"

"Family bible. It's stayed with the house all these years, believe it or not. And it dates back to the year 1700. So whether there was an actual town or not, I don't know. Probably there were homesteaders. And most definitely a plantation owner, who built himself a little beach getaway place. Pop's ancestor."

"Your ancestor, too, then," I mused. "You think Pop would let me look at the Bible?"

"Of course. A few pages are missing, though. And some of the writing is faded beyond recognition. It's really well preserved, though, considering how old it is."

Thinking of the aged book, I got a strange sense of déjà vu. "Isn't it odd to think about your ancestors from *centuries* ago? Especially the ones that lived right here? Stood in the exact same spot we're standing now?"

"Puts time in a whole different perspective," he agreed. "Justin and I never did any historical research on Rumton, other than what we learned about Pop's place. But you'll want to check with the lifetime locals and see if any of them heard tales from their parents or grandparents. Word-of-mouth stories get skewed from generation to generation, but usually there's a smidgen of truth in what filters down."

My ad seeking information in the *Rumton Review* produced zero results. Not a single phone call, even though somebody somewhere had to know something. And they all read their weekly newspaper, according to Billy at the general store. These were not proactive people. Or else they didn't believe in what I wanted to do. I needed to speak at a town meeting, present my case, and ask for help. Pop came back in the kitchen, Bandit on his shoulder and Flush at his heels. Seeing the three of them, I smiled.

"They always think they deserve more food than they get," he explained. "So they'll stick with me for the next ten or fifteen minutes. See if more chow is coming."

"Perpetual optimists," Avery said.

I told Pop I was researching Rumton's history and asked if I could look at his family Bible.

"It's tucked away, but I'll find it for you."

"What about your friends?" I had a gut feeling that learning about Rumton's past would somehow help me figure out how to revitalize its future. "Are there any locals that would be good to interview?"

"Gertrude can spin a tale. Check with her at the pharmacy.

And Mad Millie would give you an earful. But don't let on that you're there for an *interview*. You just want to stop by for a cup of coffee. The woman's not so awful once you get to know her."

I almost sneezed at the mere thought of her cats. "What if we just talk here? She's coming to get her car today, anyway. She said she'd walk over sometime this afternoon."

Pop frowned. "Coming 'ere?"

"It looked to me as if you two were getting along just fine at Duckies," I challenged. "You should be happy for her to pay a visit."

Pop harrumphed.

"So, what's the game plan?" I said to Avery. "What can I do to help?"

"Why don't you see what you can learn about the *Aldora*? Check the library; it's a small collection in the town hall, or rather the movie house. It's a long shot, but see what you can find online. And get with our research guru to see what he uncovers. If I know him, he's already made a few phone calls to various specialists, to get the ball rolling."

"Justin?"

"Unless you know any other research geniuses." Avery diagrammed something on paper while he spoke. "Meanwhile I'm going to finish your environmental survey. Finding the bell got me sidetracked, but I've got to get busy. Do a rudimentary map of developable areas. Overlay wetland areas. Get my perk test and soil compaction results. And further explore Devil's Tail. Mother Nature just might be giving you your water access back."

I asked how long everything would take.

"I passed my next contract job to a buddy. So I can stay here longer. I'll have some preliminary results for you in a week. But I'd really like to get a few satellite pictures as soon as possible."

"How does that work?"

"There are several companies with camera-equipped satellites in orbit, approximately four hundred and twenty-five miles up. You order images, which are basically aerial photographs but on a much larger, much more detailed scale. People often think that only the government uses satellite imaging, but in reality anybody can order them for about five grand apiece."

"Amazing."

"I'd like a couple of full-color shots from one of Digital Globe's satellites. And I'd want a second set from Space Imaging. They're old shots of the U.S. coastlines, originally taken by the government. That way I can compare the old one to the new ones to see an overview of what's changed. We can receive the images by e-mail in as little as three days."

"What's the price tag for your pictures of Rumton?"

"I'd want two, full-spectrum. About a sixteen-kilometer square of coverage. It'll run ten thousand dollars for both."

I dialed my boss's direct number and told him what we wanted. "I can't justify spending the firm's money on it, Jaxie, but as I told you before, this project means a lot to me. I have a vested interest in seeing you succeed. Go ahead and order what Avery wants. I'll pay out of my own pocket."

"You're sure?"

"Have Digital Globe call my secretary. She'll give them a credit card number," he said and disconnected. Getting the go-ahead was a good thing, but the fact that my boss was now investing his own money made me feel a little nauseated. What if I failed to make anything happen in Rumton? I laid my head on the table and moaned. The raccoon hopped on my back and chirped.

"Still mad at Justin, or is it pressure from work?" Pop said.

I jerked up, sending Bandit to the ground with a disgruntled squeal. "How did you know I'm mad at Justin?"

"I'm not blind, lass. But I think you might be getting all riled up for naught. Just do the best you can, and move on."

My eyelid twitched. "I think I'm in way over my head," I admitted, rubbing my eye.

"With a brilliant scientist doing your survey? And a top-notch researcher at your disposal? And Pop looking after you?" Avery said. "You got it made, sister!"

The twitching stopped and my eyes teared up. "You're right. I think I'm just tired. I didn't sleep well."

The phone rang, and Sheila's cheerful voice surged through the line when I hit the speakerphone button on Pop's new fax phone. "Hey, you! How is everything in Rumton?"

I wanted to tell her what had happened with Justin, but not in front of an audience. "Hey, back at you! I sent a souvenir . . . via the Justin shuttle. Hope you like it."

"Oooh, a present. Excellent."

"Things here are clipping right along. What's happening at the agency?"

"I think Pepsi is going to go for our campaign! They loved the idea of using jungle animals in the city to push the low-sugar, high-energy concept. Plus add a teeny bit of ginger and ginseng. And they agreed to leave out the artificial sweetener. Sales will be off the charts!"

For a microsecond, jealousy hit, and I wanted to be part of the Pepsi presentation team instead of the pro bono project lead. Then I thought of all the people in Rumton whose lives might be changed by what I did, and the jealousy vanished.

"Sheila, that's awesome!"

"Yeah, I'm jazzed about it!" she said. "Listen, I just called to say hello, but the interns have some ear food for you. They're in my office now. I'll put you on speakerphone."

Their news on grants wasn't great. They found several that

Rumton could apply for as a municipality, but only after the re-vitalization effort was already under way. It was a catch-22 dilemma—Uncle Sam didn't think it prudent to put money into a venture unless there would be a return in the way of tax revenues.

"Any good news for me?" I said into the machine.

"We did find one very promising grant that could be used to build a museum of historical significance. Since it's available from a newly formed historical foundation, there shouldn't be a lot of applicants this first year. And it's worth up to five hundred thousand dollars! But you have to show a community interest in history and have some actual artifacts to preserve. Plus, you have to prove the means to keep up the museum once it's built. Such as doing tours and charging admission, or something."

It was a start. "Good job, guys. Do it."

"Apply for it? What artifacts do you have? What history?" The two of them spoke at once, their voices muffled by the speakerphone.

"I'll e-mail you a list of historians who reside here and a syn-opsis on why preserving the history of the town is significant." I just had to get some residents on board to help with the details and to designate a few of them as historians. "Anything else you need? Make it up. Create a vision. Go for the emotional small-town appeal. This foundation has money to spend, so treat them like a client," I said. "Sell them on Rumton!"

"But, make stuff up?"

"Look," I told them, "if you're going to get anywhere in the advertising and public relations business, you can't let a little thing like a lack of tangibles hold you back. Come up with a vi-sion, capitalize on the revitalization effort, and complete the ap-plication. Throw in something extra to make it look pretty, and FedEx the thing to me. The mayor and council members will sign it, and I'll mail it in. We'll fill in the blanks later, when we need to."

"Okay," they chimed and clicked off the speakerphone.

Laughing, Sheila came back on the line. "They're about to blow a brain fuse over this project of yours." She paused to take a drink of something. Probably the Pepsi energy drink prototype. "By the way, the boss is paying you a visit soon. I overheard him telling Janice to mark a few days off the schedule because he'll be in South Carolina."

"Aaron? Here? He hasn't said anything to me." Maybe he didn't think I had it under control. Or maybe Justin had called from the road and given him dismal feedback. My eyelid twitched all the way up to my eyebrow. A headache threatened to invade my skull. I rubbed my temples in a circular motion.

"He hasn't said anything to me, either," Sheila said in a low voice. "I overheard it, so don't tell him I told you. He'll think I eavesdropped. Anyway, didn't he grow up there? He probably just wants a stroll down memory lane. And he thought it would be fun to surprise you."

"I miss you," I told my best friend. "I wish you were coming instead of him."

"If it makes you feel any better, we're planning a huge welcome back party. But don't tell yourself. It's a surprise."

I hung up, smiling, but I felt like crying.

Pop patted my hand. "Things will work out, lass. They always do."

10

After a loud and full few days, the house was suddenly quiet. I was alone. Pop left a note to tell me that he'd gone to the movie house to meet some buddies for coffee and doughnuts. Thoughtfully, he'd propped the piece of paper against a blueberry muffin, brewed a pot of coffee for me, and put the family Bible on the kitchen table.

Avery was gone, too. Out in the field, as he liked to say, my volunteer scientist was busy doing whatever it was he did. Even the animals were gone, and I missed them all. Pop, Avery, Flush, and Bandit. I missed Justin, too. I couldn't get him out of my mind, even though I was mad about being snubbed. Our last evening together, the kiss mostly, kept replaying in my head, and I wondered if he thought of me as much as I thought of him.

I set my coffee cup far away from the Bible before carefully picking up the Bible. Bigger than an Atlanta phone book and just as heavy, it was bound with thick brown leather and was in surprisingly good shape. I unbuckled its tarnished brass clasp and slowly opened the cover. An earthy smell of aged paper wafted out. It reminded me of bargain hunting in a used bookstore. Except that this book had the scent of leather and something fragrant mixed in. Lavender, maybe.

It was the standard King James Version of the Bible, printed in a fancy font that I hadn't seen before. Perusing the pages, I saw that some lines of Scripture were underlined and that notes were periodically scribbled in the margins. In the very back, pages of Pop's family tree were recorded by several different people, judging from the handwriting. Mostly, there were births, deaths, and marriages with an occasional description of the event, such as "curly red hair straight from the womb." I took notes as I pored through time-darkened pages.

April 1 of the year 1700 was the first of the entries, written in what I guessed to be a woman's handwriting. The parents' names weren't written in, but the baby was christened Mary A. Barstow. I figured the Bible had been a gift to the child, and based on what Pop told me about his house, Mary was the daughter of the plantation owner who'd built the original structure. Sixteen years passed before the next entry. A boy named Simon was born on May 14 of the year 1716. The mother was Mary A. Barstow; the father was not listed. This entry was probably written by Mary herself, and the handwriting was petite and flowery with a left-handed slant.

I sipped some coffee and absentmindedly chewed a bite of blueberry muffin. At sixteen years old, I'd been cheerleading, going to the shopping malls with my friends to talk about boys, and studying for my driver's test. This girl had become a single mother. What a scandal that must have been!

The next pages appeared to have been torn out, and the births picked up again in the year 1822. The entries were sporadic, with only a few of the death dates filled in. Yet seeing the stretch of Pop's family tree back to the eighteenth century—however incomplete—fascinated me.

Even more interesting—I came across a section of blank pages with notes jotted on them, almost like diary entries. Faded and smudged, the first was not readable. But the next page, written in the same precise, loopy handwriting as the birth entry announcing Mary A. Barstow in 1700, grabbed my attention:

> *My darling child,*
>
> *Thou have yet to come into the world. I cherrish thee alredy and wish thou hold dear this place as much as I. The cotage by the sea is built, and tho small, is my favorite place to be. I come for the fresh air and brillant sunrises. Tis a strolle to the shore, but worth the sweet voice of rolling waves. I am next to heaven here. Close to God. Thou fater comes only to trade with the seamen who saile skiffs up the canal. The joy of the land is lost to him. We speak not of it, tho. He says matters of busyness be not my concerne. He wishes a boy, tho I am certan a girl thou ar. Be strong, as he will love thee just the same. My sikness worsens with each sunset. I grow weak. I am at peace and pray for thou. I pray God see fit to keep me of this earthe til I birth thee. I pray thee a good life. I love thee alredy.*

Since the handwriting was the same as that listing the birth of the baby, I knew the woman lived long enough to deliver the daughter she named Mary A. Barstow. But I didn't know how soon after she died. Had Mary grown up without a mother? Then become pregnant and given birth to a baby boy when she was barely sixteen? Thinking of the woman who settled in South Carolina so long ago, I wondered how her daughter felt when she'd read the same message I'd just read. I stood to stretch and imagine what my life would have been like had I been born in the 1700s.

Engrossed in reflection, I jumped at the noise when Pop came through the door with Bandit perched on his shoulder. "Oh! Hi, Pop."

"Morning, lass." Bandit rappelled down his body to the floor. "Find anything to help you in there?"

"I'm not sure, but it's fascinating. And sad. The woman who had the baby named Mary but knew she wouldn't be around to raise the child."

He slowly nodded. He'd read it, too. "Aye."

"So then, the father raised the girl? The original owner of this house? The plantation owner?"

"It's more likely that the house servants raised her. Far as I can tell, she was the only child. When the mother passed on, one of the slaves would have been put in charge of the girl."

I'd read a lot of information on plantation owners in the Carolinas. Some worked with sharecroppers, but many used slaves to work their fields, whether growing rice in the low country or cotton, tobacco, and indigo elsewhere.

"So the slaves were not only fieldworkers and house servants but nannies, too?"

"Aye."

Bandit tugged on my pajama pants leg, wanting attention or food. I gave her the last bit of blueberry muffin. "So Mary grew up without a mother, raised by slaves. Then she gave birth to a little boy. But who was the father? And what happened to Mary?"

"I've oft' wondered that myself, lass."

He poured two glasses of iced sweet tea and sat at the table with me. "I've ne'er added anything to the births and deaths recordings. If you want to, write in my grandpappy. And me and my sister." He gave me the life dates of his grandfather and the birth dates of him and his sister.

"But the pages are disintegrating. Maybe I should record your information separately? In a new book? Or, better yet, I could put the family tree that's here, at least what I can read of it, on the computer. And burn it to a CD for you."

He sighed, frowning. "I reckon people are getting to where they want to look at a computer instead of reading a book."

The expression on his face made me realize the Bible was more special to him than he let on. "Why don't I do both? See, with the disk, you don't have to worry about the information getting lost. It will be like a backup. But I'll record your information in the Bible, too. In fact, I'm honored to write in your family bible. Really. It would be a privilege."

He smiled. "You have a good heart, lass. 'Twill take you far."

Knowing he was the one with a good heart, I gave him a hug. "Thanks for everything you're doing for me, Pop. Letting me live in your house. Cooking for me. Convincing Avery to help out. Everything."

He patted my back. "E'erybody needs a little help now and then."

Even though I'd eaten most of the muffin and Pop admitted he ate two jelly-filled doughnuts at the movie house, we both had appetites and decided to walk to Chat 'N Chew as soon as I took a shower.

11

Chat 'N Chew buzzed with twelve or fifteen people, and Bull tended to everyone with her usual good cheer. It was the biggest crowd I'd ever seen at the restaurant. Pop raised his eyebrows as we found a table and settled in. Seeing us, Bull carried over a pitcher of lemonade and two empty glasses.

"Howdy, Pop." She expertly poured, adding just the right amount of ice without spilling the liquid. "You're looking good, hon. Life in our little piece of paradise must agree with ya!"

"Thanks," I said and scanned the diner. A man I didn't recognize stood at the center of the crowd. Nodding and smiling, he looked like a politician. And standing beside him, Riley seemed to be playing the role of mayor, a first since I'd been around.

"Who's that?" Pop asked.

Bull waved a hand in the direction of her customers. "Some investor. Spouting off a load of crap, if you ask me. Name's Lester Smoak. He had a meeting with Riley and some of the council members. Guess their chat drew a crowd."

My ears perked up. "Investor?"

Bull nodded and yelled across the buzz of voices. "Hey, Lester! This here's Pop and the girl we was tellin' you 'bout. Jaxie from Atlanta!"

He instantly appeared and pumped our hands, sliding into the chair next to me, beaming a smile at us. "Pleased to meet you both. I've heard a lot about you."

Pop studied him. "From who?"

"Oh, everyone knows you, Pop." The man chuckled and looked my way. "And you, young lady, are popular in your own right. I understand you're doing some good work around here to revitalize this town."

He beamed another smile, and it made me squirm. All once-bright white caps, slightly stained from smoke, his teeth were too big for his mouth. And something about him reminded me of a pay-by-the-week used-car salesman.

"I'm here on behalf of Shine Advertising and Public Relations in Atlanta. Doing pro bono work," I said.

"Sure, sure. I heard about your little project. Which is why you'll be thrilled to hear what I have to say!"

I searched Pop's face for direction, but he just shrugged and leaned back to study Lester with narrowed eyes.

"And what would that be?" I asked.

Riley pulled up a chair. "Lester here is gonna invest some money in Rumton. Yer revitalization plan is done!"

People stopped their conversations to listen to ours. All eyes were on Lester the investor. He projected a smile in the general direction of everyone before talking.

"Your mayor is right! I most certainly am. I heard about Rumton's financial plight and decided there's no better time than now to jump in and help out!" When he patted my arm, I almost cringed. "See, Miss Parker, I am putting together a high-tech think tank, if you will. A team of creative programming geniuses, who will be designing some state-of-the-art security systems for computer networks across the country. I've got to put them all in one place. A place with plenty of fresh air but a place without distractions."

"Uh huh," I muttered. "A place without wireless Internet service?"

"Oh, we'll take care of that with a Wi-Fi system." His eyes swept the place to make sure everyone still listened. "Goes up pretty quick, and makes Internet service available to everyone."

"Perfect, perfect!" Billy said.

Lester's arms stretched out to his sides, revealing a rounded gut. "I'm going to buy a few parcels of land. Build a small, cozy town house community. After all, my team will need someplace to live, and we'll have a steady stream of consultants visiting, too. Heck, maybe I'll even build a quaint little bed-and-breakfast."

I guzzled my lemonade and put down an empty glass. "You're going to *build* a town house project so your programmers have a place to live? Wouldn't it be much easier to select a site that already has housing in place?"

"Of course, it would be *easier*, Miss Parker, but easy is not always best."

I wondered why he called me by my last name, when I'd been introduced as Jaxie. "So, you'll rent these townhomes?"

"Sure. Rent. Sell. Whatever is best for the people. Heck, I'd be willing to bet some folks around these parts will want to sell their houses and move into one of my town houses." His eyes grazed the small audience. "Think of it! No yard to mow or house to paint. A nice little outdoor courtyard, to grow your tomatoes and flowers. A swimming pool. Barbecue grill in the common area for cookouts."

"I might buy me one of them," a woman said. "I'm getting too old to keep up a yard."

Lester nodded. "Exactly! And I'm going to make sure we have a real medical building with a practicing doctor and dentist. We'll get a couple of sharp young fellows or gals, who have completed their internship and want to open their own practice. I'll subsidize them."

"We've been needin' something like that for a long time,"

Gertrude said, sitting down stiffly, rubbing her arthritic knees. "We need us a young doctor."

Riley slapped a hand on the table. "So, whadda ya think, Jaxie? Ain't this perfect timin'?"

"Well, it's certainly coincidental. That's for sure." It was all *too* coincidental.

At the next table, Riley nodded. "Well, me an' the town council members think it's perfect timin'. Lester's plan will perk up Rumton!"

I scanned the eager nodding faces of the town council members and felt slighted. Overnight, they'd given up on me and Shine Advertising.

"He's a godsend," one said.

"A godsend!" another echoed.

Out of the corner of my eye, I could see Bull shaking her head. She didn't agree. But then she didn't speak up, either. Probably because Lester was a paying customer. For all I knew, he'd bought everyone lunch.

I asked the stranger how he'd heard the town was in trouble.

"Why, he's one of our own," Gertrude answered for him.

"Right, right," Billy said. "We asked the same question. But see, Lester was in the army with Cappy's grandson. The two boys were best friends. Everybody remembers Jonathan coming to visit and just raving about his friend, the first sergeant."

"Cappy was our mayor," Riley explained. "I got elected when he kicked the bucket."

Lester the investor nodded solemnly. "I didn't think I was going to make it when Jonathan got killed in the line of duty. Messed me up good, losing him like that. And then, when Cappy passed away, it was another shock. Like losing my own daddy."

"We all miss Cappy," Bull said, topping off coffee cups and lemonade glasses. "But I wasn't aware he knew you. Fact, I don't recall ever seeing you around here."

Lester shrugged. "Could be because I haven't spent much time here. But it's time to change that. The last time I spoke with Cappy, he told me how Rumton's economy had all but dried up. As mayor, he was quite concerned. That was just before he died. And now, since I've decided to get out of the city, I got to thinking, why not move to Rumton and help turn things around?"

"What city would that be?" Pop asked. "The one you got out of."

Lester waved a hand. "Oh, I have business ventures in different cities. But I've been spending most of my time lately in Raleigh-Durham. The Research Triangle. In fact, I planned to set up my think tank there, but it's too noisy. My team needs solitude."

"I might want to buy me one of them townhomes, too," Riley said.

Lester laughed. "I'd better start a waiting list."

"We're right grateful you're here to revitalize the town," Gertrude said. "Jaxie wasn't making much progress, bless her heart. Were you, sugar?"

"Well, actually," I said, my cheeks burning from the criticism, "these things take some time. We've already done grant research. An environmental survey and feasibility study is under way. There is a lot going on."

"Well, nothing gets results like money on the table, does it, sweetheart?" Lester said. I wanted to tell him not to call me "sweetheart," but he kept talking. "After all, I've worked hard and invested well. The stock market has been good to me. So why not put some of that money to good use in Cappy's memory?"

Defensive, I leaned back in my chair and crossed my arms. "Out of the blue, you want to buy up Rumton?"

He chuckled. "Oh, I'm not buying up anything, Miss Parker. Just purchasing a few parcels of land. And it's not out of the blue. I've needed a change of pace for some time now. Cappy's death reminded me that sometimes you have to just go for it—or you might not get around to it. And, really, Rumton is the perfect setting for my think tank. I'll employ fifteen to twenty programmers, and with the results I expect, my team will certainly generate good exposure for the area. But, of course, I want to make things better. Not change everything. Rumton's gentle pace and charm is what makes it so great."

He showed the smile again, with just the right amount of modesty on his face. I suppressed a scream. Why were these people so gullible? The man just happens to show up and wants to buy a bunch of land? And both of his supposed ties to Rumton—Cappy and Cappy's son, Jonathan—were conveniently dead?

I uncrossed my arms and forced a smile. "It all sounds interesting, but I'd say everyone should carefully think things through. Do you all really want to sell your land?"

"Yer the one who started this whole revitalization push," Riley pointed out. "And now that somethin's happenin', you go an' get skittish."

"Yup," a man said. I think he was a council member. "We didn't even know we needed revitalizin' until you came 'round and told us."

A murmur of voices hit my ears as people agreed with the councilman. Pop leaned forward to speak, and the restaurant quieted in an instant. "Jaxie might be young, but she knows her business. She works for a top firm in Atlanta, and I think she makes a good point. You all should think about things before you make a quick decision." He leaned back in his chair. "No need to be hasty."

The murmur rose up again. Lester did a palms-down motion to quiet the restaurant. "I'm sure Miss Parker has everyone's best interest in mind. And she's right. It is important to think very carefully about financial decisions before you commit to something. If I hadn't made wise decisions in the past, I'd be broke right now, instead of a multimillionaire."

Silence ensued while everyone pondered Lester's net worth.

Billy cleared his throat. "I've already thought long and hard about what you want to do for Rumton, and I'm signing my option papers right now. Signing 'em right now."

"Option papers?" I said.

"Lester is buying options," Riley said. "You get upfront money that's yers to keep. Whether or not he actually buys yer land. An' if Lester does buy it, the price is already set. The selling price on my option is more'n fair. How kin anybody go wrong?"

Lester had already bought options? Hadn't he just gotten to town?

"Why, heck, Lester," Riley continued. "With your grand ideas, you ought to run for mayor when my term is up. I ain't gonna run for a second term."

Lester modestly nodded his head, and his eyes glimmered at the suggestion: Yes, he would entertain the idea of getting in on the upcoming mayoral race. Shaking his head, Pop dropped a few bills on the table for our drinks. We excused ourselves and left without eating.

"Think you can whip up a few of your famous deli sandwiches?" he said as we were walking home.

"Of course."

"With your signature slice of pickle?"

"Sure."

"Good. I'm still hungry."

We walked some more, quietly, mulling over what had just occurred at the Chat 'N Chew. We both frowned.

"I suppose he mailed the option to buy contracts out to landowners," I mused. "Did you ever get an offer to buy your land, Pop?"

He shook his head. "If I 'ad, it would've gone straight to the trash. I'll ne'er sell."

"What's your take on Lester?"

"I have the feeling that e'erybody is being snowed."

"Me, too. A stranger shows up out of the blue to save the town?"

Pop shrugged. "Sort of what you did, lass."

"Oh, c'mon. That was different. My intentions were pure."

His left eyebrow shot up and arched wide over the green eye.

"Okay, I didn't want to be here. So my intentions were forced. But they were still pure."

The eyebrow went down.

"Anyway, this guy gives me the creeps," I said.

"Let's get some food in our bellies before we talk 'bout it," Pop said. "I can't think on an empty stomach."

"Not only did this guy appear out of nowhere with plans to buy land and build condos," I explained to Avery, "but now Riley is telling everybody that when his term is up, they should elect Lester mayor!"

Avery shared a bite of his sandwich with Bandit. "And this guy Lester says he was best friends with Jonathan?"

"Yeah," I said, munching a pickle. "Lester Smoak. He said they were like his family."

"Then how come I never heard of him?" Avery said. "He'd be about the same age as me and Justin. We spent a lot of time here as kids. And played with Jonathan."

Pop saluted my cooking effort by holding up the last bite of his sandwich before popping it into his mouth. "Lester says he was Jonathan's first sergeant in the military. They didn't know each other as kids."

"But people remember Jonathan talking about Lester when he came home on leave?" Avery asked.

Pop shrugged. "Jonathan used to talk 'bout lots of people he met in the military."

"But when did Lester have time to buy options?" I said. "You have to do research to find out who owns what and determine fair market value of the properties. So he planned this a while ago. He hooked everyone and reeled them in."

"Why?" Avery said. "What are his motives?"

We finished our sandwiches and tried to guess all the reasons why a wealthy man might want to get his hands on a small, economically depressed town. After we'd brainstormed and eaten peanut butter cookies for dessert, we were no closer to having a hypothesis. As an investor, he'd face all the same roadblocks that the town had faced for years. A weak infrastructure. Lack of young people, a labor pool, and amenities. Plus the fact that the town was sandwiched by inaccessible water. What did he know that we didn't?

"Back to square one," I muttered. "But here's another question: Why would Riley suggest that Lester run for mayor unless the two of them had already discussed it? And if that's true, why on earth would Lester want to be the mayor of Rumton?"

"For the power, I suppose," Pop said, and gave me a quick lesson on South Carolina politics. Local governments operated under one of three different setups, one in which the mayor was just a figurehead and had no real power. But Rumton was incorporated under the strong-mayor form. The council consisted of five members, but ultimately one person controlled the little town: its mayor. Outright, he or she made all the important decisions, including those regarding town assets, budgets, and zoning ordinances.

It was information I should already have gathered. "You mean to tell me that Riley completely controls what happens in this town? And if Lester became mayor, he would run things?"

Pop nodded. "He'd rule the town."

"That's crazy," Avery said.

"System works okay, long as people are smart enough to elect a good mayor."

"Like you, for instance," I said, thinking out loud.

"Ne'er thought 'bout being mayor. Nobody else did either, after Cappy, because nobody ran." Pop shrugged. "Riley's not so bad at it, really. He's just a little too trusting at times."

As I cleared away our plates, Flush materialized to wait for leftovers. There weren't any, but I gave him a dog biscuit and he nuzzled my hand in appreciation. I wondered how it would be to lead such a simple life. As long as Flush's food bowl was filled a couple of times each day, and he received some attention from Pop, he was perfectly content.

"Well, I've got some news for you," Avery said, after I'd finished the dishes. "Somebody already did some surveying. It was recent, too. I found some markers."

Things were getting weirder by the minute. How could surveyors traipse around Rumton undetected?

"Could have been somebody that lives 'ere," Pop said. "Or surveyors could've come through, quietlike. We get visitors e'ery so often. Grandkids and such. So it wouldn't be all that unusual to see out-of-towners."

"True." Avery smiled. "Two buddies of mine are at work right now on the shipwreck site."

The news caught me by surprise. "They are?"

"Brent and Tom. You'll meet them later. And by the way, their bags are in the two rooms next to yours, so if you see Bandit hightailing up the hall with something in her paws, try to get it back."

"Are they volunteering?" The additional help would be great, but I worried about paying them.

"Of course, they owe me one. Besides, the promise of Pop's cooking hooked them. Checking out the shipwreck is just a bonus."

"Excellent! I can't wait to meet them." A diversion of two

shipwreck-hunting masculine hunks would surely take my mind off Justin. Plus, having the extra manpower was a good thing. With Lester in town, I was up against the clock. The more people working, the better. Especially since somebody had been doing some land surveying. I asked Avery where he'd found the markers.

"Area bordering the Intracoastal Waterway on the north end of town."

"Be willing to bet it's the same land the town owns," Pop said. "Riley mentioned selling some land a while back. But he's always rambling on 'bout something they discussed on the council."

An already bad feeling in my gut suddenly got worse. "So not only is Lester acquiring options from individuals, but he's already spoken to Riley about buying the town's assets. But why would he want it? I've seen it on the charts, but what exactly *is* the waterway?"

Avery explained that the waterway ran a north-south route along the East Coast. A string of both natural and manmade channels that periodically dumped into the ocean, it was basically a three-thousand-mile-long "highway" for boat traffic.

"The original purpose was to move supplies during wartime," he said, "but today the Intracoastal Waterway has grown into a playground for pleasure boaters and a cash cow for land developers."

"Well, assuming Lester is behind the property markers, why would he survey the land near the waterway?" I said, thinking aloud. "He can't build anything there because of the wetlands. That's why the town never put in a public boat ramp."

We moved outside and spread out in the courtyard. Avery studied some hand-drawn sketches he'd made. "It wouldn't be difficult to fill in wetlands and create developable property. It's just a matter of moving dirt around to create high and dry areas and low-drainage areas. Then, you stick fountains in the water-retention ponds, import some ducks, and call the ponds lakes. You'd elevate the houses on pilings, like beach houses. It would be one heck of a view, too. Imagine your house backing up to the marsh, with the waterway just beyond. You could sit and watch the boats go by. In fact, you could build your own pier right across the marsh that led to your own boat dock."

"But filling in wetlands is illegal." Even I knew that. Messing with estuaries upset the delicate balance of the ecosystem. "And you said that environmental protection regulations are super strict."

He shrugged. "They are. But developers will fill in wetlands all day long if the numbers mesh. Waterway property is the next best thing to oceanfront right now, and it brings astronomical selling prices! Three, four, even five hundred thousand dollars for a residential patch of dirt. We're talking a lot that is only, say, seventy or eighty feet wide."

"So how do people get away with screwing up the environment?"

"They'd have various authorities to deal with including the Army Corps of Engineers. But theoretically, a person could do what he wanted. Especially if he controlled the town. If he got caught and the authorities came after him, he'd claim ignorance. Say his surveyor told him everything was a go, and he didn't know he was breaking the law," Avery theorized. "He'd take a slap on the hand and pay the fines."

In business, everything always boiled down to the numbers. That much I knew. "So he just figures the fines as a cost of doing business. And has a good lawyer to keep him out of jail."

"Exactly. Once construction is under way, he could even apply for permits to build a community dock and marina. Say it's for the public good and all that."

"Which would allow a boater to go anywhere," I said, the picture coming together.

My brain raced with possible scenarios as I wondered why Lester was interested in Rumton and how long his eye had been on the small town.

12

Keeping the handset cradled between my head and shoulder, I made angry doodles on a scratchpad and relayed the Lester situation to my boss.

"This could be good timing, Jaxie. Perhaps some interest from an investor is just what the town needs."

The doodles grew larger and darker as my frustration grew. "But the timing is too coincidental. Lester is already acquiring options from residents to buy their property, plus Avery found markers near the waterway that appear to be from a recent survey. Pop just called Riley, uh, I mean the mayor, and he confirmed that Lester offered to buy the town's land. They're going to vote on selling it."

"The waterway property?"

"Right. It's about a two-mile stretch."

The door opened and a couple of guys bounded through toting supply bags and diving gear. Figuring them to be Avery's scientist friends, I waved hello and did a quick survey of my own. Handsome in an athletic way, they sported the same hip outdoor gear that Avery wore.

Aaron's tone became rigid. "You're smart to be cautious, but you might be overreacting. Lester is a businessman. If he's considered Rumton for his think tank venture, he would be smart to do survey work in advance. The same goes for buying options. That's an insurance policy for him."

"I understand what you're saying, but I've got a bad feeling about it," I persisted, even though I had nothing concrete to back up my reservations.

Suddenly sounding tired, Aaron sighed. "I'll see what I can find out about Lester Smoak. Meanwhile, you just sit tight and keep doing what you've been doing."

I hung up with a curse and decided to forget Lester and my boss for the time being. There were two very interesting newcomers standing in front of me who were much more deserving of my attention. I unleashed my best smile, relieved to realize that I hadn't totally forgotten how to flirt. "You guys must be Avery's friends."

I automatically scanned their hands when they introduced themselves. Brent wore a wedding band, but Tom didn't. Aiming the smile in Tom's direction, I teasingly asked if they'd dug up a buried treasure chest.

Flirting back, Tom returned the smile and stole a look at my chest. "No signs of an actual treasure yet, but it sure is fun to look."

I closed the notepad and made a show of sliding my bright orange Waterman pen into a front shirt pocket. "So what are the possibilities, do you think?"

"Very good," he answered in a voice thick with double meaning. He was a player, it seemed, who liked to have fun.

As I mixed glasses of powdered Gatorade for my thirsty newcomers and continued to check out the single one, a memory of Justin's kiss washed through me. It left me unexpectedly drenched with desire and then anger. What the heck was he doing in my head? Justin shunned me, and besides, he wasn't even my type. Plus, there was a gorgeous, straight, single, and willing researcher right in front of me.

Tom saw the confusion in my face. "Something wrong, Jaxie?"

"No, no. I just remembered something I have to do."

"Okay. Well, thanks for the drinks. We came back to get a new snorkel and some equipment, but we're heading right back out."

Brent guzzled his drink and grinned at the interaction between me and Tom. "Ready, partner? Let's roll."

I took their empty glasses. "Be careful out there. And thanks for everything you're doing."

Backing through the door, Tom graciously bowed. "Glad to be of service. See you tonight."

The second they were gone, I silently scolded myself for allowing Mr. Research Analyst to force his way into my thoughts. In a moment of weird timing, the phone rang. I knew Justin was on the other end before I picked up. I wanted to answer with, "*Will you please get off my mind?*" But I said hello instead.

"Got some news for you, Jaxie," he said. "One word: nothing. I can't find anything on a ship named *Aldora*. Trying to determine what she might have had on board when she sank is a dead end. We'll just have to wait and see what Avery's guys turn up."

My hope for a sunken treasure fizzled. "Thanks for trying."

Dead airtime ensued, during which neither of us said anything. He waited for me to say something and I stubbornly didn't. After all, he had called me.

"This isn't all bad news, you know," he finally said.

"Really? Why is that?"

"Because it tells us some things. One, the *Aldora* was not a famous ship with a famous captain, per se. Unless, of course, it had just been bought or stolen right before it sank, and the new captain renamed her first."

"Interesting."

"Also, I found out that Aldora was a somewhat common name for a woman in the 1700s. English origin. Means 'noble.' Chances are, your sunken ship was named after a woman. Could have been a father naming it after his daughter. More likely, it was a lovesick man naming it after the girl who stole his heart."

As if someone changed my mind's channel by remote control, the late-night walk with Justin replayed in my memory, uninvited. The scene fast-forwarded to his declaration of interest in me: *Jaxie, I've been crazy about you for a long time. Ever since you came to work at the agency.*

"Great!" I said brightly, shaking my head to clear out all thoughts of him and me together. It would never work. "Maybe I'll find out something from the locals, on a woman named Aldora from the eighteenth century. It's a long shot, but you never know. Besides, word has spread about your brother's find. Everybody knows about the shipwreck. Pop said you can't keep a secret around here."

"True."

"So, uh, thanks for checking on the *Aldora*."

Another brutal silence hit my ear and memories of Justin's visit to Rumton pushed their way back into my consciousness. I wondered if his thoughts mirrored mine: being in his arms, in the middle of the street, bathed in blue moonlight. And the possibility for more of the same.

"Well, how are you?" he said.

Pissed off, I wanted to answer. *For letting you get into my head.* "Look, Justin, you know I don't do long-term relationships," I blurted out, and my eyelid twitched hard enough to force itself shut for a moment. "I, uh, just want to make sure you know that. So it's probably for the best that we didn't, uh, you know . . ." *Sleep together.*

He cleared his throat but didn't say anything.

"I had a great time with you driving to Myrtle Beach and going out to Duckies for the karaoke." I plowed on. "I think it might even be fun to go out sometime, when I'm back in Atlanta. But I'm not looking for a serious relationship. I just thought you should know that. You know, to be fair."

A long pause traveled the line before he said, "I understand everything perfectly fine, Jaxie."

"Okay, right. Good."

"Now, back to my original question. How are you?"

My resolve dissipated. I wanted to get his take on the Lester situation. I relayed the entire story about coming across Lester at Bull's place and how Lester planned to save the day. And how Aaron seemed to be siding with the people. And I finished by admitting my suspicions. "It's not that I'm taking this whole thing personally, because I'm not. I mean, I'm the first to agree that results are what matter—not how you get there. If I thought this guy was legit, I'd be thrilled that he waltzed in here and saved my butt. But he's hiding something, I just know it."

"Why are you so sure?"

"I may not know much about small-town life, and I don't understand why in the heck these people choose to live here. But I do know big-city businessmen. I deal with them all the time. And this guy is not your average businessman or investor. He says exactly what everyone wants to hear. Gives me the willies."

"Willies?" Justin chuckled. "I don't have enough information to make an informed decision on the matter. But I am curious. Why do you care?"

"What do you mean, why do I care?"

"Why do you care who Lester Smoak is or isn't?"

Bandit climbed into my lap and for once sought attention rather than food. I petted her back. "Because if he's not telling the truth about his real intentions, then he has something to gain at somebody else's expense. He wants to keep it a secret because if Rumton residents knew the real story, they'd chase his ass out of here."

"Okay," Justin said. "Let me ask again. Why do you care?"

"Because I don't want these people to be hurt!" I almost shouted.

"You've developed a *conscience* about the assignment? I thought you just wanted to slap something together and get out of there."

"Oh, go analyze some spreadsheets or something!" I slammed down the phone for the second time in half an hour. My only regret in doing so was that I hadn't thought of a better exit line.

I rubbed my eyelid with one hand and Bandit with the other while I pondered what to do next. It occurred to me that Aaron was supposed to be visiting soon. Sheila said so. But he had still not mentioned anything to me about traveling to Rumton. And in hindsight, he hadn't seemed shocked at the news about Lester Smoak, almost as if he'd known about the man in advance of my phone call. Had someone else already told him?

Not only did I feel inadequate, but I also felt paranoid. Aaron was a fair boss. I'd never had reason to distrust him before, and I felt disloyal to second-guess him now. Maybe I was not being impartial. Regardless, I was not one to sit back and wait for answers. I checked my electronic organizer to find the number I wanted, grabbed the telephone, and dialed Atlanta.

"Chuck, hi. It's Jaxie."

There was an annoying pause while he determined who was on the other end of the line before he spoke. "Well, well. Jaxie Parker. Haven't heard from you in a long time."

"Right, well. We've both been busy" was all I could think of.

"What can I do for you?" His voice sounded formal, as though I was an old business acquaintance instead of an old fling. We'd had utterly amazing sex for two solid months, in fact. Once in his motor home while doing an all-weekend stakeout to watch a police captain who'd been suspected of dealing cocaine. Chuck was older than my usual boyfriends, but he looked exactly like Harrison Ford and had a smile that made my legs wobbly. And he never went anywhere without a gun, which made him dangerous in a sexy sort of way.

"I need some help, and you're the only ex-cop and private investigator I know . . . personally."

He sighed. "Lay it on me. Whatcha got?"

I gave him a day-in-the-life-of-Jaxie, over the past weeks, starting with me getting sent to Rumton and ending with the mysterious investor. "I have no idea what to look for, but can you try to find something on this guy Lester? I don't want my boss to know I'm checking the guy out, because he said he'd take care of it. But I want a second opinion and I'll pay your usual rate. By the way, what is your usual rate?"

He laughed. "You can't afford me, babe. But give me everything you've got on this man, and I'll do some digging. On the down-low. And, don't worry about my fee," he added. "I may need a favor from you someday."

I smiled. "A public relations favor?"

"You never know."

"One more thing, Chuck. It's important you know how serious this is. The future of a town may be at stake here. A town with a lot of . . . well, quirky, crazy people. But really good people. I mean, this isn't just some snubbed wife who wants to get the dirt on a cheating hubby, you know. It's really important to me. Are you any good at what you do?"

"Yeah, I'm damn good at what I do. And just for the record? I take on very few domestic cheating-spouse investigations. Can't stand to see women cry."

I laughed. Chuck had always enjoyed his image as a stereotypical tough guy.

"Now, about your man. Get his license plate number and the make of the car. Get some digital photos without being obtrusive about it. E-mail everything, along with any information you have, including the cities where he says he has businesses. Also, try to send a copy of the option offer that the residents received. You have my e-mail address?"

I was a fanatic about keeping the contacts database current in my Palm handheld. "Of course."

"If the opportunity comes up, get his fingerprints on a glass or something else that's relatively smooth and clean. Put it in a plastic Baggie and overnight it to me. Lastly, keep your eyes and ears open. Meanwhile I'll see what I can find out from this end." He hung up without waiting for a good-bye.

Suddenly, the house felt stifling. I had to get away from the phone and the computer and my thoughts about men I'd dated in the past. I found Pop shelling peas and asked him the best way to hook up with all the town council members. I was way past due in having a talk with them about the future of their town.

"A few of them were at Bull's earlier. But now e'eryone will be at the town hall," he said. "Judge is holding court today."

"Town hall being the movie theater?"

"Aye."

"Why would the council members be there unless one of them had to go in front of the judge?"

"It's a big event 'round here. E'erybody will be there."

"You mean, for the entertainment value?"

He nodded. "Right-o. C'mon, I'll take you. Might even buy you a popcorn, if you're lucky."

"With butter?"

He winked the green eye. "Why not?"

13

Gertrude spotted us and waved as soon as we walked into the movie theater's lobby. "Yer birth control pills are in, sugar!" she yelled in a decibel level much higher than an eighty-year-old pharmacist ought to be able to produce. "You kin pick 'em up any time!"

Conversations stopped as people followed the direction of Gertrude's voice until their gaze settled on me. I hurried to the woman in an attempt to ward off further outbursts about my medical profile. "Uh, thanks, Gertrude. I'll stop by your place tomorrow."

Cackling, she patted my shoulder. "Come tell, who is it? You musta found yerself a hot beau around here," she said loudly enough for everyone to hear, and twenty or more people milled around. "I'll bet he blows away those prissy city boys yer used to!"

I'd simply stopped by the Always Open Apothecary to get a prescription refill. After I woke Gertrude up and told her what I needed, she explained that nobody in Rumton had used birth control pills for umpteen years and that she didn't have them in stock. The only hormones on her shelves were for menopause. But the drug wholesaler she ordered from could have my pills to her in a few days, she'd said. We agreed I'd drop back by.

"It's okay, sugar, I know how to keep a secret," Gertrude yelled. "Now who is he?"

Thankfully, Pop came to my rescue. "Time to replace your 'earing-aid battery, Gertrude. You're shouting."

She pulled the device out of her ear to look at it. "Really?"

"Jaxie will see you later for her prescription." He clapped his hands and turned toward the concession stand. "Now, how 'bout some popcorn, lass?"

Pop joked with the volunteer firefighters as they served our popcorn and Pepsi sodas. Looking around, I was amazed to see the lobby fill with still more people. Propped on an easel, a large dry-erase board served as a marquee. Five names with corresponding offenses were scrawled on it. An Ohio man was charged with driving past Rumton while intoxicated. Two drivers, both from Virginia, had the bad taste to speed through Rumton jurisdiction while heading south on Highway 17. A local woman was charged with violating a restraining order. And another local was charged with shooting his neighbor's goat.

"That goat deserved to git shot," Riley mused, walking up behind me as I stood gaping at the sign.

I turned to him. "Mr. Mayor—"

"When did ya quit callin' me Riley?"

"When I found out you were the mayor. Listen, Riley, do you think I could talk to you and the town council members tonight? After court is out? It'll just take a few minutes."

"Sure. I'll let everybody know. Might have to buy us a drink, though. Once the judge finishes up, you can git rum in yer Pepsi, for an extry three dollars."

I had some bills in my purse. "No problem."

The crowd migrated through the double theater doors. It was showtime. A large desk on wheels rested center stage, flanked by stands holding the South Carolina and United States flags. Looking uncomfortable in a starched uniform, the police chief sat to one side. Smacking chewing gum, a court reporter sat on the other. Sporting a long black gown that may have been a church choir robe, the judge took his seat without any fanfare.

A gavel rapped. "Quiet down, people. This ain't no movie show."

"He says that e'ery time," Pop whispered from the seat beside me.

"Every time," Mad Millie seconded, sliding into the vacant seat beside Pop. The two of them had become quite cozy.

"Every damn time," Riley agreed from my other side.

If Justin had been with me to share the craziness of the event, we'd laugh about it later back at the office in Atlanta. I wished things had turned out differently after our late-night walk. I wished he wasn't so hung up on meaningful dating. I wished I could quit thinking about him. What did I want from him, anyway? The thoughts playing out in my head against my will were maddening.

"Let's get down to it," the police chief said. "First up! Manny Blake Ledsetter, for destruction of his neighbor's livestock. Allegedly put a bullet between the eyes of a prized goat, to be exact."

While people munched their popcorn and leaned to whisper comments in one another's ears, the chief went through the swearing-in process, using a Bible. The judge asked Manny how he pleaded.

"Not guilty, judge. It was self-defense. That damn goat was just askin' to get itself shot!"

There was a murmur of agreement from the audience.

"Manny, you're a piece of work!" a woman shouted, standing up. "Elvis was the sweetest goat on this planet, and you killed him in cold blood. Out of pure meanness."

"That goat wasn't right in the head," Manny argued back. "Even for a goat!"

"Elvis had more brains in his head than you do in yours!" the woman rebutted.

An aisle in front of us, Gertrude stood up, shaking her head side to side. "That goat didn't have nothin' upstairs, Jane. It ate my patio table last year. And it tore up the passenger door of Walter's truck from buttin' it. You ever catch a ride with Walter? You have to climb through the driver's side and scootch over because the other door won't open."

Another murmur of agreement came from the audience.

Encouraged, Gertrude continued. "Elvis needed medicatin'. That's what that goat needed."

The gavel rapped again. "Quiet down, people. Everybody will get a turn to talk. And Gertrude, your hearing aid has gone out again. You're shouting. Now, sit down," the judge said.

Fidgeting with the device in her ear, Gertrude sat down.

The judge did a pretty good job of getting both sides of the story, and he managed to extract the pertinent information from both Jane and Manny. He did want to know why Manny had a pistol on him while pulling weeds. Manny explained that the goat had attacked him before, and the gun was for protection. Before ruling, the judge opened up the floor for five minutes of public input. Anyone with something to say about the matter was allowed exactly one minute, and the police chief, using a standard rotary-dial egg timer, doubled as the timekeeper.

"Is that normal?" I whispered to Pop. "A judge asking for public input?"

"Don't think so, lass. But he likes to hear what folks think before making a decision."

"What do you think about Elvis?"

"Damn goat should've been shot months ago."

Everyone who stood up to say his piece in sixty seconds or less agreed with Pop. And the judge agreed with them.

"I hereby find that the accused, Manny Blake Ledsetter acted in self-defense when Elvis butted him while he pulled weeds. On the charge of destruction of property, not guilty!" A short round of clapping ensued. With narrowed eyes, the judge pointed the gavel at Manny, and everyone quieted down to hear what came next. "The neighborly thing to do, though, would be for you to buy Jane a new goat."

The judge's stare got sharper as his eyebrows went up. Manny visibly shrunk down under the piercing look. "Okay, judge. Sure. I'll buy her a goat to replace Elvis," he mumbled.

"And you'll take care of this neighborly reimbursement by next week?"

Manny sighed, straightened up. "Yes, judge."

The gavel rapped.

In similar fashion, the judge heard the remaining four cases. It was determined that the driver charged with DUI had a medical condition, which caused him to talk with slurred speech. The two speeders were given reduced fines in return for a promise to obey speed limits in the future. And the local woman was found guilty of violating a restraining order when she broke into her estranged husband's wood shop. She thought he was having sex with his mistress at the time because Gertrude let it slip that he'd picked up a prescription for Viagra. During public input, the alleged mistress declared that the affair was over, the wife admitted that she didn't want to end her fifty-year marriage even if her husband had been unfaithful, and the husband asked the judge for leniency because the restraining order would be removed anyway. The husband had plenty of Viagra pills left and wanted to give it a try with the woman he loved. People clapped when the gavel rapped to conclude that case, too, and the court reporter had to stop for a minute to wipe a tear from her eye.

As we filtered back into the lobby, I realized that my contacts had dried out from not blinking enough and dug some rewetting drops out of my handbag. A line immediately formed at the concession stand, and I wondered how many of the people were going to whip out an extra three dollars. I also noticed some bills changing hands among several people, as I'd seen at the country club in Atlanta after a golf tournament.

"People *bet* on the outcome of these court appearances?"

Pop nodded. "Aye."

Mad Millie appeared and playfully punched him on the arm. "You win, Cuddles," she said, snuggling up to him as she handed over a dollar. "And I always pay my debts."

Cuddles?

Grinning, he pocketed the money.

I couldn't believe what I'd heard and saw. "*You* bet on the outcome of these court hearings, too?"

"Aye."

"Sweet Jesus."

Riley gathered up the council members and told them to get a drink on me. They did, and with Pop as my moral support, we returned to the theater. I borrowed the folding chair previously occupied by the police chief and placed it to face the front row of seats, where Riley, three men, and one woman waited to hear me out. I cleared my throat, willed my eye not to twitch, and thanked them for agreeing to meet with me.

"I didn't know there was going to be a second show tonight," someone said from the back of the theater. A group of people returned to their seats. They didn't want to miss anything.

"Come on in," Riley said. "Jaxie Parker wants to say her piece to the council. Everybody's welcome to listen."

"Get up on the stage," Gertrude shouted. "We can't see you."

I looked at Pop. He shook his head no.

"What if I just speak up, Gertrude? So everyone can hear me better."

She waved a hand at me, as though shooing away a fly, and

plopped down. I faced the council and did my best to speak loudly without shouting. "First, thanks for agreeing to meet with me on such short notice. As you all know, I'm in your town on behalf of Shine Advertising and Public Relations, doing this work for free. Trying to come up with some ideas on how to revitalize Rumton and get some money flowing into the town again. I think most of you know my boss, Aaron Ackworth, who grew up here."

A few Pepsi cups rose up in acknowledgment. "Good man," someone said.

Nervous, I took a deep breath. I wanted these people to like me and, more important, believe in me. I gave them a brief update on what had been done so far and where things stood regarding a revitalization plan, leaving out nothing except the part about the submerged shipwreck. "So with all that being said"—I paused to look at each council member directly—"I'm here to ask that you give me some time to finish what I've started before you make a decision regarding Lester's investment offer to buy the town-owned plot of land near the waterway. Let's wait and see what I come up with first. That way you will have some options, and you can choose what's best for the town."

Their expressions were set, as though the issue had already been decided. They were going to take Lester's money for the till, gratefully, as though he was doing everyone a big favor.

"We're appreciative of your efforts and will pass along our gratitude to Aaron," the councilwoman, Delores, said. "But Lester's offer for what is essentially worthless land is quite generous. It will give us enough money to make some improvements to our downtown."

"And now that Lester is here," one of the men said, "seems to me like you ought to be helping him out, not doing your own thing, like finding a shipwreck and sending your boys out there without telling anybody about it."

My face flushed. They'd heard about the boat, along with

everyone else who knew the secret, but had waited to see when I would tell them. Maybe that's why nobody responded to my *Rumton Review* ad seeking historical information. They thought I had held back and they didn't like it. "Look, there's really not much to tell yet, which is why I didn't bring it up. It's just an old boat, submerged right on the shoreline. Avery has some marine archaeologists checking into it, to see if there is any historical value."

A few of them shrugged. A few drank. Still, nobody offered anything to make me feel better. Tough crowd.

"I'll keep you updated on the ship and let you know what we find out," I promised. "But back to Lester. None of you really knows this man personally, right? So why is everyone so quick to buy into his plan? What if it's not the best thing for Rumton?"

"None of us knows you personally, either," Delores said politely.

"Right, but you know my boss very well. And we have nothing to gain by being here, other than the satisfaction of helping the small town where he grew up. This place is very near and dear to his heart. So I'm just asking that you give me some more time before you start selling land. The land the town owns near the waterway *and* any of your personally owned properties that Lester inquired about." I paused to breathe. Their expressions were not softening. "May I ask how many of you have been contacted regarding selling property that you own?"

Several hands went up. Riley, two council members, and four or five people who sat in on our meeting.

"And options? Has anyone besides Riley already signed options to sell?"

With the exception of one person, all the same hands stayed up. My heart dropped into my stomach with dread. I might have been too late. I stood up to unroll an area map that Avery gave me and whispered to Pop to have one of the firefighters bring more drinks and some bags of pretzels. He left to do so while I went around and asked people to point out where there parcels of land were. I wrote on the map how much acreage they had, along with the option purchase price, if they were willing to say. When I finished, it was apparent Lester Smoak meant business. He already acquired options for more than sixty acres of Rumton soil. I also learned that he mailed letters to everyone about the same time I'd arrived in town.

Apparently, letter recipients got a follow-up phone call from Lester the day after their option contracts arrived. All they had to do was sign and return a single page in the postage-paid envelope, and their check arrived a week later. The buyer was not listed as Lester Smoak but what I assumed to be one of his businesses. Gertrude had a copy of her contract in her purse and told me I was welcome to take it.

"You kin just bring it back to me when you come pick up yer birth control pills," she near-shouted, even though I sat right next to her at the time.

Stunned at the speed with which things were happening in sleepy little Rumton, I resumed my place before the council to see if I could change their minds. But, ultimately, I couldn't come up with any concrete reasons why they shouldn't sell their land. Most of it had been farmland that was no longer cropped. And most of the sellers could use the money.

"So what about the town's land? The strip by the waterway?"

"We've already gotten an independent appraisal and had a first reading on the issue at the last council meeting," Delores explained. "I don't think any of us sees a reason to hang on to it. We'd never use it for anything. But we can use the proceeds for several things."

I scanned their faces. "Aren't you concerned about what he wants to do with it?"

"Not much he can do with it," Delores answered for the group. "A lot of the acreage is wetlands."

"We know you mean well, Jaxie," Riley said. "But Lester has

said that he's willing to run for mayor, since he'll have such a vested interest in seeing us succeed. And his plan is gonna bring people and money to town. Ain't that what you wanted?"

"But elect him mayor?" I countered. "You'd give control of your town to somebody you don't even know."

"We got a good feeling about him," Rusty, one of the council members, said. "And we do know all about him. He sent a sheet telling about himself in the letters that went out."

My eyelid went wild. "Not only did he send actual option contracts, ready to be signed and returned, but he also sent you a bio on himself?"

"Sure. Even had a photo on there."

I sighed. "Gertrude, do you have one of those in your purse, too?"

"Sure do, sugar. You want it? You kin bring it back when you—"

"I know, I know"— I sighed, interrupting—"when I come to pick up my birth control pills. Sure, I'll get it before we leave."

"Besides," Rusty said, "it will be good to have a businessman with a vision as mayor. He can take us places, without changing Rumton. That's what he promised. To keep things laid-back and quiet, the way we like it. But better. Why not sell the man some land and let him fulfill his dream to look after a small town? What's the problem?"

A few more people sauntered in to the theater to see what was happening. "It's too sudden," I countered. "And it doesn't make sense that Lester wants to spend money here if he's not going to get a high return from it. That's the reality of business. An investor doesn't spend money unless he's going to make money."

"You're a thick-headed one, that's for sure," Rusty said. "He *is* going to make some money from that high-tech think tank of his. He'll make lots of money from that security system thing they're going to develop."

Frustrated, I paced while I spoke. "First of all, he could put his think tank anywhere, if that's truly what he intends to do. There are a lot more suitable places for something like that. And second, why does he need so much land?"

"As I've already told you, sweetheart, I'm just an old eccentric with money to spend," Lester's voice boomed from the rear of the theater. He walked down the aisle as he spoke. "This is the place I want to make home! And why wouldn't I want to own land in my own hometown? I love Rumton and everything it stands for. Beautiful country. Great fishing. Old-fashioned values."

Stopping to stand beside me, he spoke to our audience, arms outstretched. "And wonderful, warm, friendly people. That's the main reason I want to help this town and call Rumton home."

Thwarted and feeling ridiculously incompetent, I didn't know what to say. Maybe there wasn't anything else to say.

Lester patted my shoulder; his touch was revolting. "You might just be a bit upset over the good things happening because it wasn't all your doing," he said. "But don't feel bad because everybody knows that you've tried your best."

As several white heads nodded, my cheeks burned.

"Pop, can't you talk to Riley and get him to wake up?" I asked later, in the lobby, as we waited for Gertrude to come out of the bathroom. She had copies of the option paperwork, and I was going to hold her to lending it to me, despite the fact that Lester had crashed my party.

"I already planned to, when it's just me and him. Maybe o'er a game of chess. I want to make sure he's thought of all the consequences of letting Lester take over before he allows it to 'appen."

That was something. "Thanks."

"Probably won't change anything, though. When Riley gets his mind set 'bout something, it's hard to change it."

I managed to obtain Gertrude's paperwork without getting another reminder about my birth control pills, paid the volunteer fire department for everyone's drinks, and we left. I would have been totally dejected driving home were it not for the fact that I had managed to snap a few digital photos of Lester on my camera phone to e-mail to Chuck. Even though there were no wireless signals in Rumton, the phone wasn't rendered totally useless. I was glad I carried it in my purse, out of habit.

Even better than the photographs, we'd secured Lester's fingerprints. I had told Pop about the background check on Lester, and Pop had casually retrieved Lester's discarded plastic water bottle from the garbage can. As an added bonus, on the way out I was able to snap a picture of his car, a white Lincoln, and jot down the plate number. I also took a shot of the item hanging from his rearview mirror, just because it caught my attention and I wondered what it was. A round loop with feathers and beads, it resembled Indian artwork, which seemed like an odd adornment for a man like Lester.

Feeling like a sleuth eager to transmit everything to Chuck as soon as possible, I had to force myself not to speed. Pop had caught a ride with Millie, and I drove myself home, absorbed in thought. Regardless of what everyone else thought about Lester, I had to trust my instincts and do whatever it took to protect the people of Rumton. They might not yet believe in me, but I couldn't help having become enamored with all of them.

14

Buttering a piece of toast, I studied my hands and realized it was the first time in a long time that my nails weren't painted. Since Rumton didn't have a salon and there was no place nearby to get a manicure, I'd just removed the old polish and filed my nails short. Oddly, au naturel nails didn't bother me as much as I would have thought. Probably because I had too many other things to worry about.

I spread a spoonful of peach jam atop the already buttered toast, not caring about calories, and bit in. Chewing, I spoke through a mouthful of food, not caring about bad manners, either. "Everybody knows about the sunken boat. Everyone in town. So much for keeping it under wraps."

Avery took the jar of jam and doctored up his toast. "That's okay because there is nothing of monetary value down there, anyway."

"For sure?" I looked at Brent and Tom, who took their turns at the peach jam. Mad Millie had made it. It was really good jam. I told Pop he should have become friends with her years ago, and he agreed.

"Are you guys done exploring?" I asked.

Tom nodded. "Yep, and sorry to say we've got to leave today."

Oh, well, I thought. *No sunken treasure and no time for a fling with Tom.* "There was nothing at all? I don't know what I expected, but that's disappointing."

"We can say with confidence that the boat was in use between the late sixteen hundreds and mid-1700s. Based on what's left of it, we did a sketch of what the original ship looked like, and we think it was big. Possibly a three-masted square-rigger. And we found a few cool artifacts," Brent said. "Some ceramics and carpentry tools. There is also an anchor that appears to be intact and in good shape, but it's still half-submerged and covered with barnacles. Too big to get out of there without using heavy equipment."

"A ship of that size would've had several anchors, but only one stayed with our wreckage," Tom added.

"The items we recovered are in Pop's shed on the workbench, if you want to take a look," Brent said.

"No doubloons? No pieces of eight?"

He laughed. "Spanish explorers and conquistadors certainly traveled the Gulf Stream, returning to Spain with treasure-filled loads. And pirates certainly ran these shores to steal from the Spaniards among others. But if the *Aldora* was a pirate flagship, and if there was anything valuable on board when she sank, it's still out there somewhere."

I asked why they didn't want to look for a possible treasure.

Tom shook his head. "Probably, the *Aldora* went down offshore but didn't fully sink and was washed into Devil's Tail during a storm. If there's no historical documentation to indicate that valuables were on board, and where the ship traveled from when it sank, it makes no sense to search the ocean floor. Without knowledge of what you're looking for, doing that would be a real waste of time and money."

Brent smiled. "We knew it was a long shot to begin with. But *not* knowing what you'll find—even if what you discover is nothing—is what it's all about. We had fun looking. Besides, we got to see a ghost. Well, we felt one at least."

"You're kidding!"

"Seriously. I got the feeling that we were being watched out there. But not a threatening kind of thing. More like a curious ghost who wanted to know what we were doing."

I pointed at Brent. "He's messing with me, right?"

"Crazy as it sounds," Tom said, "I felt it, too. We joked about it and even checked to see if somebody was offshore, watching us with binoculars. Nobody was, but the sensation didn't go away. It's almost like there's an energy field around the site."

"Huh," I said.

"Huh," Pop and Avery said.

Brent shrugged. "Some things can't be explained. But Tom is right. It has been a fun three-day distraction. And I haven't eaten this well in months. Thanks for all the great cooking, Pop."

"Anytime."

"Don't forget to thank Jaxie, too. It's almost artistic the way she layers sliced turkey and Swiss together on wheat," Tom teased. "She's mean with that mustard squirt bottle, too."

"Gimmie a break. I'm trying to learn how to cook!" I'd offered to cook the night before in fact, but the men turned me down. My reputation in the kitchen had leaked out.

After finishing breakfast and recovering a handheld sonic device that Bandit had swiped and stuck in the spittoon, Brent and Tom gathered their gear for the road. Pop, Avery, and I headed to the shed to check out the ship's artifacts. It looked like a bunch of old, rusty, broken junk to me, but at least it was something to put in Rumton's museum if the grant money came through. Not that the townspeople would even want a museum if they knew it was my idea.

I felt sluggish and knew I'd soon start feeling sorry for myself if I didn't do something to ward off the blues. "I need a spinning class," I muttered.

"Eh?" Pop said. I had to laugh at the look on his face.

"It's a type of exercise done on a stationary bike," I explained.

"I'm feeling antsy or something. We're not making any progress, and this whole Lester thing is blowing me away. I can't think straight. I need a workout."

Avery put an arm across my shoulders as we walked back to the house. "Don't let it get to you. Life's too short. Besides, I have some good news for you."

"You do?"

He explained that water was regularly flowing in and out of Devil's Tail with the tides and that the spot was definitely where shrimpers used to move their boats in and out of Rumton, back when it was an actual inlet. Before shifting sands, and possibly storms, filled it in. He could tell from information he'd gathered on foot, combined with data he'd just received from the satellite imaging company. Like me, Avery used satellite Internet access since he traveled so much, and the images with corresponding reports had been sent to his laptop.

Inside, we all crowded around the computer to look, while he toggled between different screens and explained what we were seeing.

"Amazing," I said when he finished. "But how does it help us now, other than we know for sure where an inlet used to be one hundred years ago?"

"If the trend continues, Rumton may very well have inlet access to the ocean again. Of course, it could be a while before there's enough water depth to move a boat in and out. Hard to say, but it could happen in seven, maybe eight years."

"Oh, great. Seven or eight *years*? That's not going to help anything right now."

"Whyn't you go for a jog?" Pop suggested. "Or if you want to ride a bike—what did you call it? Spinning? I've got one you can ride. Just pumped up the tires a few days ago."

"I'm used to working out in air-conditioning," I said, knowing how absurd it must have sounded.

"No better air than here. Go spin the road I took you on when we went crabbing. Always a good breeze blowing. And the smell of the salt marsh makes you feel good. Flush might even join you."

Flush did join me and easily loped along beside the single-speed bicycle, as I furiously peddled to expel some energy. Once I got the initial burst of frustration out of my system, beautiful weather and flat land made for a very pleasant ride. I easily found the road that led to Pop's favorite crabbing spot and kept going until the trees cleared. The sprawling marsh view and glimmering ocean beyond was as magnificent as it had been the last time I'd experienced it. Pop was right. Breathing in the aroma of salt marsh did make me feel good. It was so pure and unpolluted and *simple*. Totally unlike anything anywhere near the city.

I pulled a bottle of water from the bike's handlebar basket and drank half before pouring the rest into a plastic bowl for Flush. He gulped noisily while I put down an old blanket and stretched out to enjoy the solitude. I felt so peaceful that I wasn't bothered by being totally alone, even though it was a new experience for me. My mind ran in reverse, and speeding through past years of my life, I couldn't recall ever being anywhere without other people in my immediate vicinity. I stretched, filled my lungs to capacity, exhaled, and did it again. I felt good, more relaxed than I'd ever been after a yoga class at the spa. Hoping a revelation would come to mind, I reviewed events since my arrival in Rumton. Whatever Lester had up his sleeve wouldn't be good for Rumton, but I still couldn't pinpoint what the man wanted. The townspeople were ready to put their future in his hands, but I had to find a way to stop them before it was too late.

Lying back, arms folded beneath my head in lieu of a pillow, I stared at the sky through ultra-dark Maui Jim sunglasses. Scattered puffy clouds periodically blocked the sun. Each time the sun popped out, my eyelids shut reflexively while brief patterns of what might have been miniature blood vessels danced in my vision. I'm not sure how much time passed—I might have dozed—when loud barks caught my attention.

I sat up to look. Flush stood in one of the shallow canals thirty or forty yards away. Excited, he intermittently barked at something in front of him.

"Oh, hush," I said. "It's probably just a blue crab. Try to catch it if you want to get your nose pinched!"

The sharp barks turned into whines. Agitated, Flush danced in front of his find. He wouldn't come when I called him. I scrambled to my feet to explore.

When I saw the object of his attention and realized what it was, I could only scream, even though there was nobody to hear. It was the first dead person I'd ever seen outside a funeral home. The lifeless, distorted face of Riley stared up at us through half-open eyes.

15

The police chief wasn't as shocked to see a dead body as I had been. Because the population was an elderly one, folks died every so often, he told me, adding that I shouldn't let my imagination run away with me.

The fact that Riley's deathbed was a spread of marshy grass and tidal salt water was certainly unusual, he explained, but Riley died peacefully. There were no signs of struggle, no trauma to the body, and no evidence that anyone else had been with the mayor. Riley had probably been out catching baitfish because a water-filled bucket and net were found nearby. He suffered a heart attack and must have died suddenly, the chief surmised, because Riley hadn't tried to get to his truck, which was parked just off the main road. The chief saw no need for an autopsy, especially since Riley told Billy he was going fishing the same day I'd found the body. He'd stopped by the general store for a cup of coffee. Besides, the chief said, Rumton wasn't like my hometown. Burglaries and assaults and murders might be commonplace in Atlanta but not in sleepy little Rumton. People here didn't worry about crime because there wasn't any. To think that Riley's death resulted from anything other than natural causes would be downright silly.

Walking downtown, Pop, Avery, and I discussed the police chief's conclusion. Flush came along for the walk, and Bandit hitched a ride on Pop's shoulder. Pop reached up every once in a while to rub her chest.

"Does Riley have any family? And what will happen with the mayor's vacant position?" I said.

"As far as filling the position, there will be an election," Pop said. "If Lester hangs 'round, he's a sure bet to replace Riley."

Avery threw a stick into someone's front yard, and Flush bounded after it. "Riley's only family is a son and daughter-in-law in Pennsylvania, and one grandkid that just got married. They'll come in for the funeral and bury Riley at the Methodist church cemetery."

"Aye. Chief already spoke to the son, assured him that Riley died peacefully."

"So, just like that, everyone is certain Riley went to catch bait to use fishing? And then died of a heart attack?"

Pop nodded slowly. "That's what the chief and coroner say."

"Rumton has a coroner?"

Avery smiled. "Gertrude."

My jaw dropped in amazement. "Rumton's sleepy pharmacist beekeeper is also the coroner. This town gets weirder by the minute. What do you think of it all, Pop?"

"I think I'm going to miss the old coot."

To me, Riley's death was another spark of suspicion surrounding Lester's arrival. I'd forgotten that, for Pop, Riley's death meant losing a lifelong friend. "It's a sad time for you."

"It is. But I've got a few questions of my own."

Avery threw the stick again, sidearm. "Like what?"

"Sure, Riley liked to catch live baitfish before he went fishing. Always said he caught more fish with them than using blood-worms. But why would he go to the crabbing spot to catch bait-fish? That meant getting back in the truck to drive to his fishing hole."

Panting, Flush brought the stick back and shoved it into my hand. Avery could throw it farther, but the dog wasn't choosy. With a big windup, I threw it overhand. "So?"

"Riley ne'er did anything extra he didn't have to. Liked to conserve his energy. So he would've caught his live bait in a spot right near the fishing hole, like he always did."

"Maybe he decided to fish the crabbing spot for a change," I said, playing devil's advocate.

Pop shook his head. "Can't catch any good eating fish there. Besides, I don't recall Riley e'er fishing alone."

"So you think his death is suspicious, too! Did you tell the chief?"

"He thinks I'm upset because I've lost a card partner."

"Gertrude said he hasn't refilled his blood pressure medication in two months," Avery added. "He was supposed to be taking a pill every day."

I brought up the subject of Lester, and as we headed toward the Chat 'N Chew, we discussed him and his possible evil motives for the umpteenth time in the past few days. The fact stubbornly remained that Lester had nothing to gain from Riley's death, and neither did anyone else. Nothing we could see, anyway. Riley had already publicly said that he wouldn't be running for a second term as mayor. Everyone liked him well enough, and he didn't own much, other than his house and small plot of overgrown farmland, which he had optioned to Lester. His son would inherit the house, as well as any money received from the land sale. Riley didn't even have life insurance.

Changing humans, Bandit gracefully leaped from Pop's shoulder to mine and stuck a perfect landing.

"Can't the son demand an autopsy?" I asked.

"Sure, but he probably won't."

We got to Chat 'N Chew, which was empty except for Gertrude and Mad Millie, who ate pie at the counter. Fluttering her lashes at Pop, Millie explained that Bull had run home for a few minutes. That was okay with us, Pop told her. Other than the animals, which were perpetually hungry, nobody wanted anything to eat anyhow. The raccoon still on my shoulder, I rummaged behind the counter to find three glasses and brought everyone an iced tea. Returning the serving tray to the counter, I couldn't help but overhear Gertrude.

"Maybe she takes the pill to regulate her cycle," she said way too loud for a conversation with someone seated on the next barstool. "I read in a pharmaceutical journal that women do that now for convenience."

"I haven't had a cycle in so long, I forget what it's like." Millie clacked her teeth. "But we didn't have no pill to regulate nothing. It just came 'round when it came. And if it was late, you prayed like there was no tomorrow and swore to God Almighty you'd never bump bellies with anybody again until you was married."

Gertrude shrugged. "Probably she takes it so as she don't get pregnant."

"Hey," I said from behind the counter, "has anyone ever heard of the medical privacy act? Can we please quit discussing my sex life?"

They looked at me, surprised.

"Then you do have a sex life?" Gertrude said. "What's it like?"

Rolling my eyes, I gave them coffee refills.

The door opened and a puff of pungent cigar smoke drifted in, along with a chuckle from my boss. "Moonlighting as a waitress, Jaxie?"

"Aaron!" Coffeepot in hand, hair piled sloppily on top of my head, and a raccoon perched on my shoulder, I was entirely out of character for a Shine Advertising and PR professional. I wasn't even wearing good shoes. I'd given them up on my second day in Rumton, after unknowingly pushing a strappy Cole Haan slide into a pile of horse dung. In Atlanta, you could get away with wearing the most casual clothes, as long as you carried a designer handbag and wore great shoes. Here, though, nobody cared what you put on your feet or carried your lipstick in. "No, I'm not working a second job. Just filling in for Bull."

My boss made the rounds to give his aunt a big hug and say hello to Gertrude and Avery. He pumped Pop's hand a few times before giving him a quick man-hug and spent a few one-on-one minutes with Flush before turning to me with a grin. "Since Bull is missing in action, would you mind bringing me coffee?"

"Of course not." I detached Bandit from my shoulder, brought an ashtray for the cigar along with his coffee, and joined everyone at the table. Even dressed casually, Aaron exuded an executive's aura. I immediately shifted into professional mode. I'd been e-mailing regular updates, but our sudden face-to-face meeting caught me off guard and I didn't want to come across as anything less than the successful senior account executive I was.

He made pleasant chatter with everyone, finished his coffee and asked if I'd like to go for a drive. It was his way to talk in private, so we could get down to the business of why he'd come to Rumton.

"I had Lester Smoak checked out, and everything looks fine," he said, when we were in his Mercedes. I noticed a pack of Marlboro Lights in the console, but Aaron didn't smoke cigarettes. Just cigars. He caught me looking at the Marlboros. "I brought a CPA with me to meet Lester and go over everything. In fact, Marty's inside with Lester now."

"Lester checked out? Who's Marty? Does he contract for the firm?"

"Lester is who he says he is, Jaxie. Just a businessman. Why he wants to drop money here, I don't know. But since he does, we'll take it." We made a few turns and ended up in the residential area. People in their yards waved as we cruised by. "And Marty's an old friend. He knows his way around a financial statement better than anybody I've ever known."

We pulled into the driveway of a house I didn't recognize. A white Lincoln sat in the driveway. I recognized it as Lester's because the feathered circle hung from the rearview mirror. A FOR SALE sign rested against a trash can in the open garage.

"Whose place is this?" I said.

"Lester Smoak's. He just bought it from Joanne Singer, who moved up north to live with her daughter. She's getting up there in years and couldn't take care of a house anymore."

"Great," I muttered. "Lester is a resident. Now that Riley is dead, he'll be mayor soon."

My boss killed the engine and turned to me. He looked drawn, as though he hadn't had a good night's sleep. "Jaxie, you're one of the best we have at Shine, and we're lucky to have you on board. But I'm afraid you might have become too personally involved with this project. Maybe I should have listened to your protests and sent someone else."

I shook my head, disagreeing. "I didn't want this assignment when I found out I actually had to stay here. But things are different now. I see what's at stake and know I can do some good. I just need the townspeople to give me more time before they jump on board with Lester's vision and sell out."

He stepped out of the car and I followed suit. Standing in the driveway, he sighed deeply, before formulating his words. "Jaxie, the decision to give you more time in Rumton is your employer's. Not the townspeople's."

"Right, of course. So is the company going to let me finish what we've started here?"

Uncharacteristically, he sighed again. Aaron did not usually sigh, even when delivering less than favorable news. "The outcome wasn't as you expected, but our revitalization plan is a success. It doesn't matter how it happened. It just matters that we got results. And an economic push from an eccentric investor qualifies as results."

"But I—"

"You should be thrilled that the project is over and you can head back to Atlanta."

"Over? As in concluded?"

"You've done a good job and were on the right track. But once Lester joined the picture, there was no need to keep pursuing a revitalization plan. He's legit. The townspeople are happy. So yes, your assignment is over."

"But I think the—"

"Shine will stay on in a pro bono capacity as a consultant. However, your work here is done, and I've already got a new assignment for you." He paused to make sure he had my attention. "We got the Georgia Association of Realtors account. You're coleading the team."

A month ago I'd have drooled at the opportunity. But right now it was a hollow consolation prize. "Have you met him? I mean, spent any time with him?"

"Lester? Yes."

"You don't find anything odd about the man?" I said, noticing that my boss stared down at his feet. He never did that. He was so self-assured that people often thought him arrogant. "You think he is totally legitimate and has everyone's best interest in mind?"

Aaron looked up, shrugged. "I don't have feelings one way or the other about the man. But he did check out, and the people around here are behind him. That's all that matters. Let it drop."

It would do no good to argue because the decision for me to return to Atlanta had already been made. Resigned, I nodded my acceptance.

He smiled. "Well, then. Let's go inside. I'd like you to share your Rumton experience with Lester and Marty before you go.

They may have a few questions for you about the survey results and such." He paused in thought, turned. "Before we go, though, why don't you tell me about the sunken boat?"

My face grew hot, and I hoped my cheeks weren't visibly red. I didn't know why I'd kept it from the townspeople and my boss. Not that it made a difference because everyone had heard about it anyway. But I should have included it in my daily updates, and we both knew it. "I was waiting to see what Avery's guys found before I updated you. But they didn't find anything except the ship's bell, engraved with her name: *Aldora*. Oh, and a big anchor that is half buried in sand. And a few artifacts, which they put in Pop's garage."

"Nothing of value?"

I shook my head no. "Historical value, maybe. Monetary value, no."

"Shame."

"Justin checked to see if there was any information out there on the ship, but that was a dead end. Bottom line is, it's an old boat of unknown origin that sank and washed up here."

We went inside the house, where, remarkably, Lester already looked at home. He would use the furnishings that came with the house, he said, until he got a chance to buy new stuff. I met my boss's accountant friend, whose occupation I'd have guessed as anything other than a bean counter. A cigarette hung from his mouth, unlit, and despite the gold Rolex watch and diamond pinkie ring, he had rough edges, like someone who'd grown up on the street. Short and stocky, he looked like an ex-fighter. Or maybe an ex-con. His accent placed him from somewhere up north. Aaron told the men I'd be returning to Atlanta but that Shine Advertising and PR was happy to share the results of our revitalization efforts. Not that there were any results. It was more like a briefing of what had been done so far.

They asked questions. Trying to conceal my irritation, I answered as succinctly as I could without elaborating. The third degree lasted half an hour until Lester stood up to indicate that the meeting was over.

"Well, we've got a funeral to get to," he said. "Are you going, Aaron?"

"Of course. Marty will probably just want to rest up at my aunt's place, though, since he's driving us back tomorrow." He grinned, nodding in his friend's direction. "Lost the bet on who had to chauffeur."

Marty shot Aaron a dirty look.

"Miss Parker?" Lester said. "You going?"

"Yes, I'm going with Pop," I replied. "But speaking of chauffeuring, I noticed the unusual artwork hanging from your rearview mirror, Lester. What exactly is it?"

His eyes narrowed in irritation for a split second before he smiled broadly. "Oh, that? It's called a dream catcher. Just a little artifact my father gave me. See you all at the funeral, then. And Marty, nice to meet you. I'm sure we'll talk again."

Marty grinned, and I caught a flash of silent communication between him and Lester. I had the distinct feeling that the two men had met before today. But then, I questioned everything Lester said.

Aaron drove Marty to Mad Millie's and left me at Pop's before heading to the church by himself.

Pop's face looked worn, and sadness had driven the usual sparkle from his green eye. He played with Flush while he waited for me to change clothes. When I returned, Lester sat in the living room with Pop. Seemingly enamored of Bandit, he fed her pieces of a pretzel stick and laughed each time she snatched the food from him.

"Hello, again," I said, annoyed that Lester had intruded on my time with Pop. It was Friday and I had only one more day in

Rumton. Saturday marked the end of my small-town adventure and a failed assignment, at least in my mind. Sunday, I'd drive back to Atlanta. Monday, I'd be dressed in my usual attire, back in my usual office. "I thought you were going directly to the funeral, Lester."

"Miss Parker," he answered in greeting. "I was passing by on my way to the church and figured I should stop by to offer condolences in person. After all, Pop and the mayor were the best of friends."

Neither Pop nor I had anything to say to that, and taking his cue, Lester left. I hugged Pop, and together we picked up Millie before heading to the church to witness Riley's casket being lowered into the ground at the small graveyard.

It was a dignified affair that, by the looks of it, every single person in Rumton attended. Luckily, the preacher had a loud voice that carried through a still afternoon to reach the ears of a few hundred people. When the service was over, most everyone stayed to talk about Riley and share stories. A steady line of folks spoke with Riley's son and wife, who looked uncomfortably stiff and out of place, as though they couldn't wait to get on a plane back to Pennsylvania. When the townspeople finished with the son, they all said a few words to Pop while Millie stood possessively by his side. It was a beautiful outpouring of support that made me almost like Riley. I would miss him, too, a little. And when I left the following day, I'd miss Pop a lot. A hollow feeling unsettled my stomach.

16

The beggar sat quietly, wrapped in a jacket even though it was the first week of September and a hot day in downtown Atlanta. At his feet, a small cardboard box held some coins and a few crinkled dollar bills. As we walked by, I dropped in a five.

"What are you doing?" Sheila said. "We never give money to homeless people. You know it just goes to buy meth or booze!"

It was lunchtime and we were on our way to eat at Max Lager's on Peachtree Street. "Maybe not," I said. "Maybe he's hungry and needs the money to buy a meal."

"Jax, what's got into you? I practically had to drag you to the salon yesterday. And then you didn't want to hit Nordstrom's fall shoe sale!"

"I'm not in the mood to shop. And anyway, I've got all the shoes I need. I've got shoes I don't even wear."

"You can never have too many shoes!" she said, eyeing me. "You're acting weird around Justin, you won't shop, and now you're giving money to a street person. I just hope you snap out of it before your welcome-back party tonight."

"I'm not really up for a party. Maybe we should call it off."

Sheila stopped walking, blocking the foot traffic behind us. "Oh. My. God. Jaxie Parker would never say she's not up for a party. Aliens abducted my best friend and invaded her body!"

Hands on my hips, I frowned at her.

She grabbed my shoulders, shook me, and shouted up to the

tall buildings. "What have you done with Jaxie? Where is my friend? You give her back right now, or I'll . . . I'll tell the *Enquirer*. The government will quarantine her body, they'll dissect her piece by piece, and your cover will be blown!"

Most people walked by us, ignoring the show, but a few stopped to watch. Undeterred, Sheila continued to shout at imaginary aliens until I burst out laughing. "Okay, you're right. The party will be fun, even though it's a day late."

We continued on to the restaurant. "Hey, you just got back yesterday, and, besides, nobody knew you were done in Rumson until you showed up at the office yesterday morning."

"Rumton," I corrected. "And why didn't you guys know I was coming back? Aaron drove in to tell me the assignment was over."

She shrugged. "Why would he drive seven hours to tell you that? He could have just called you."

I had wondered the same thing. "He wanted to bring his CPA friend to meet with the investor guy. And he has an aunt there. Mad Millie. I'm sure he wanted to visit her, too."

Sheila shrugged again. "Okay, back to more important things. What are you wearing to the party? And speaking of tonight, Justin said he might stop by. Acted all nonchalant and shit. What's up with that? Did something happen in Rumsley?"

"Rumton. Not really."

We arrived at Max Lager's and slid into an open booth. Sheila couldn't stop grinning, knowing I had something juicy to share. We ordered diet sodas and decided to split a wood-fired veggie pizza. Her grin grew bigger. "Well? Spill it!"

"There's not much to tell."

She stared at me, eyelids closed to near slits, not buying it.

"I hung out with him a little, and it was really weird seeing him away from the office. In shorts. He's actually got pretty nice legs."

Our drinks arrived. Sheila sipped hers through a straw. "Uh-huh . . ."

"And I had fun with him. Go figure."

"I am figuring! Give me the rest, girl."

"Then we went out to a little club with Pop and Avery, and I drank too much rum, and then we came back and went for a walk. And I kissed him or maybe he kissed me. I'm not sure."

Sheila let out a squeal of delight, and her eyebrows arched so high they almost met with her hairline.

I frowned. "Then he confessed that he's always been interested in me, but I had a habit of blowing him off."

She slapped the table. "I knew it! I told you he was hot for you. Our boring vice president, Justin Connor, and the renowned social queen, Jaxie Parker. Together. Imagine that."

I sighed. "Then he blew me off."

"What!"

"I was up for a little fun and kissed him again," I said, remembering. "Wanted to keep it going, you know?" She motioned for me to keep talking. "But he pushed me away. Said that I go through men too quick. He's heard our famous motto: If you dig 'em, do 'em, and ditch 'em. Told me he couldn't bear to be dumped by me."

Sheila sat back in her chair. "Wow."

I nodded.

"That's heavy."

I nodded.

Our pizza came. While we ate, Sheila filled me in on her Pepsi energy drink campaign, and I tried not to think too much about Justin.

"So what are you wearing tonight?" she said, as we walked back to the office. "Might stop by, my ass. Justin will *definitely* come to the party after what happened between you two in Rimtown."

"It's Rumton. And *nothing* happened. That's the whole problem."

Thanks to Sheila's efforts, my mood was much improved by the time the party revved up. As she predicted, Justin showed up. Sheila threw the bash at her place. Everyone from the office, as well as all our close friends, were invited. Most everyone came except the partners, who never attended unofficial social functions, even though it was customary to invite them. Although Sheila's condo was much larger than mine, people crowded the oversized kitchen, living area, and balconies. Strung across one wall, a giant banner read: WELCOME BACK TO HOTLANTA!

Below the banner hung a "before and after" poster of me. The "before" photograph was the same headshot used on my business cards. The "after" photo was done by someone in the graphic art department. They took an old picture of actress Donna Douglass as Elly May with her *Beverly Hillbillies* television family and superimposed my face on her body.

Party favors consisted of key chains shaped like miniature wooden outhouses and individual bags of pork rinds. A giant bowl of pickled pigs' feet replaced a flower arrangement on the living room coffee table. It was all in good fun and reminded me how much I'd missed my friends, but it also reminded me how flawed my notion of small-town living had been. Pop led a wonderful life. He enjoyed advantages I'd never have in the city—like seeing the stars at night or catching fresh blue crabs for dinner.

Justin's voice snapped me out of my reverie. "Welcome back."

My lower lip tingled at the sound as though we'd just kissed. "Thank you," I said, thinking I needed to get a grip and forget about our late-night walk in South Carolina. He was a bore and, up until that night anyway, completely predictable.

He sipped what was probably a club soda and studied me through the thick-framed glasses. "You don't seem as thrilled about getting out of Rumton as I thought you'd be."

"I'm happy to be back, but I don't feel victorious."

"Why not?"

I didn't want anyone to overhear me giving a less-than-favorable report of the pro bono project and led Justin out the front door. We stood on the walkway for a moment without talking and listened to the chorus of night sounds a city makes. I drank some of my cosmopolitan from a plastic throwaway martini glass. "I'm competitive and like to win," I finally said.

Justin laughed. "That's why you're so good at what you do."

"Most projects, you meet with the client, come up with a plan, and work your ass off. Solve problems or, at the minimum, overcome challenges. In the end, when the campaign is working and the client is happy, you feel damn good. Victory is the jackpot. The payoff for all your brilliant scheming and seamless implementation."

He took a drink, and as his head tilted back, I caught a glimpse of the amazing green eye beneath the reflection of a streetlight in his glasses. If he knew I was staring at him, he didn't let on. "This project was different?"

I nodded. "*Way* different. I'm not feeling the victory. I'm not even sure there has *been* a victory in Rumton. To the contrary, I've got a sick feeling that Lester is going to do something really bad."

"But you have no proof?"

"None," I said and finished my drink. I immediately wanted another one. "Just a feeling."

"Guess you can't help what you feel," he said levelly.

His words may have held a double meaning, but I played it straight. I refused to get involved with a man who wanted a commitment. "Guess not," I said. "But what can I do? Aaron says it's over, so it's over."

He took my hand to lead me back inside. "Let's forget about

work right now. We'll talk about Rumton tomorrow, when you're doing your final report. What do you say we enjoy your party?"

Inside, I'd barely had time to get another cosmopolitan when Mark bear-hugged me. "Welcome back. Miss me?"

"No." I smiled. "But I hear the outhouse key chains were your idea. Nice touch."

"Thanks. So, now that you're a small-town girl, you ready to be barefoot and pregnant? Be my little missus?"

"Do you ever give up? No!" Pregnant was the last thing I wanted to be. Barefoot was kind of nice, though. I'd acquired a taste for it, padding around Pop's house and yard. My feet were starting to complain from the Moschino high heels I wore.

Laughing, Mark moved off to circulate.

I made the rounds, caught up on the latest office news, flirted, gossiped, drank a lot, and laughed more. At the end of the evening I found myself face-to-face with Justin on the balcony. I'd been so busy talking to everybody that I'd forgotten to eat. Although my stomach growled from hunger, my entire body buzzed with a pleasant sense of levitation.

"Those glasses you wear really suck," I said.

"Don't beat around the bush, Jaxie. Out with it." He smiled.

I realized it was no way to talk to a company vice president but felt too good to care. "Really, Justin. You've got this amazing green eye, and the brown one is pretty awesome, too." I reached up and slid the eyeglasses off his face. "But you cover them up with these ugly things. Do you really have to wear them?"

"Only if I want to see."

"Maybe you should think about contacts."

His mouth twitched as he tried to hold back a smile. "I hate wearing contacts. But I'm scheduled for Lasik surgery next month. So I won't have to wear those horrendously ugly glasses anymore."

I moved in for a closer look at his eyes. "Oh. Excellent. Just make sure the doctor doesn't make them match." My words might have been slurred. "The color, I mean."

"I didn't see you eating anything tonight. Are you hungry?"

"Yes."

We were standing close together, and food instantly fell to the bottom of my priority list. Through the French doors, Sheila made a kissy face and gave me a thumbs-up sign. Thankfully, Justin's back was to her.

"We should probably go inside and eat something," he said, taking back possession of his ugly glasses. "There's plenty of food left over."

"Okay," I said and didn't move.

Sheila pointed at us and started grinding her hips to an invisible lover. Trying to ignore her, I moved in to nuzzle his neck, but watching my best friend through the glass made me laugh out loud. She froze the second Justin turned around to see what I was looking at, which made me laugh even harder.

"You probably do need something to eat," he decided, and led me inside without any further discussion.

We shared an entire plate of miniature pimento cheese sandwiches, and I guzzled two or three glasses of water. When I realized that everyone had gone home except one of Sheila's current boyfriends, I pulled out my mobile phone to call a cab. Since guest parking at Sheila's building was nonexistent, I rarely drove. Even if I had driven, I wouldn't get behind the wheel to go home. After all the drinks, I could barely trust myself to keep my hands off a company vice president, much less keep a vehicle between the lines.

"You're calling a cab?" Justin said.

I nodded.

"I'll give you a lift."

I agreed, we thanked Sheila, did the nice-to-meet-you thing

with her newest boyfriend, and left. The food and water dampened my booze buzz but did nothing to quench the desire I felt for the man sitting in the driver's seat. The more I studied him, the more I realized how little I knew about him. When we reached my building, I invited him up. He declined, but when I took off the glasses to look into his eyes, I could tell his resistance factor rapidly approached zero. Mine had hit the same mark hours ago on Sheila's balcony.

"Just walk me to my door. That's all I want," I lied. We found a parking space in the garage, stopped to speak with the night-shift doorman, Scott, who welcomed me back to town, and were in each other's arms before the elevator doors fully shut.

"Jaxie, this isn't a good idea," Justin said without much conviction. "I really am just going to walk you to your door and head home. After all, it's midnight, and we both have to be at the office early."

I took one of his hands and studied his fingers. They were neatly manicured but strong. His were the hands of a man who was as comfortable behind a desk as he was on a tennis court. Or maybe a golf course. Or in a boat. I still wasn't sure what he did with his free time.

The elevator doors slid open. When we arrived at my door, I put his hand to my mouth and slowly kissed the tips of his fingers, one at a time. The same fingers that I'd seen for years—clutching spreadsheets as he pored over data, holding a cup of coffee during a late-afternoon strategy meeting, or unconsciously rubbing his temple while he studied something on a computer screen. The same hand I'd seen but never really noticed.

I wasn't sure if I heard him moan or just imagined it, but when I unlocked the door, he followed me in. As he looked around to take in my furnishings, I sensed approval. But when he looked back at me, there was more hesitation.

"Look Justin, if you want to go, then just go."

"Jaxie, how do you feel about me?"

"Confused. You're not my type, but I can't quit thinking about you."

"But you still want to sleep with me?"

"Yes."

"You realize that we take our jobs seriously, and whatever happens here, stays here."

"Yes," I repeated.

"What about your no-dating-coworkers rule?"

I went into the kitchen and poured us each a glass of water. I was still thirsty. "You know about that, too?"

He nodded.

"To heck with my no-dating-coworkers rule. Besides, you're not really a coworker. More like a superior. Anyway, what about your don't-want-to-be-dumped hang-up?"

"I've decided to take my chances," he said in a voice that induced a shiver.

"So can we go to bed now?"

"Yes."

We did, and in an instant all the previous men in my life melted into a hazy, meaningless memory.

17

Sheila's head appeared in my office doorway. "What happened last night?" she demanded in a whisper. "Did you two . . . you know, *connect*?"

I rolled my eyes at her.

"Well, did you?"

"I don't want to talk about it. I've got a lot to do."

Arms folded across her chest, she copped an attitude. "Since when don't you want to talk about something with me? Hello?"

"Since last night."

She did a sharp intake of breath as realization dawned. "You had meaningful sex! That's never happened before!"

I had to laugh. "Sheila, hush. I don't want him to think I'm talking about him." I lowered my voice, face flushing just from the thought of Justin lounging in my bed. "And yes, he was fabulous. He *is* fabulous. That's all I've got to say."

She did a spin and tangoed her way out of my doorway.

Forcing myself to focus, I reviewed my new project assignment and made some phone calls. During a lunch meeting, I did a final evaluation with the interns, who had just had word that the grant application to build a museum in Rumton was accepted for review. Not that it mattered now, but I praised them for a job well done and thanked them for all the research questions they'd tackled for me.

I worked nonstop into the afternoon until the last thing I had to do was complete my pro bono project final report. Aaron was out playing golf with a client, his assistant told me, but I should leave the report on his desk. Procrastinating, I decided to do it at home. It would still be in his in box first thing in the morning.

As I automatically merged into traffic on I-85 North, windows rolled up tight and air-conditioner blasting, I thought of Pop. Riley's death must have hit hard, and I hoped Millie would offer him some comfort. They certainly seemed to be hitting it off, despite their notorious disdain for each other. I laughed out loud at the memory of him calling her Mad Millie and her referring to him as Pompous Pop on my first day in Rumton.

I was about ten minutes from my building when my mobile phone rang. "Don't forget about the final report," Justin said when I answered. "The partners are going to want it tomorrow."

"Hello to you, too."

"Just wanted to remind you, since I didn't get a chance to see you before you left this afternoon."

A succession of brake lights lit up in front of me, and I automatically slowed down. "Thanks, and I didn't forget. I just decided to tackle it at home. I may need your help with the feasibility study results. Heck, I may need your help with all of it. Can I give you a call later?"

"Of course. Better yet, why don't I just come over and we'll do it together. No fooling around. Just work. And maybe some food. You buying any groceries on the way home?" In search of something to drink, Justin had looked in my refrigerator the night before. He was rewarded with bottled water, a carton of clumpy milk, and one beer. The shelves were devoid of food, but then I *had* been out of town. Usually there were a few cartons of leftover Chinese and a pack of lunch meat or two.

"I wasn't planning to. But I will if you're cooking."

His laugh, long and slow, rolled into my ear. "Pop says you really can't cook worth a damn. You weren't pretending."

"Don't beat around the bush, Justin," I said, mimicking his words to me when I'd criticized his glasses. "Out with it."

"Tell you what. I'll pick up some groceries and meet you at your place. You can work on the report while I cook dinner, and if you have questions, just fire away."

"How long?" Traffic had slowed to a near-dead stop. I couldn't see any flashing lights, but from the look of things, there was a wreck ahead.

"Half hour, maybe forty-five minutes," he said.

"I should beat you there. If not, the doorman will let you in. He takes care of my plants when I'm gone and he has a key. I'll give him a call to let him know."

"Same fellow who was there last night? Scott?"

"Good memory. A walking encyclopedia who is a sucker for lists and also remembers people's names."

"I never forget anything. As I told you before, it's a curse. But not necessarily a bad one."

"So then, you'll remember last night forever?" I said, smiling even though I was stuck in a massive traffic jam and had to pee.

"Longer."

The accident, which involved a number of cars, blocked four lanes of traffic. An hour passed before I rushed into my building, bladder ready to burst.

"Your personal chef is here," the doorman said with a wink, as I practically ran by him.

"Thanks, Scotty!"

He followed me into the lobby. "I like this one."

"You never like any of them," I countered, waiting on the elevator.

He shrugged. "Always a first time."

My mouth watered from the cooking smells when I opened my front door. Looking completely at ease, Justin stood at the stove stirring something in a skillet. I detected garlic, lime, and a spice that might have been oregano. When I got past the delicious aroma, I devoted my attention to the chef. Faded black jeans, leather belt, ribbed white cotton shirt and Nike sport sandals. I'd have never figured him for a sandals type of guy.

"You look like a different person out of your office duds," I said, rushing past him to the bathroom.

"Thanks . . . if that was a compliment," he said, when I returned. "This oven and range is like new. Do you *ever* cook?"

"Yes, it was a compliment. And, of course, I cook," I said. Skeptical, he turned around to look at me, his eyebrows way up. I might have blushed. "Well, I usually use the microwave."

He laughed. "Dinner will be ready in about forty-five minutes. Meanwhile, why don't you start on your report? Any questions I can help with, just ask."

I arranged the laptop on the breakfast bar and situated myself on a barstool. He set a stem glass in front of me and poured some white wine. I took a sip. It was cold and refreshing and just right. I almost told him I could get used to being pampered, but I stopped myself. No need to sound as if I was into the domestic scene. "Thanks for all you're doing to help," I said instead.

Slicing what looked liked zucchini on a cutting board, he nodded. I didn't even know I had a cutting board. "No problem."

Due after every assignment, project final reports were the responsibility of the team leader. I hated paperwork, and the Rumton report would be especially difficult since I had nothing positive to say. Other than that a stranger waltzed in and threw some money on the table to save the day. Which wasn't a positive to me. Staring at the computer screen, I sighed.

Sensing my distress, Justin poured himself some wine and joined me at the bar. "You need to come up with only two pages. Might even get by with one. You know the drill. Just write something to make the partners feel good and back it up with enough substance to justify your time."

Frowning, I looked at him. The computer screen remained blank. My fingers rested on the keyboard but didn't move.

"Okay," he said. "Let's try this. Forget the report for a minute, and we'll sum up the Rumton situation. Organize what was done on behalf of Shine. That way you can clarify what you want to say."

As something sizzled in the oven, we started by naming all the setbacks Rumton faced, such as its lack of infrastructure. The list was long. Next we reviewed results of the development feasibility study that Justin had overseen from the office. It was just as dismal. Even with its proximity to water and neighboring towns, Rumton was too remote to attract developers or businesses. People wanted activities, choices for recreation, quality schools, shopping, and medical facilities. If Rumton weren't landlocked, it might have been a different story. Developers would dish out big bucks to put in the amenities, knowing they could turn the community for a nice profit.

Then we made a list of everything we'd done. Avery's environmental study and satellite photos. Justin's feasibility study for both residential development and corporate appeal. Grant money research. A town profile. Resident interviews.

My fingers finally started punching keys. Fifteen minutes later I'd condensed my Rumton ordeal into one page. All that remained was a concluding paragraph. When Justin stood up to serve our food, I realized the table wasn't set. I started to do it, but he waved me off.

"Just point me in the direction of plates. And the flatware, which hopefully is not plastic."

I pointed. "Stainless steel, thank you."

Telling myself to forget about Rumton, I typed furiously:

No immediate avenues for the revitalization of Rumton were apparent. In what was coincidental timing, an investor with ties to the town displayed an interest in purchasing several parcels of land. Lester Smoak recently bought options and purchased a primary residence in Rumton. He promises to build public amenities at his own expense, including a medical office. The majority of the townspeople and the town council fully support his efforts. Therefore, the 2005 pro bono project has reached its conclusion. Information gathered during Shine's studies and surveys will be made available at the request of the town council, and Shine will remain involved in an advisory capacity.

I stood, stretched, sighed. "It's done," I announced, struggling to ignore gnawing thoughts of looming calamity that nagged at my unconscious. I was just a worker bee, after all. Not the queen. I was paid to do what I was told, and that was that. Rumton wasn't my problem anymore.

Justin put two plates of food on the small kitchen table. "See? That wasn't so bad." He added water glasses garnished with lemon wedges, refilled our wineglasses, and put a bread basket between us. Finally, he placed a single yellow tulip on the table. Its stem cut short, it stuck out of a Coors Light bottle.

"I didn't see a vase anywhere," he explained.

"I don't keep them," I said, and immediately wished I hadn't. Not only did it sound snobbish, but it also reminded him of my track record with men. I'd had my share of flowers but always threw away the cheap vase along with the blooms when they dried out. Which typically took as long as it took for me to tire of the individual who'd sent them.

Justin didn't reply. I turned the television to a jazz channel and we sat down to eat. Stomach rumbling from hunger, I unceremoniously dug in. "I had no idea you could cook like this!"

"Just one of many things you don't know about me," he said, saluting with his wineglass. "To being officially done with Rumton!"

He'd made a roasted pork loin topped with a garlic, red pepper, and pineapple sauce. The vegetable was seared zucchini. The bread was fresh and hot enough to melt butter. I slowed down to enjoy both the food and the man sitting across from me. I'd worked with him as long as I'd been at the agency, but knew nothing about him. Now I yearned to learn everything there was to know. Weird.

"This is amazing," I said, sipping the wine and letting it roll over the back of my tongue. "I didn't know you could cook. You could open a restaurant."

"Thanks. I just might do that someday, when it's time to retire from the research grind."

We ate in silence, enjoying the smooth sound of Kirk Whalum flowing from the speakers.

"I know it's a done deal and all," I said, when my stomach was comfortably full, "but I can't help wonder why Lester wants to buy up Rumton. In essence, he's buying a small town. Why?"

"Well, he's not buying the entire town. Just pieces of it. People have bought towns before." Justin went on to mention a few examples. Kim Basinger bought Braselton, Georgia, and later sold off most of it when she declared bankruptcy. Much more recently, an engineering school bought Playas, New Mexico, to create an antiterrorist training ground for Homeland Security. The possibilities for Lester's interest in Rumton were endless, Justin told me.

"He's a slimeball," I replied. "His interest is greed. Somehow, it boils down to the land. He's going to do something with the land."

Justin rolled the tulip back and forth between his fingers. "You're not going to let this drop, are you?"

"Look," I said, unable to conceal my exasperation. "A man who doesn't know me invites me to live in his home. Cooks for me. Shows me around town. Knowing he's not getting anything in return. He wouldn't even accept the daily stipend the company offered for room and board."

Justin smiled. "That's Pop for you."

"And Rumton wasn't the hellhole I imagined it would be. It's bizarre, no doubt about that. But the people are . . . well, they're just genuine, I guess. No pretenses. You have to admire that."

"True."

"So maybe it has become personal. I've become fond of these people, and I feel as if I ought to still be there, trying to figure out what Lester is up to. Somebody needs to look out for them."

Justin wiped a napkin across his mouth, pushed his plate back a few inches. "Jaxie, they've been taking care of themselves for a long time. They got along before Shine ever stepped into the picture, and they'll get along just fine now."

Suddenly the food in my stomach, previously settling beautifully with the music and the company, hit a wave of discord. Agitated, I straightened in my chair. "You think I'm blowing everything out of proportion? Like, who the hell am I to think I know what's best for Rumton?"

His gaze dropped, paused, moved up to meet mine. "I wouldn't have put it quite that way, but yes. I agree with Aaron. You might be personalizing this assignment because it didn't turn out as anticipated. As you said, you're used to winning. But you can't win every single time. Maybe this one was a draw."

"Yeah, and maybe you should just go," I said miserably, my mood shattering faster than a dropped glass.

He stood casually. "No problem."

"I'm grateful for your help. Dinner, too. But you just don't get it!"

"I get it, Jaxie, but you are being unreasonable. Pop is my uncle. I love him. I love Rumton. And I don't see this grave danger or impending doom that you keep talking about. Maybe your ego is in the way."

"My ego?" I wanted to slap him. "I don't know why I even bothered with you. You . . . you're . . . you're not worth it!"

He didn't say anything. Part of me wanted to quit talking, quit *thinking*, and just . . . kiss. Or more. But another part of me wanted to slap him.

He read the latter emotion on my face. "I'm going, I'm going," he said, palms up and facing out in a surrender motion. "If it will make you feel better, give Pop a call tomorrow to say hello. See what's going on."

I closed the door behind him with a feeling that was part lust, part anger, and mostly frustration. The result was a churning in my stomach that did total injustice to the incredible meal I'd just eaten.

"Why can't anybody else see the obvious?" I said to the walls as I moved dishes from the table to the sink. In answer, my mobile phone rang. Disgusted, I dug it out of my purse. "Hello."

"Your investor with small-town political aspirations?" It was Chuck. "He has quite an interesting track record, babe."

My heart did a somersault. "I *knew* it! What did you find?"

"The gentleman's name used to be Spear. Not Smoak. He had it legally changed. And before that, he went by at least one other alias. He never served time in the military, at least not that I could find. He owns a majority share of a development company that specializes in master-planned communities. They do the groundwork, acquire land, and deal with local municipalities to get things approved. Layout the design, put in water, sewer, roads, and such. Then they use very expensive and very splashy marketing to promote the community but sell out to another developer before the first house ever goes up."

"High-tech think tank, my ass," I muttered.

"He was busted for fraud three years ago but was acquitted. Apparently, he took a lot of money from a lot of old people under the pretense of building an amusement park that never happened."

I sat on the sofa and flipped open a pad to jot some notes. "A real upstanding citizen."

"But wait, there's more," Chuck said, mimicking a TV commercial announcer. "He keeps some interesting company, according to my pal in the bureau who spoke to me off the record. They're watching Senator Wands, who incidentally, is quite active on the Indian Affairs Committee. And Wands has been seen playing golf with your man on several occasions." Chuck paused, and I heard papers shuffling.

"Where is Wands from? And why are they keeping an eye on him?"

"Wands is a democrat from South Carolina, and my source wouldn't say why they have an interest in him. Other than that it has to do with accepting kickbacks."

"Huh," I mused.

"Huh?"

"It's a small-town thing," I said. "Means I was thinking."

"Huh," he said, while he thought about it. "You might also find it interesting that one of Lester's business partners won't be winning any congeniality awards. He has known affiliations with one of the mob families and is not a nice guy."

"Huh," I said again. My brain attempted to make sense of it

all. "Ties to Indians and mobsters. I wonder if the Indians know that Lester's other friends are bad guys."

"First," Chuck said, "I don't believe Senator Wands is of Native American Indian heritage. He just serves on the committee. He serves on three different committees. But he spends a lot of time and effort on Indian affairs issues. That's one of his main campaign platforms."

"What's second?"

"Second, this information doesn't prove anything."

"It proves Lester is hiding things. And that he made up his military experience." I felt as if I'd just hit the jackpot. "How'd you get all this?"

"As I told you, I'm good at what I do. And the fingerprint helped. Nice job in getting that." He paused to sip something. "Oh, and that feathered ring hanging from the rearview mirror of his Lincoln? It's a dream catcher. A Native American Indian artifact."

"Yeah, I asked him what it was. He said his father gave it to him but didn't elaborate. It's rather coincidental that he's been playing golf with an Indian Affairs Committee guy and he has a dream catcher in his car."

"I thought the same thing, but nothing came up in the background information to indicate his heritage. Although anybody can claim to be just about anything these days if it suits his purpose, so I rarely look into genealogy. Criminals invent family backgrounds every day."

I thought about that while I paced in front of my kitchen table, looking at the bloom sticking out of the beer bottle and wishing Justin hadn't left. "What the heck is Lester up to?"

"Don't know." Chuck sighed. "But keep in mind that none of this information proves any harmful intent on behalf of Lester Spear."

"Maybe not. But what does it say of his interest in Rumton?"

"That's for you to figure out."

Chuck gave me some more details, but ultimately we con-cluded that Lester was free to do what he wanted. Being shady wasn't illegal. And keeping company with mobsters wasn't ille-gal. Other than some gossipy information, I had nothing to stop the man from taking over Rumton. The more I thought about it, the more I knew Lester could talk his way out of accusations that he'd been dishonest. The townspeople thought he was a savior. After all, he'd say through his big-toothed smile, there was noth-ing wrong with changing your name. And the bust? All a misun-derstanding, he'd say. He'd been acquitted. As far as his alleged military service, he'd explain that the records were sealed or he'd make up some other nonsense. The town council would probably assume he'd done top-secret work in the military.

I wasn't sure if the townspeople would listen to me, but they deserved to know something about the real Lester Smoak, whether or not they chose to believe it.

"You're the best," I told Chuck.

"You're welcome," he said.

"Before you go, answer this for me. My boss said Lester checked out. How did that happen?"

"Either he did a sloppy Internet background check that cost thirty dollars or he didn't do a check at all. Or maybe he uncovered everything I did but saw no reason to make a big deal out of it."

"I get the feeling my boss knows something about this whole mess. Something he's not sharing with me."

Chuck took a sip of something and swallowed. "Are you still in Rumton?"

"No, I'm home in Atlanta. The pro bono project is officially over. I've been told to let it drop."

"Are you going to keep digging?"

I wasn't sure myself until I said it. "Yes."

"Be careful, babe. Spear keeps some dangerous company."

I disconnected and immediately dialed Justin's mobile. Like most people I worked with, Justin's was in my speed-dial list. I couldn't wait to tell him I'd been right.

"Justin here," he answered.

Changing my mind, I hung up. He didn't deserve to know the truth.

18

Flush pulled himself off the front porch and ran to greet me when I opened the car door. I hadn't told Pop I was coming and hoped his greeting would be just as enthusiastic. Aside from Sheila, I didn't tell anyone where I was going. I took off work by using a vacation day, and since it was Friday, the personnel guy assumed I just wanted a long weekend. The seven-plus hours on the road allowed me to think about Lester and his motives. Unfortunately, I hadn't reached any conclusions. Maybe Pop's insight would help.

I knocked on the front door, even though it stood open. "Pop? Are you here?"

He appeared with Bandit on his shoulder, and when he saw me, a smile spread across his face. "Back so soon, lass? You must've missed me."

Pointing at the raccoon, I smiled. "I'm here to recover the mascara she swiped. Took it right out of my makeup bag. It came from the Clarins counter, you know. That stuff's not cheap."

He put Bandit on the floor before squeezing me tight. "Need your room again?"

"Yes, I do."

"You paying the same rate as before?" he teased.

"Zero works for me."

Chuckling, he carried in my overnight bag and asked if I'd been tracking the hurricane.

"Hurricane?" I hadn't watched television news or read a paper in weeks.

"Hailey. She's almost a cat three and growing. Moving fast. Formed in the South Atlantic and nearly hit Cuba before turning toward the States. Yesterday, forecasters said it would hit land somewhere between Little River and Beaufort. Which is basically the entire South Carolina Coast."

"That can't be good."

"The projected path tightened up last night and we're still right in the middle of it."

"I had no idea. I haven't been keeping up with the news lately."

"Could hit as soon as Monday afternoon, if it doesn't stall," Pop said. "You might ought to head back tomorrow. Get out of here, just in case."

"Trying to get rid of me already?"

We went inside and Pop let Bandit climb back onto his shoulder. " 'Course not. Just that most people head away from a storm. Not straight into it."

"It's definitely going to hit Rumton?"

"No way to know," he said. "Usually can't tell exactly where a storm will run ashore till the last minute. You just keep an eye on it and get ready."

I stretched and dropped into a chair. "Well, I'm not leaving in the morning. I just got here!"

Looking at the kitchen, I realized that things were messy to the point of being near trashed. Broken and stacked on the floor, drawers had been pulled from their slots. Ripped, the kitchen curtain hung sideways from its rod. Big jars of flour and sugar and other cooking ingredients were broken and piled into a cardboard box. Propped in a corner, as though for easy retrieval, a shotgun stood on its end with the barrel pointed up.

"It looks like Hurricane Hailey already hit," I said. "What happened?"

Pop shrugged at the mess. "Somebody wanted something more than I did."

"What does that mean?"

Carrying two glasses of sweet tea, Pop joined me at the table. "I think you city dwellers call it a break-in."

Shocked, I leaned forward and almost knocked over the tea. "Somebody broke into your house? When? How?"

" 'Twas not a true break-in, I reckon, since my doors weren't locked. But somebody walked in and sifted through the house while I was o'er at Millie's. Day after you left."

"What did they steal?"

"Nothing, far as I can tell," Pop said, looking tired. "Sure made a mess, though."

Pop had no ideas about who'd come into his house and rummaged around or what they were looking for. The police chief said there wasn't much to be done, other than write up a report. But everyone knew about it and the whole town was on alert for a trespasser. Lester did his part by putting a full-page ad in the *Rumton Review*, which offered a reward for any information. Billy got the newsletter out on time for a change, and Pop slid it across the table for me to see.

I read the ad with distaste. "It's a campaign message."

Pop frowned, and his green eye went dark. "Don't know why he's bothering to campaign for mayor. People 'round here have already elected him. They're just waiting for the election to make it official."

Flush nosed up to Pop and laid his large head on the leg that wasn't occupied by Bandit. It was as though the animals sensed his distress and tried to comfort him.

An hour later we nursed the same iced teas, and our topic of conversation remained on Lester. I'd passed along the information from Chuck's background check, and Pop, while disturbed, wasn't shocked. We tossed possible scenarios back and forth, brainstorming. Finally, Pop asked what my boss thought about it all.

"I don't know," I said. "I haven't told him. Nobody knows I'm here, except Sheila. I took the day off."

Pop's forehead wrinkled in worry. "What 'bout your job? When Aaron finds out you went behind his back, and you didn't share what you found out . . ."

Pop was right. It wouldn't sit well with my boss. I tried to convince myself that I hadn't made a stupid move. "It should be okay. I did take a vacation day. My personal time is mine to do whatever I want. My visit has nothing whatsoever to do with the pro bono project."

He shook his head, and the green eye sparkled. "Whate'er you say."

"I'm amazed every time I look at your eye. It's very cool."

"Aye. And I'm amazed at yours."

I was confused. "What do you mean?"

"It's not twitching anymore." He got to the end of his tea and chewed a piece of ice. "The first time you got to town, it looked like you were in a convulsion, much as your eye tic came and went. After the first week, I didn't notice it too much. Now, it's gone altogether."

I had to laugh at his reference to a convulsion. My left eyelid always got a tic when I stressed over something. But I hadn't noticed it lately, so maybe he was right. Maybe it was gone for good. Odd, because there'd been more stress in my life post-Rumton than before. Reflexively, my hand went to my face and I rubbed my eye, just below the brow bone. "I didn't realize it was that obvious."

He asked me if I was hungry. As usual, I was, and he pulled a plate of leftover meatloaf from the refrigerator. Millie dropped by with a homemade lemon pie just as Pop served me a plate of food.

She seemed stunned to see me back in town. I told her I was visiting Pop, and not in town on official Shine business. Then she shrugged, as if it made no difference to her either way. Anyone could tell she wondered what I was up to.

"If you just happen to talk with Aaron . . ." I began.

She waved off my concern. "Your whereabouts is safe with me. I don't hear from my nephew much anymore, nohow. But why *are* you here?"

I told her over a fried meatloaf sandwich and dill potato salad. Her eyes grew big, and she almost stopped breathing to concentrate on the information.

When her body reminded her to breathe, she suddenly inhaled. "I know Pop isn't a fan of Lester's. Now I'm not, either." Her eyes moved to Pop. "I guess you got a better sense about people than me, Cuddles."

I gave Pop a look, and grinning, he answered with a mini-shrug. I giggled, he made a funny face, and soon we both laughed uncontrollably.

"What's so funny?" Millie demanded.

"Cu-Cud-Cuddles!" I managed to get out. "It's a far cry from what you used to call him. Pompous Pop!"

"Well, he has a nickname for me, too," Millie said.

Pop nodded. "Right-o, Maddie."

"It's short for Mad Millie," she said, pleased rather than offended.

With Flush leading the way, we took a walk and debated what I should do. I could put the word out about Lester by telling a few people at Bull's place and let the grapevine take over. Or I could gather residents together for an informal meeting and confront Lester outright, publicly. Or I could do nothing and quietly hire an investigator to uncover enough dirt on Lester to shut him down. Option A would be easy, option B would be risky, and option C would take both money and time. All three courses of action could put me in hot water with Shine Advertising and PR. The partners were all about teamwork. Renegades were not tolerated.

"Council votes on selling the waterway property after second reading, tonight," Pop said. "Might be best if you go to the council meeting and say your piece there. Or I could do it for you to keep you out of the doghouse with Aaron."

"Oh, no! I forgot there'd already been a first reading. I can't believe how quickly things are moving."

Millie took Pop's hand, and without trying to, they began stepping in unison. "Aye," he agreed. "Unusual for anything to 'appen quick 'round here."

"So everyone's come together to push through an ordinance to sell off land. This is crazy." Feeling way out of my league, I sighed. "I should have obtained a schedule of all public sessions when I first got here, instead of aimlessly roaming about."

"Don't be so hard on yourself," Pop consoled me. "You had no way to see what Lester was up to. It's obvious he's had his sights on Rumton for some time now."

"But what if the council won't listen to me? They wouldn't the last time I tried to reason with them."

"True. Lester got e'erybody worked up, but at least he's motivated them to rally for a cause." Pop put his fingertips together while he thought about things. "Might be a good thing. Folks 'round here haven't come together over an issue in a long while. You just need to aim their energy in a different direction."

"I don't have a direction for them. That's the whole problem! I just don't want them to sell to Lester."

Pop squeezed my shoulder. "Maybe all that brainstorming you did might mesh out to an idea for revitalizing Rumton. What you came 'ere for to begin with."

I looked at my watch. It was already four thirty. "What time is the meeting?"

"Five thirty."

We returned to Pop's house, and while I figured out what I wanted to say to the council, we dug in to Millie's lemon pie. The filling was creamy and tart, and the sweet meringue topping was superb. It was the best lemon pie I'd ever eaten. Savoring each bite, I thought about discussing the situation with Aaron before I did anything. But there wasn't time. And when he learned that I'd spoken out against Lester, I'd be in trouble.

I thought about taking Pop up on his offer to deliver the news, but third-hand information wouldn't pack the same punch. Besides, I wanted to see the reaction on Lester's face, just for the satisfaction. He'd swatted me away like a pesky fly, but soon he'd know that I wasn't through buzzing around in his business. Scooping up the last bite of pie, I decided I'd deal with the consequences at Shine Advertising and PR later. Worrying about it now wouldn't help a thing. Using Pop's new fax machine, I made copies of some detail sheets that I'd printed at home and prepared my plan of attack.

The movie house lobby was less crowded than the last time I'd been there. Sitting in the ticket window, Amy surfed the Internet on her dial-up connection. Waiting for a page to load, she looked up and waved when we walked by. Since the break-in at his house, Pop told me, they'd been keeping the police station open later in the evenings. But there was no purpose to that, in his opinion, since anyone who needed the police chief could just call him at home or knock on his door.

In the theater Councilwoman Delores called the meeting to order. The mayor pro tem, she had taken over Riley's role when he died. A smattering of people occupied the first few rows of seats, but it was nothing close to the crowd on hand for last week's court session with the judge. Since everyone supported the council's intention to sell off town assets, there was no need for them to attend. We slipped into seats near the aisle, and I scoped the rows to see who had come. A few volunteer firefighters who worked the concession stand hung out in the back of the theater, along with the police chief. Elwood and Gladys sat with five or six of their neighbors. Holding a notepad and pen, Billy was present to take notes in his official capacity as *Rumton Review* reporter. Walter and a few of his bar buddies sat clumped together. Chin on her chest, Gertrude dozed next to them. In the front row, Lester relaxed, arms outstretched and resting on the chair backs beside him.

The only item on the agenda was the land sale, which meant town leaders scheduled the meeting solely to accommodate Lester. Council was intent on pushing it through quickly. They'd already obtained independent appraisals, which came in at a ridiculously low estimate, averaging a mere six thousand dollars per acre. The town also publicly offered the parcel for sale but received no bids, a fact I found hard to believe. During discussion or, rather, brainwashed testimonials, Lester sat quietly, nodding. He had the smug look of a puppeteer as he controlled the strings of his marionettes.

When it was time for public input, I raised my hand. Once Councilwoman Delores recognized me, I pushed my shoulders back and walked to the front of the theater. Lester's face flashed a look of surprise that instantaneously morphed into anger. But I'd done my homework, and I was prepared to give the presentation of a lifetime. I'd probably be in hot water later, at work, but saving a small town had become bigger than a simple job assignment. It had become personal.

"I'm no longer here on behalf of my company," I began, "but rather as a concerned individual. I'd like to explain to you why selling this parcel of land to Lester *Spear*, whom you know as Lester Smoak, would be a tremendous mistake."

A collective murmur came from the sparse audience, and I couldn't resist turning around to catch Lester's expression after he heard his real name uttered. Hatred emanated from his eyes, which, oddly, induced a small thrill in me.

I paused to let my opening sentence sink in and decided to save the best for last. The dirt on Lester could wait. I started by questioning the council's appraisal and listing methodology. I already knew which appraisers they'd used because Millie was friends with Delores and had kept copies of the paperwork. Handing each council member a list of every company in coastal South Carolina that specialized in commercial land appraisals, I explained that the market value estimates the town obtained were flawed. None of their appraisers specialized in commercial land, and in fact one of the three I'd tried to contact had a disconnected phone and was already out of business.

Next, I explained that to get the best price for any sizable parcel of land, the town would need to list it for sale with a real estate company, which in turn would advertise it statewide and in some instances nationwide. At the minimum, it would go on the Internet, for viewing by any number of investors with money to spend. I passed out another handout to the council and the audience. It showed the selling price and dates of comparable plots of land in the Carolinas.

"We might do things a little different than yer used to, but nothing was done improper-like," Rusty said when I'd finished. "The point is, we feel it's a fair price." The other men nodded, their minds already made up on how they would vote. But I could see that Delores was thinking about what I'd said.

I smiled. "I certainly did not mean to insinuate anything was done improperly. I just wanted to bring it to your attention that you might be selling yourselves short. Way short. Imagine what you could do with an additional six or seven hundred thousand dollars. I'd be willing to bet you could get that much more if you marketed the property, rather than just taking the first offer."

"They don't *want* to market the property, Miss Parker," Lester said tightly, standing up. "That's the whole point. The people of this town don't want to sell to a big land developer who will put up ugly condominiums. They don't want traffic and noise and criminal activity. By selling to me, they know the integrity of their town is protected."

I turned to face him. "What exactly are you planning to do with the property?"

Frowning, he shook his head from side to side, as though disappointed in me. It was an intimidation tactic. "Miss Parker, city living has made you cynical. I have no immediate plans for the land, other than to do a little duck hunting."

"Then you wouldn't mind signing a legal agreement to restrict what you can do with the property?"

He laughed, but it came out as a snort. "Land-use restriction agreements aren't worth the paper they're written on. Any good lawyer can see to that."

I smiled, slow and calculating. It was time to sling my mud. "Gosh, Mr. *Spear*, you seem to know an awful lot about land development for just an old eccentric."

Lester's hand clenched into a fist at his side. I continued before he had a chance to say anything. "That's probably because you *own* a land development company, which specializes in master-planned communities," I said very slowly and very loudly, to make sure everyone—even Gertrude—heard me clearly. Awake and sitting forward in her theater seat, she hung on every word.

I handed out a third sheet that outlined what Chuck had learned about Lester's company, including names and locations of the master-planned communities he'd started. Before Lester had a chance to backtalk his way out of that revelation, Delores took the bait.

"Why do you keep calling him Spear instead of Smoak?"

I explained that Lester changed his name shortly after being charged with fraud for taking people's life savings to build an amusement park.

"This is outrageous!" Lester bellowed. "I was acquitted on that ridiculous charge. I was found not guilty. It never happened and the whole thing was a misunderstanding."

Hoping my voice wasn't shaking as badly as my insides were, I thanked the council members for their time and returned to my place between Pop and Millie. Victorious, I'd accomplished what I'd come for, but the high was suddenly weighed down by worry over the repercussions that were sure to come. Lester was not a nice man.

"I'd say you just kicked some arse," Pop said when I sat down. Patting my knee, Millie agreed. Gladys turned around to wink her approval at me, and I realized that she and Elwood had come to speak out against selling. But since I'd just lit the spark of suspicion about Lester's benevolent nature, there was no need for them to add anything.

Led by Delores, the council shot a barrage of questions at Lester, and overall, he did a decent job of keeping his cool while dismissing their concerns, even though fury radiated from his eyes. When I caught his piercing glare, my palms grew sweaty, and I realized I'd unconsciously been clenching my hands with trepidation, wondering what Lester would do to retaliate.

When the interrogation was over, council delayed their vote. Another week or two certainly wouldn't hurt anything, they said. I wanted to smile in victory, but my mouth had gone dry.

19

My mood shifted between elation at what I'd accomplished and anxiety over what I'd tell my boss. Millie assured me that another piece of lemon pie would make me feel better, and not one to argue with a pastry chef, I obliged. We ate pie and drank coffee and kept an eye on the Weather Channel, which gave periodic hurricane updates. Pop taught me how to play gin rummy, and we played hand after hand, until Millie convinced him to turn off the weather and watch a television movie with her.

"Can't believe you ne'er played gin before," he said, putting the deck of cards into a wooden box. "You know how to play any card games?"

"Poker. I'm pretty good at that." Women's poker groups were the hot new trend, and Sheila and I had taken some lessons from a pro gambler before forming a club. Women only, we met once a month and had a blast.

"You bet high stakes?"

"Of course. We bet all sorts of things. Last time I played, I won movie passes and a twenty-five-dollar prepaid phone card."

Chuckling, he commented that women were more inventive than men.

"Every *once* in a while, you need a girls' night out without any men."

"Maybe I should start one of those," Millie said. "I'm getting sick of the ladies auxiliary. We need some excitement around here."

Pop shot her an incredulous look, his green eye glaring.

She seemed flustered. "I mean after the storm passes, and we figure out who burgled your house, and this whole Lester mess is settled."

I decided to read and leave Pop and Millie to their movie. Realizing it had grown dark, Pop got up to lock the doors. He also took the animals outside to do their business before securing the doggie door, effectively locking Flush and Bandit inside for the evening. He made the rounds a final time to check that all windows were shut tight and locked. I noticed the shotgun resting against a wall in the den, where they'd watch TV. Without being obvious about it, he kept the gun within easy reach.

"Is there something you're not telling me, Pop?"

He shook his head. "Just a feeling, lass. Whoe'er went through the house looked for something specific. The random trespasser theory doesn't fly with me."

Chuck's warning to be careful rang in my memory, and a jolt of fear made the fine hairs at the back of my neck stand on end. I thought about getting in the Range Rover and heading back to Atlanta until it dawned on me that Pop was in danger, too. For that matter, everybody in town was in danger if Riley had really been murdered. "Do you think we're in jeopardy, Pop?"

"Aye. I'd have told you not to come, if I'd known you were coming. Like I already said, be best if you head back at first light."

Hunched on the end table next to him, Bandit held a morsel of something in her paws and prepared to dunk it in Pop's coffee. He shooed her away. When she scampered off the table, a photograph behind her caught my attention. Framed in red antiqued wood, it was me and Flush. Smiling into the camera, I held an empty net. Pop had taken it when we went crabbing, after we realized there would be no blue crabs on our plate that night. Seeing my picture in his living room stirred up an unfamiliar emotion. It was a sense of belonging to a family. A taste of what it might feel like to have a set of traditional parents and be doted on by a caring father. Nobody had ever put a framed photo of me in their living room before. Strangely sentimental, I told Pop I'd think about leaving first thing in the morning, even though I'd already made up my mind not to.

I decided to go to bed early, stretch out, and read the dossier on my new project, the Georgia Association of Realtors account. Pop and Millie remained on the sofa with Flush sprawled between their feet.

"Night, Jaxie," Millie said, snuggling closer to Pop. It was apparent she planned to stay overnight, although I hadn't seen her carry in a bag. Which meant she must have already left a few belongings in Pop's room. Which meant that Pop was getting more action than I was lately. And much to my distress, the only male in my thoughts lately was Justin.

I headed to my room. "Good night to you guys, too." Flush jumped up to follow me.

"He probably wants to get on the bed with you, lass," Pop called.

"No problem." I was happy for some male company, even though it had four legs and drooled.

Startled, I woke instantly. I couldn't make out the words, but I'd felt a woman whisper in my ear. Sitting up, I switched on a lamp. Other than Flush, who happily snored away beside me, the room was empty. The woman must have been a dream, I decided, and reached for my wristwatch to check the time. It wasn't on the nightstand where I'd left it.

"Bandit, you little thief!" I said to the house. "What did you do with my watch? If it wouldn't be animal cruelty, I'd kick your ass. With one of my pointy-toed Kate Spade slides, which I just happen to have in the car! Brand new, in the box. I planned to return them, but I'd just as soon use one on you instead!"

Roused by my voice, Flush opened an eye to look at me, yawned, and turned to lie on his other side. He stopped midway over for several seconds, all four legs sticking up in the air. Realizing he wouldn't get a belly rub, he flopped the rest of the way over and started snoring again.

I fished my Palm handheld out of my purse to see that it was barely after three in the morning. Stretching, I sensed the presence of somebody else in the room. Thinking it was the raccoon, I got up to look for Bandit. She wasn't under the bed, or in the closet, or behind the door. I thought about tracking her and my watch down but decided the hunt could wait until morning. I figured that the strange sense of being watched was residual memory of the vivid dream.

The house was quiet when I padded to the kitchen to pour myself a glass of milk. Through the window, I saw Millie's car in the driveway and smiled at the image of her and Pop together. They acted as if they'd been together forever, instead of just a few weeks. Watching them gush over each other, I couldn't help but cheer them on. As I drank the milk, my thoughts turned to Justin and that single wonderful evening we'd spent together. It wasn't likely ever to happen again for a lot of reasons. Still, though, I wanted him. And hated him. All at the same time. It was maddening.

The milk did nothing to cure my insomnia, but I crawled back into bed anyway and listened to Flush snore while I tried to go to sleep. Ten minutes later and still wide awake, I turned on the lamp and my laptop. I found the Georgia Realtors Web site and figured I'd take a look at their past ad campaigns. If I still had a job when I got back, at least I'd be up to speed on my new assignment.

An hour later and no closer to being sleepy, I spotted Pop's old family Bible on the dresser. I decided to read the genealogical entries again and look through the page margins to see if there were any scribbled notes I'd missed the first go-round. Without getting out of bed, I stretched to retrieve the huge book, but just as I was about to swing myself back against the pillow, it slipped out of my hands. Heavy, it fell fast and landed on the hardwood floor with a thud.

Appalled that I'd just dropped a three-hundred-plus-year-old book, I hopped out of bed to look at the heirloom. It appeared intact, but when I picked it up, the sound of ripping leather made me cringe. The back cover broke loose from the spine and remained attached by a single dangling corner. "Oh, no." I said to the sleeping dog. "This is not good."

Carefully putting the Bible on the bed, I sat down to assess the damage. When I unlocked the clasp and opened the cover, something tickled my nose and I sneezed hard, eyes shut tight. Opening them afterward, I saw the edges of a folded paper sticking out from inside the cover.

It was a letter or some type of document, folded in half. My heart did a double beat. Had someone purposely hidden it between the seams of the thick cover and leather binding? If so, how long had it gone undiscovered? I gingerly unfolded the dry age-yellowed sheet and immediately recognized the petite left-handed slant. It was the sixteen-year-old girl who'd documented the birth of her baby boy in 1716 without listing a father. Based on the date, she'd written this letter six months before her baby was born. Heart slamming against my chest, I heard the words while my eyes devoured each line, as though the woman who wrote them centuries ago sat beside me now.

> *I love him, despite my will to not. He is dangere, to be sure, yet he has the heart of one thousand men. He loves me as well, sufficient to forgo his pirating ways. Noble*

blood pumps threw him, but life on the sea is the only life he lived after seised when a boy. It has not damaged his soul, tho, for he is beutiful.

What an outrage when I told Father of the burning in my heart. Why must a hypocrite he be? He commissions them to steale, the pirates who rest in Rum Towne. He is a thief surely as they, he hides it better.

Never have I been so delited and so sad. I love Father but love Emerald Eye more. Not a soul knows, save God, within me a baby gros. Tonite I go to Rum Towne in the cover of darknes, where my love awaits. We shall marry and set sail, gone from this coast to find another. For months I have secrettly transport chattels to the summer cottage. Now I go with just a mare.

How I wish Mother were of this earth, for she would see the man, not the existence. May God protect us both.

Mary Aldora Barstow

My lungs cried for oxygen, and I realized I'd held my breath. I sucked in air and let it out with a shout. "Pop! Millie! Wake up!"

Startled, Flush jumped off the bed and stayed on my heels as I headed to the kitchen, flipping on lights along the way. Instantly, Pop was there, in pajamas. He held the shotgun with both hands, pointed at the floor but ready to take aim and pull the trigger. His eyes darted around the kitchen to take inventory of the situation. "Da hell's going on, lass?"

"I'm so sorry. I didn't mean to scare you. It's just that I found something!"

"It's okay, Maddie," he shouted back to the bedroom. "E'erything's okay."

Not sure why all the humans were awake, Bandit hid behind the doorway and peeped in to take a survey, while Flush stood at attention near his food bowls. He figured it was time for breakfast.

"The ship, *Aldora*? It was named after the woman! Mary A. Barstow. Aldora was her middle name! And get this: Rumton used to be called Rum Towne, probably because people came here to buy rum from the pirates. Mary Aldora Barstow married one of them—the pirates—or at least she was running away to marry Emerald Eye when she wrote the letter." I paused to breathe and another piece of the puzzle swooshed into place. "Emerald Eye! Her lover must've been given that name because he had a green eye and a brown eye, just as you do! When she ran off to meet him in Rum Towne, Aldora was pregnant with Emerald Eye's baby. . . ."

"Take it easy, lass." Pop led me to a chair, but I was too excited to sit.

Another deep breath fueled my brain with enough oxygen to make a startling connection. "The baby! Aldora and Emerald Eye's baby was your ancestor, Pop! That means you're a descendant of the pirate. It's why you've got the green eye."

Wrapped in what had to be Pop's robe, Millie joined us, just as another revelation floored me. "Justin has it too! He's carrying the gene from Emerald Eye."

A simple chunk of DNA on a chromosome, creating a recessive gene that stubbornly hung on to the branches of Pop's family tree, captured my imagination. Placing Aldora's letter on the table, I dropped into the chair, a flood of scenarios churning in my head. Had the girl's pirate looked at her with the mesmerizing green eye in the same lustful way Justin looked at me when I'd kissed his fingertips? Had she been just as enchanted by the gaze?

Carefully picking up the letter with both hands, Pop sat down to read. Millie asked if we wanted some milk.

"A glass of whiskey would be good, Maddie," Pop said. "With a milk chaser." As he held the paper gingerly by its edges, eyes moving slowly across the longhand, I knew he envisioned Aldora while he read. Running a hand through thick white hair, he read it a second time. "Where'd you find this, lass?"

Apologizing for the damage to the Bible, I told him.

He smiled. "You hadn't dropped it, we wouldn't have seen this."

Millie wanted to know what had caused me to be so wound up. I told her about the birth and death entries in the old Bible. Together, Pop and I pieced together the story of the young girl, a plantation owner's daughter who fell in love with a pirate and had his baby. But we had to assume that she didn't run away as planned. Had Emerald Eye been at the helm of the *Aldora*, sailing to pick up his bride in Rum Towne when the ship sank? If so, had the wreckage been submerged at the shoreline for the past three hundred years and just recently worked its way to the surface?

"Who do you think Aldora wrote the letter to?" I wondered aloud.

"Probably the slave who took care of her, since she didn't have a mother or any sisters," Millie surmised. She snapped off the corner off a dog biscuit and gave it to Bandit before giving the remainder to Flush. Both animals happily munched. She asked Pop if he'd like some more whiskey or a snack, and watching her fuss over him, I couldn't help but grin. She caught my look. "You won't tell our little secret, will you?"

"That you and Pop are an item? Of course not. But your car is parked in the driveway. And there are no secrets in a small town. I learned that lesson after the whole shipwreck thing."

She sighed, but it was a happy sigh. "You're probably right. We'll be the talk of the town soon."

Steering the conversation away from his sex life, Pop brought up some theories on how the town's name changed from Rum Towne to Rumton. We decided it had to have been a slow progression. Over time, people probably quit calling it Rum Towne, when they no longer bartered for liquor.

"The wooden barrels!" I said loudly enough to make Millie jump. "They're all over town. Billy keeps iced drinks in them at the general store. There's a few in Chat 'N Chew. Elwood sits on one while he carves. Heck, you've got one outside the front door as an umbrella stand. I bet they're old rum kegs."

Pop nodded. "Ne'er thought much 'bout it, but I'd bet you're right. Barrels have been 'round long as I can recall. They come in handy."

It all made sense. The town's slogan, Ya'll Hideout, which started out as Yawl Hide, referring to a place for seamen to secure their small boats out of view and unload goods. And Rum Towne, where settlers traveled to get their rum.

"You think it was just one shipload of rum, probably from the Caribbean, that pirates seized and dumped here?"

"Good question." Millie frowned in thought. "I wonder how many kegs of rum one cargo ship would have carried?"

Pop's eye sparkled. "Maybe," he said, "the rum was made in Rum Towne, and pirates came 'ere to get it."

We all thought about that. Millie read the letter again, after which Pop told me to bring him the Bible. With a sharp kitchen knife, he quickly sliced the strip of leather that attached a dangling cover to sever it from the book. Next, he cut around the edges and peeled back the thin leather binding to see if anything else had been stashed in the hiding place.

I held my breath but involuntary sucked in some air when the edges of another folded piece of paper appeared. "There's more!"

Millie and I huddled around Pop, as he read the words aloud with fascination.

> My beautiful Aldora,
>   The place is found, a peaceful sound. Until we go, I give thee bolle. A sign, soon thou are mine. Like the serpents, we are strong. As two, there is no wrong.

The writer signed it Emanuel Anthony, beneath which he'd written, *your love, Emerald Eye.*

"Huh," everyone said.

Millie took Pop's hand. "What does it mean?"

"I'd say he 'ad a place picked out for them to live," Pop said. "A sound. An open stretch of calm water."

Millie drank some of Pop's whiskey and chased it down with a sip of his milk. "You mean like the Pamlico Sound or Albemarle Sound?"

"Right-o. A pirate, even gone clean, wouldn't stray too far from the seas."

Millie ran a hand through Pop's hair before rubbing his back. "So he gave her some sort of bowl. But what did he mean by the serpents?"

"I don't know, but the ending is beautiful. He told her to be strong. That their love for each other wasn't wrong." I rubbed Flush's chin with my toe. "It's fascinating. An educated boy of noble blood, who ended up on a pirate ship and became a pirate himself. But then fell in love."

We sat talking until the sky above Rumton lightened in promise of sunrise. Since it was already time to start the day, Millie busied herself making pancakes.

"Got my curiosity up, lass," Pop said. "I left the Bible on your dresser in case you want to look through it some more. But what were you doing up in the middle of the night?"

I told him about the dream of the woman whispering in my ear and asked what it could have meant.

Staring into his milk glass, nodding to himself, he contemplated his answer for a long minute. "Don't know what it meant," he said, looking at me, his expression incredulous. "But I've had the same dream. Se'eral times."

20

Saturday was perfect: cloudless, vivid blue sky, mercury barely above seventy, and just a hint of breeze. Were it not for the Weather Channel's steady flow of hurricane reports, I'd never have guessed a 250-mile-wide destructive monster spiraled our way. In the lower latitudes, a television meteorologist explained, hurricanes traditionally gained speed as they approached land. Not only had Hailey gained speed, but she'd also gained strength and would soon upgrade to a category four. Like a bullet headed for a target, this storm had Rumton in its sights. It hadn't bothered to zigzag as many hurricanes did.

Pop returned from Millie's house, where he'd boarded windows and helped move patio furniture inside. "I'll say it again, lass. You really need to leave. Drive back to the city."

I rinsed out Flush's water bowl in the kitchen sink and refilled it. Bandit stood by, waiting while I did the same with hers. I looked at Pop. "I appreciate your concern. I do. But I want to stay with you. Besides, it may not even hit here."

"Or it might," Pop said. "If it does, it's going to do some serious damage. You won't want to be 'ere."

"Are *you* leaving?" I challenged, though I already knew he wasn't.

He shook his head.

"What if the governor orders a mandatory evacuation? They're saying she will, later today, for everybody east of Highway 17 and east of the waterway."

He shook his head again. "I won't leave. But that doesn't mean you ought to follow suit. A storm of this size is deadly."

"So why don't you evacuate, then?"

"I ne'er do. I'm stubborn. Or stupid. Not sure which."

Pop said if Hailey continued on her current path, probably half the townspeople would evacuate. Some already had. Others had packed up and were prepared to go. American Red Cross chapters were in the process of opening shelters at schools and churches in neighboring cities, but they were a good drive away. Shelters were to be avoided if at all possible, Pop said, unless you enjoyed sleeping on a hard floor with an untold number of strangers.

"But the other half will stay?"

"Like me, they're stubborn. Or stupid." He smiled. "We're far enough away from the ocean to give us a false sense of security."

Somebody knocked on Pop's back door. "Jaxie? You here? I got your birth control, sugar." Gertrude walked in before Pop could answer her knock. "I heard you were back in town. I wasn't sure if you'd be needin' these or not. Jane said she saw your car here."

I took the prescription refill and thanked her, no longer self-conscious that everybody in Rumton knew I was on the Pill. "You always deliver door to door?"

"Only if somebody's out of sorts sick—and during hurricane watches. It's my way of doin' community service. Now come, tell. Who is it? Is he here?"

Moving stiffly because of her arthritis, Gertrude scanned Pop's place, figuring I had to be bopping someone. Disappointed at not spotting the male in question, she was heading out the back door when Justin walked in. *What was he doing here?*

The pharmacist squinted up at him as she passed and gave him the once-over, clucking her approval. "I figured it might be you!" she told Justin, patting his arm. "You're all set, dear. She's good to go."

We watched Gertrude wobble-walk to her car with a side-to-side motion, as though her knees wouldn't bend. She was off to make more drug deliveries.

"What was she talking about?" Justin said, dropping his luggage on the floor.

"You don't want to know."

The men hugged. "You shouldn't have come," Pop told him.

"Figured you could use some help, since you have absolutely no intention of evacuating."

"True."

Justin turned to me. "Since you're still here, I assume you're not leaving, either?"

"You knew I was here?"

He smiled. "Sheila."

"I'm going to kill her. So much for secrets."

"I'd have told him, anyhow, lass," Pop said.

Before I could argue, Justin hugged me tight. He took my face in his hands so that I had to meet his eyes. "You're not *my* type, Jaxie Parker, but I can't quit thinking about you, either."

He let me go just as quickly and my whole body warmed. Looking around, Justin stopped in place when he noticed the disarray. Pop and I had repaired and cleaned what we could, but damage from the break-in was still evident. After grilling Pop for details, Justin checked to see that the shotgun was loaded. Satisfied, he propped it back in the corner. "Your forty-five automatic where you normally keep it?"

"Aye."

"Loaded?"

"Aye."

"Where would that be?" I wanted to know.

Pop nodded toward an antique piece of furniture in the den,

on which the television sat. "In the slide-out, where a VCR is supposed to go. Just beneath the squawk box. Whoe'er came through 'ere didn't look in there. Probably would've taken it, if they 'ad."

"You know how to shoot?" Justin asked me.

"I can make a tight pattern in the center of a paper target from thirty feet with a short-barreled thirty-eight automatic." Both men looked at me, astonished. I shrugged. "Sheila and I took a gun safety course for self-defense. Instructor said we were naturals."

"Well then," Justin said, "let's get to work."

He pulled pieces of precut plywood from the attic. They'd been used before, and Hailey was the fourth major storm they were meant to protect against. The boards custom-fit all the large windows; it was just a matter of attaching them on the outside of the house with a cordless drill. Next, they moved patio furniture and outdoor plants into the garage. Justin placed the grill near the garage door and disconnected the propane tank to refill it.

"I'm feeling kind of useless here," I told them. "What can I do?"

"You can get started on some dinner for us tonight," Pop said. "Pull the steaks out of the freezer to thaw. Probably lose power anyway, so we need to eat what we can."

"Bourbon and Coke okay for the marinade?" It was all I knew.

"Rather drink me bourbon, but go ahead, I've got plenty. Pull out some of those frozen rolls you bought, too. We'll let them *thaw* this time. And see if you can make us a salad or some such. Just don't do anything that requires using heat. Me and Justin will do the actual cooking."

I made a face at him. "Ha, ha."

"Wasn't joking, lass. Those are the last four steaks."

When they'd finished prepping the old house and it was time to go shopping, I offered to drive. I couldn't cook, but two things I could do well were shop and drive.

People buzzed jovially around Billy's store, talking and filling their carry baskets as though Hailey were an upcoming social event instead of a natural disaster. Batteries, jug water, canned goods, and Bud Light were in high demand, as were Slim Jims and Moon Pies. Billy gave away propane free, and a short line of people waited to fill tanks outside the general store. Others waited to fill their cars with gas at the single pump, and several filled gas containers to use for their generators.

Equipped with a full propane tank for the grill, groceries, and dog food, we headed to the Chat 'N Chew to see if Bull needed any help.

"Justin! Good to see you," Bull said. "Hey, Pop. Ya'll help yourselves to some coffee and a slice of pound cake, on me. And Jaxie, nice job at the council meeting. I heard what you did. Sorry I missed it!"

Justin gave me a sharp look. "What did you do?"

"Tell you about it later," I said.

"Stopped Lester in his tracks, that's what she did!" Bull said. "Gladys told me all about it."

I tried to act modest, but I relished the praise. "I simply gave the council some information they were not aware of. They decided to postpone their vote on selling to Lester."

Festive as the general store was, Bull's place buzzed with animated conversations while people watched Hailey updates on a single wall-mounted television. We settled onto swivel stools at the counter for coffee and pound cake. I gave Justin a nickel version of the information I'd obtained on Lester.

He frowned. "So your gut feeling about Lester was right."

"Yes, it was. But that didn't come through as a genuine pat on the back," I said, feeling shortchanged. He should have been impressed by my initiative. He should have congratulated me. He should have apologized for doubting me.

"You need to tell Aaron."

"I did it on my personal time. And I was right all along about Lester hiding something. What's the big deal?"

Justin did the frown thing again. "They know each other. Aaron and Lester."

"What? How?"

He slowly chewed a bite of cake and swallowed before speaking. "I don't know how. But Aaron's assistant took some calls from a man named Lester in the past few months, before you ever went to Rumton. It's got to be the same person."

"I don't get it," I mused. "Why didn't Aaron just tell me he knew Lester?"

"Don't know who knew what, but right now we've got more important things to worry 'bout." Pop pointed to the television, where a weatherman delivered the latest Hailey update. "She's a cat four now. Justin, I want you to take Jaxie and get out of 'ere."

We studied the small screen. The funnel of projected landfall had tightened as Hailey closed in on the coast. Rumton still sat at the center of it. Sixty miles of coastline would get battered, but we would take a direct hit if the storm continued on its current path.

"I've never been through a hurricane before," I said.

"No reason for you to start now," Pop said. "You both did what you came to do. It's time to head on back."

"I'm not going anywhere," I said stubbornly. "I'm taking Monday as another vacation day. I already called the office."

Pop looked at Justin, who said, "Can't make her go if she doesn't want to. And if she's staying, I am, too."

We both looked at Pop.

He sighed, relenting. "Lord Almighty."

Walking past us to deliver an armload of plates loaded with fried chicken, Bull dropped a cordless phone on the counter in front of Pop. "Avery's lookin' for you."

Pop took the phone, listened for a minute, and green eye sparkling, passed it to Justin. Justin listened, asked a few questions, and passed the phone back to Pop, who assured Avery that all was well before disconnecting.

I felt left out. "What was that all about?"

Pop stirred some cream into his coffee. "Danger aside, Avery thinks Hailey might be a good thing."

"What?" I said. "That's crazy."

"If we take a direct hit, especially at high tide, Mother Nature might open up Devil's Tail for us," Justin explained, excitement causing him to stand. "The storm surge could be huge. Maybe twenty-five feet, even thirty feet. But we'd need to help her along. Get the shipwreck remains out of there, so more than a trickle of water is flowing between Skirr Creek and the ocean before Hailey hits."

"So the shipwreck is like a giant plug that has stopped up the inlet?" I asked.

Justin sat back down to think. "Something like that. If we get the wreckage out of there, it would allow for a bigger flow of water. At which point, theoretically, the storm surge could completely open it up."

"It's a major powerful storm," Pop said. "Could 'appen. Heck, it happened at Hatteras in 2003 with Hurricane Isabel. That storm opened up enough of a channel to get small boats through."

Energized, they discussed the possibilities and envisioned what Rumton would be like as a water town.

"We don't have enough time. We'd have to get a permit to get heavy equipment out there. Not to mention that we'd need manpower." Frustrated, Justin shook his head. "All we've got is one day. Tomorrow. There's no way."

"No way what?" Bull said, retrieving her telephone.

Justin relayed Avery's phone message.

"You mean we'd have a way for boats to get in an' out of Rumton, like they used to?"

"Well, theoretically, it's possible. But, realistically, there's no way we can get that wreckage out of there in one day." He sighed, and I could almost see his enthusiasm dissipate. "Not to mention, we'd destroy any historical value by randomly digging it out of there."

"The *Aldora* was my ancestor's. Way I see it, she belongs to me now. What's left of her, anyway. And I've got all the historical value I need right up here." Pop pointed to his head.

Justin's head snapped around. "Your ancestor's? How do you—"

"Jaxie found a letter. And a poem."

Justin's head snapped the other way to look at me. "Written by whom?"

I removed the thick glasses from his face and stared straight into the green eye. "Your ancestors. Aldora and her lover, Emerald Eye."

21

Dusk had settled over Rumton by the time we reached Pop's house. Millie was nearly hidden in the shadows of his front porch. When we came to a stop in the drive, she jumped up and made a smooching gesture at Pop.

"They're an item now," I said to Justin.

"An item? Millie and Pop?"

"Mmm-hmm."

"Didn't think they even liked each other," he mused. He suppressed a smile, the corners of his lips just barely curving up.

I unloaded groceries while he attached the propane tank to Pop's grill. Informing Pop that she planned to stay through the storm, Millie carried in bags of baked goods, a litter box, a bag of cat food, and two cats.

"No worries," Pop said, obviously pleased she'd invited herself to our hurricane party. "Need a fourth anyhow if we're going to play cards. You're welcome to take shelter here, Maddie."

"Thank you. After all, your house is the oldest one around. I figure if it has withstood three hundred years of storms, it'll keep standin' for one more."

Pop nearly strutted, like a peacock trying to impress the female. "Right-o."

"Did you have to bring the cats?" I whined.

Affronted, she blinked at me. "I can't leave my babies at home by themselves during a hurricane!"

My eyes watered and the sneeze erupted. A chorus of "bless you's" came my way. "What about all your other cats?" I asked, wiping my nose on the back of my hand.

"Only got these two."

I eyed Pop. "*Somebody* told me you had ten or fifteen of them."

"That's ridiculous. You'd have to be mad to have that many cats!"

Pop looked sheepish. "It's what Riley told me. Ne'er been to Maddie's house myself. Well, until recent."

I told Millie I was severely allergic to cats and was relieved to hear that her babies would be perfectly content in the garage until bedtime, at which point they'd stay in the room with her and Pop.

"You'll be fine," she told me. "Here, have a brownie. I made them with pecans and coconut."

With the windows boarded up, the house was eerily dark inside. Justin left a few uncovered so that we'd have some light; just a splash of fading daylight filtered through. I ate a brownie.

Pop switched on the TV just in time for us to hear a news anchorman announce that the storm had not changed course and mandatory evacuations were now in effect. About that time, the police chief knocked on the door. He wore jeans, old boots, and a baseball cap. Were it not for the badge affixed to his T-shirt, a stranger never would have guessed he was the law.

"You heading out?" he asked.

Pop told him no. Millie offered him a brownie.

"I'm supposed to make you leave," the chief said through a mouthful of brownie.

"Aye."

"It's going to be a bad one. Might be a few news crews drive through to take a look-see tomorrow."

"But they won't stay. They'll head to the beach towns for their live reports. Ocean makes a better backdrop."

Bandit stood on her hind paws and stretched up to look at the chief's badge, deciding if she could find a way to steal it. He reached down to give her a pat. "True. There's nowhere here for them to stay anyhow, even if they wanted to."

Pop nodded.

"What's this I hear about Devil's Tail," the chief asked. "Avery says the storm surge could blow it open?"

I was amazed at how fast gossip traveled in an otherwise unhurried town. Pop told the chief of Avery's conclusion and finished by adding that we couldn't get the wreckage cleaned out in time. There was no way.

The chief adjusted his baseball cap. "Lot of old farm and tractor equipment around here. There's even a dragline parked behind Duckies. Some of it might still work."

"Nobody to man it, though. Just us. Avery's on a job and can't get 'ere. Folks are busy preparing for Hailey." Pop shook his head. "Half the people are already gone, anyhow. And the rest of us aren't supposed to be 'ere."

The chief nodded. "So you're staying, then?"

"Aye."

"Need anything, give me a shout. I'll be at the station till this thing's over."

Pop agreed and the chief continued on his rounds. We couldn't help but wonder what would have happened if we'd removed the ship wreckage out of Devil's Tail when we first found it. But Pop was right. Now was too late.

Justin tried to lighten the mood. "Hey, Pop. Maybe you should offer a few bedrooms to the storm chasers. You can open a boardinghouse."

"What you ought to do, Cuddles, is turn this place into a bed-and-breakfast," Millie said. "It's sure big enough."

"*Cuddles?*" Justin burst out laughing.

"That's a great idea, Millie," I said. "*Cuddles* B and B. The cozy place to stay."

Pop pointed a finger at us. "Don't you two start, or I'll sic my attack dog on you."

Flush stretched out on his stomach near Justin's feet, occasionally sniffing the air in hopes of a fallen morsel. "Your attack dog seems a tad lackadaisical this evening."

"Pop's a good cuddler," Millie said, defending the nickname. "What's wrong with calling him Cuddles?"

Justin finished chopping vegetables and stirred something on the stove. "Not a thing. It's just, ah, a surprising pet name, is all. Speaking of surprises, where is that letter you found, Jax?"

It was the first time he'd ever used the short version of my name, and a sense of warmth flowed through me upon hearing it. I pointed to the kitchen table, where we'd left the old papers.

While Pop grumbled about everyone making fun of his nickname and Justin read with obvious awe, I opened a bottle of cabernet and Millie decided to feed the animals. "Hey, I've seen something like this in a magazine," she said, holding one of Flush's big bowls up to the light with both hands. "A vase. Ivory white with dragons stamped in it, just like this. And a band encircling the rim."

Justin finished the letter and read the poem aloud, perhaps envisioning its green-eyed author. "The place is found, a peaceful sound. Until we go, I give thee bolle. A sign, soon thou are mine. Like the serpents, we are strong. As two, there is no wrong." Justin rubbed a temple. "So he had a place picked out for them to live. And told her to be strong, like the serpents on the bowl . . . what did you just say about dragons, Millie?"

"I saw a vase in a magazine that looked just like these dog food bowls," she repeated.

"Which magazine?" I asked.

"Don't recall. One of those antiques magazines. The article was on old porcelain from China, and how it's going for big bucks at them auction houses in New York, like Chrissy's."

"You mean Christie's? And Sotheby's?"

"Yep. Picture of that vase looked just like this bowl." She dumped in two cupfuls of dry food and returned it to the floor. Flush shoved his snout in and chomped away. Like magic, Bandit appeared, waiting for her food. Millie fed the raccoon, too, before leaving to check on the cats.

"Pop," Justin called. "Where'd those bowls come from?"

I answered. "They've been around forever. Pop said they came with the house."

Justin watched Flush eat. "Emerald Eye gave her a gift of a bowl, or perhaps a set of bowls . . . and wrote, 'Be strong like the serpents. . . .'" He looked up sharply. "Jaxie, a serpent is the same thing as a dragon."

Flush finished eating from one bowl and slurped noisily from the other. I grabbed the empty one and brought it to the table. While Justin examined it, I powered up my laptop and went on-line to some high-end auction sites. After ten minutes of searching under porcelain, I found a photograph of pottery that looked just like Flush's bowl, except that it was a slightly different shape. A glassy-looking pale ivory piece decorated with dragons and flowers, and rimmed with a metal band, it was known as "Ding" ware. The description said the porcelain was made during the Northern Song Dynasty in southeast China. It came from a private collection and sold for $1,121,000. I aimed the screen toward Justin and pointed. He looked back and forth between the bowl and the computer screen as I gingerly picked up Flush's water bowl, dried it, and set it next to the first one. Fingers flying, Justin searched Yahoo! for Ding ware to learn more.

"Could they be?" I whispered when he'd finished and leaned back to drink his wine.

"They fit the description of Ding ware. The markings on the bottom, the engraving, the color, the copper band around the rim. If they are, they're several hundred years old and they're certainly worth some money. It's unbelievable, but there's not even a chip on these bowls."

"So maybe Emerald Eye thought they were pretty and presented them to Aldora as a gift. But where did he get them?"

"I'd imagine they were plundered from a ship. Or he may have bartered for them. Trade goods from many countries, including the Far East, were brought to the New World to decorate homes and use as barter." Justin took another look at the bowls, shook his head, and stood up. "Care to join me outside while I cook the steaks?"

We sat in folding patio chairs and drank wine while he tended the grill. The night was strangely still, but the air between us almost vibrated with a tension caused by words unsaid. I certainly wasn't going first.

"I need to apologize," Justin finally said, and the discord evaporated like helium from a popped balloon. "I dismissed your feelings about Lester because I took the position of a company executive instead of a friend. But I'd much rather have you in my life as anything *other* than an account executive!"

"Anything?"

He laughed boyishly, as though unsure if his apology would work, and I wanted to wrap myself around him. It was working.

"Okay, not *anything*. I wouldn't want you to be just a good friend who fed my fish while I was out of town, for example."

"You have fish?"

"A saltwater aquarium. But my point is that I want to be much more than friends, Jax. And much more than just coworkers."

"How big of an aquarium?"

He started to answer but pulled me to his chest instead. The embrace felt good, and we stood entwined for several delicious seconds before he stepped back to look at me. "Aaron told me he felt you'd become too personally involved here, and he asked me to help get you back into the groove at work. He wanted the old Jaxie back. The one who worked hard and partied hard and never questioned a directive."

I did a half-hearted shrug in acknowledgment but wanted to hear more.

"I still don't know what we've gotten ourselves into, but I do understand why you couldn't just ignore it. Hell, I can't ignore the information you found on Lester. Pop is the closest thing to a father I have."

I smiled. "Oddly enough, me too. I feel as if I've known him for years instead of weeks. And if I had a father, I'd want him to be somebody just like Pop."

"If he had a daughter, he'd want her to be just like you."

I drank some wine. He flipped the steaks. Flush came outside to investigate the tantalizing smell of sizzling beef.

"I'm sorry, too," I finally admitted. "I owe you an apology for being such a standoffish bitch for so many years. In retrospect, it was really unnecessary."

"Yeah, I'm not so bad once you get to know me. Am I?"

"You're pretty great." I actually thought so and wasn't just flirting. "By the way, what did Aaron say when he found out I came back here?"

Under the watchful eye of the dog, Justin turned off the gas and removed our dinner from the grill. "I didn't tell him. I'm not sure he knows either one of us is here. We'll deal with that when we get back. But you do realize that we aren't going anywhere for a few days, don't you? A storm of this size hits, the roads will be blocked with trees and downed power lines. Not to mention flooded out."

"We could flood here? Pop's house is on a hill."

"Possibly, depending on the surge and how much rain Hailey dumps." He studied me and must have seen worry reflected on my face. "There is still time for you to get out of here, Jaxie. Nobody is going to think any less of you for evacuating. In fact, Pop would be relieved if you were on the road tomorrow morning. So would I."

"What—and miss the hurricane party?" I said. "Besides, I can think of worse things than being stuck in the same house with you for a few days."

I stood close enough to see his pupils dilate.

Inside, Millie had cleared off the table to set it. Flush's bowls were back in their regular place on the floor, one filled with water. And the three-hundred-year-old letter was on the counter, stuck inside a recipe book. Justin served the steaks, along with sautéed asparagus, baked potatoes, and a loaf of French bread. I poured more wine, and we all sat down to eat. Without any preamble, I told Pop and Millie what we'd discovered about the bowls.

"Huh," Millie said. "So them bowls could be worth a few million dollars? You think we ought to put them away so they'll be safe? I can find something else for Flush to eat out of."

"They're safe right where they are, Maddie," Pop said. "Dog's been eating out of those bowls since he was a pup. And they didn't get broken when somebody rummaged through my house, either."

He had a good point. We left the bowls where they were and forgot about the impending storm and enjoyed our steaks.

Afterward, the four of us played poker. Eventually, Millie and Pop said good night and disappeared to his bedroom. On the other side of the house, Justin and I went into mine. I took off everything except my undies and a cotton tank top, and he stripped down to a pair of boxers. Although we were nearly nude, a yearning to know more about each other overrode the desire for sex. Lying in bed, we laughed and talked for hours, probing each other's thoughts and dreams until I dozed, wrapped in his arms.

I'd just fallen into a deep sleep when Pop rapped on the door. It was one thirty in the morning. My boss was on the phone, he said, and wanted to talk to me. Wrapped in a robe, I took the handset and sat in a chair, near Justin. Pop didn't seem surprised to find the two of us in the same bedroom.

"Aaron?"

"Jaxie. I'm sure I've awakened everyone by calling at this hour. I found out what happened at the council meeting. I must say I wasn't entirely surprised to hear that you'd returned to Rumton."

I knew my boss would learn of the meeting sooner or later and wondered who'd called him. It was probably Lester, since the two of them had struck some sort of agreement after Lester showed up to save the day. But I never would have guessed the news would make Aaron angry enough to call in the middle of the night. He must have been fuming. "Aaron, I should have told you what I did at the council meeting. I didn't even realize I was going to stand up and talk, until the last minute. But the information I learned about Lester kept weighing on me, and I *had* to come back to Rumton to do something." I took a deep breath, wondering if I'd be looking for a new job next week. "I hope I haven't . . . well, I just hope my job isn't in jeopardy over this."

"This isn't about losing your job, Jaxie. That's not what's at stake here." He sounded both agitated and tired. Maybe worried, too. "I never should have given you this revitalization assignment to begin with." I heard a sucking sound as he took a long pull from a cigar. "It never should have come to this."

"Come to what?" I asked, but he didn't answer.

"Aaron? What are you talking about?" I persisted.

Hearing my worried tone, Pop remained in the doorway and Justin pulled on a pair of jeans and came to stand beside my chair. Aaron's sigh traveled through the line. "I had other reasons for suggesting the pro bono project, and it should have been a win-

win situation. Good for everyone. I believed what Lester told me and had no idea what he was really up to. It isn't good."

So he'd known Lester all along, before he ever sent me to Rumton, just as Justin thought. "I don't understand. Lester is a friend of yours?"

"No, not what you'd call a friend." He laughed, but it came out as an ugly snort. He spoke slowly, deliberately, like someone who'd drunk too much booze and was making an effort to speak clearly. "It's true that Lester is a businessman. But he's also a con artist."

"Aaron, would you please tell me what's going on?" I felt agitated.

He snorted again, took a drink of something and another pull from the cigar. "Ah, hell. I've already written a resignation letter, anyway. The other partners can split my share of the firm. Doubt I'll even be missed all that much."

He stopped speaking, but I just waited. Finally, he took a deep breath. "I had good intentions, Jaxie, I did. I sent you in to stir things up and generate some interest in the town to increase property values. I knew Lester planned to buy land for a residential development. At least, that's what I thought he wanted it for until Riley told me otherwise. Anyway, in exchange for me running interference with the people, we were going to work out a pre-agreed-upon price per acre that he'd pay. A fair price. A win-win. But then I learned that he'd gone behind my back and started acquiring options at ridiculously low prices. I fired back by sending you in. I told Riley to keep an eye on you, but at the time I didn't know that he was already helping Lester." He sighed. "It's all complicated."

I still didn't quite get it.

"The best way to increase market value of any property, Jaxie, is to increase the number of buyers interested in acquiring it. I knew that if anybody in the firm could do that, you could. And in the process, maybe do some good things for the town. But mainly, I wanted to make sure that everybody who hadn't already sold would get the best price for their land, including me."

I sat up straighter. "You?"

"To begin with, I'm the one who told Lester about Rumton and its development potential. Hell, it's an undiscovered gold mine, really. I run across a lot of people with money, and they're always on the lookout for the next foreclosure, hot stock tip, or land deal. When I learned that Lester wanted undeveloped property in South Carolina, thinking of the money I'd make on the deal made me too blind to see him for what he is—a crook."

Justin studied my face to get a read on the conversation, but I couldn't look at him. Had he known all along that our boss was using me? "Why didn't you just tell me the truth?"

Ice cubes clinked in a glass before he swallowed. "That I wanted to use the firm's resources to put more money in my own pocket?"

My stomach churned. Aaron had been my mentor, and I always thought I wanted to be just like him one day. "Did any of the partners know what you were up to?" I demanded. "Or Justin? Did he know?"

"No, of course not," he answered, his words thick.

"What *does* Lester plan to do with Rumton, Aaron?"

"We can talk about that later. It doesn't matter now anyway because it won't happen. I'll see to that. What does matter is that you and Pop both are in danger, and you need to get out of there right now. Tonight."

I pounced with blatant sarcasm. "Oh. Well, then. Thanks so much for your concern, Aaron. It's mighty righteous of you to call and let us know we're in danger. Here in backwoods little Rumton, we don't watch the news, you know. I mean, who would've ever guessed that a giant hurricane is coming if you hadn't called?"

"I'm not talking about the storm, Jaxie." He swallowed some more of whatever he was drinking and by the sound of it, he'd reached the bottom of the glass. "I need to talk to Pop. Pass the phone to—"

It sounded as if he hiccupped; he never finished the sentence.

"Aaron?" I said, forgetting to be mad.

I heard a gurgle or perhaps a choking sound, and then nothing as the line went dead.

Confused and visibly shaking, I relayed the conversation to everyone. We'd gathered at the kitchen table, where poker chips and cards were still spread out.

Since we had no idea what type of danger Aaron was referring to, we unanimously decided to stay put. We could only guess it had to do with Lester and his associates, but we couldn't figure out what they wanted with us.

Nobody had seen Lester since the governor ordered a mandatory evacuation. We assumed that he'd headed inland to weather the storm. Even though they were supposed to leave immediately, Justin said, old-timers often waited until the last minute—or didn't leave at all. But apparently, Lester booked out of town without bothering to tell anyone good-bye. Some leader.

Pop called the police chief to let him know about Aaron's phone call, and Lester's possible involvement in something shady. Then Justin got on the phone and tried calling all of Aaron's numbers to see if we could get an answer. We didn't. He made another call to a cop friend and requested a courtesy check on Aaron's residence. An hour later Pop's phone rang.

Aaron had been found in a chaise longue on the back deck of his house, unconscious. A near-empty bottle of scotch sat on the table next to him, along with a smoldering cigar, the cordless telephone, and his wife's prescription bottle of Valium. But nothing was amiss, and the house appeared secure. They'd pumped out his stomach in the hospital and were running tests to rule out something like a stroke. The doctors figured that he'd simply taken too many pills and drank too much alcohol, and if the paramedics hadn't found him when they did, he would have been dead within hours. The unspoken concern was that Aaron may have intentionally tried to kill himself. They couldn't ask him, though, because he was still unconscious and they couldn't question his wife because she was out of town.

After conveying the horrible news to us, Justin called the hospital to learn that Aaron was stable, but not yet awake. Next, Justin dialed one of Shine's partners and without repeating all the details, explained that Aaron was in the hospital. That done, I called Sheila, knowing she wouldn't mind being awakened. I didn't want her to find out on Monday through the grapevine that our boss may have tried to kill himself.

Not knowing what else to do, we drank the glasses of milk Millie served and went back to bed, Pop toting the shotgun and Justin carrying the .45 automatic he'd retrieved from Pop's hiding place. We felt sure that the information Aaron discovered, the real reason Lester sought Rumton real estate, had something to do with why Aaron had called to tell us that we were in danger.

22

We awoke Sunday morning to news that Hailey, still on her same course, had progressed to a category five storm. One of the most powerful hurricanes in history, she moved fast and steady at twenty-two knots, which Pop said was almost twenty-five miles an hour. Forecasters said Hailey was even stronger than Hurricane Hazel, which hit the North Carolina/South Carolina border in 1954.

Nobody had slept well, and we were all up at sunrise. After a breakfast of toast and coffee, we headed to Devil's Tail. Even though there was nothing to be done, something drew us to the shipwreck site. It may have been the thought of what might have been if we'd dug out the wreckage days ago. Or perhaps we just needed something to do, since all our storm preparations were finished and it was now a matter of waiting for the inevitable.

We piled in my Range Rover and went as far as we could without burying ourselves in mud. Millie stayed in the vehicle, but the rest of us put on bulky hip waders and worked our way to the spot. Tranquil, almost surreal, an outline of the ship's hull just barely stuck out of the sand, as though skillfully painted into the landscape. It was a lovely morning, and the sky was nearly cloudless. The current weather certainly didn't indicate that a massive storm approached steadily.

"So this is where the inlet used to be. I can almost see the boats going in and out, winding their way to Rum Towne," I said.

"As Avery discovered from the satellite photos, it's shifted a bit from the original inlet, or outlet, to be technically correct." Justin explained that water always flowed toward the ocean. In the case of Devil's Tail, the stretch was fed by Skirr Creek, which in turn was fed by the waterway. Our problem was that the flow of water through Devil's Tail was a mere trickle instead of a deep-water canal.

Encapsulated by our rubber waders, we stood together, breathing the heady marsh scent and pondering Rumton's past. Suddenly I felt a tickle, as though a breeze had caressed my face. Only it was an uncharacteristically still morning and the air wasn't moving. In fact, no breeze blew at all.

"Do you guys feel that?" I whispered. "Remember how Brent and Tom joked about a ghost? I just felt an energy or something. Maybe I'm imagining things."

Justin closed his eyes, aimed his face at the sky, and breathed deep. After a moment, he let the breath out. "No, you aren't imagining things. I feel it, too."

"Aye," Pop said. "It's Aldora, I think. Same woman in the dream, who whispered in my ear. And your ear, too."

I laughed. "Surely you don't believe in ghosts?"

Pop speculated, "Aldora was cheated out of the happiness she would've 'ad with Emerald Eye. She might've lived her whole life heartbroken, waiting for him, haunted by love lost."

Something in me tingled at possibilities of the unknown.

Justin swayed in place. "I hate to think of the damage and possible death toll from this storm," he said. "But wouldn't it be amazing if she did open up Devil's Tail?"

"Aye. We'd have our ocean access back. Be like a bird dog set free after being kenneled 'is whole life."

A thought made me shiver. "Or like a buried shipwreck being uncovered to set free the romantic pirate who died when it went down."

"Huh," Pop and Justin said.

My feet sank into the silt, and I shifted my weight to keep them from going deeper. "I wish we had a week to get your ship out of here, Pop, instead of just a day. We might have done it."

Justin pointed. "Maybe we still can."

A rumbling of diesel engines flowed across the marsh and some sort of big tractor with a boom moved toward us, leading a parade of trucks and smaller tractors.

"Well, I'll be damned," Pop said under his breath.

I jumped up and down and almost fell when my foot stuck. "People are coming to help! I bet Bull spread the word about Avery's call!" I almost fell again and Justin righted me.

As the lead tractor moved closer, I saw that Elwood sat in the cab, surrounded by a bunch of controls and joysticks. The machine dwarfed his lanky eighty-two-year-old frame. "What *is* that thing?"

"It's an old dragline, used for dredging and excavating," Justin explained. "See that long arm? It swings the clamshell bucket out and plunges it into the sand or debris to be removed. Cables pull the bucket back and forth, to and from the machine. The whole thing rotates on its base."

"Elwood's the only man knows how to use it," Pop said. "He used to work for a heavy equipment company before he retired."

"Where'd it come from?"

"Been parked behind Duckies for years and years. Belonged to Walter's pappy, I think."

The parade stopped where we'd parked, and we started the process of trudging back across the span of marsh. "Speaking of heavy, how will they get it out here? It'll sink in this sludge."

"They're going to lay planks to make a track," Pop said, more to himself than to me. "I'll be damned."

Draglines typically floated on a barge to do a dredging job, but we didn't have that luxury, Pop told me, and laying the track

would be exhausting work. We returned to the staging area to find
even more people arriving. Bull brought thermoses of coffee and
bags of biscuits to feed people. Billy and Walter organized the
troops and divvied up duties. Several grandchildren of some of
the locals drove in to help. Three of the town's preachers had
come, deciding that removing the wreckage was more important
than delivering a sermon.

"I wonder if this is legal," I said, watching all the activity.

"Probably not," Pop said, his green eye flashing mischief. "But
then pirates ne'er were ones to follow the rules."

After collaborating with Pop, the men decided to pile all the debris in a clearing off to one side. If Hailey didn't carry it off,
they'd let it dry out, and the town would have a bonfire in com-
memoration of the *Aldora* and its captain, Emerald Eye. The first
order of business was to get the dragline in position; doing so took
hours. The track had to be laid in front of it, and as the giant
piece of heavy equipment moved forward, the track behind it was
rotated to the front. A group of men, utilizing a system of ropes
and pulleys and a four-wheel drive ATV, did the labor-intensive
work without complaining. While that project was in progress,
other people formed a human chain to the site and passed back
what they could dig out and lift by hand. Another group, led by
the judge, found the giant anchor and secured it with ropes. Once
the dragline was in place, its clamshell bucket would dislodge the
anchor, at which point trucks would pull the thing inland. A
trailer hitched to a farm tractor stood by to tow it to Pop's house.

"That's one piece of the ship that won't go anywhere with
the storm," I said. "It would be cool to use that in the museum if
the grant goes through. If the town would even want a museum,
that is."

In a symphony of coordinated efforts, everyone did his part, as though they dug out shipwrecks every day. Gertrude delivered a box of supplies from her drugstore, and Millie and I set up a makeshift first-aid station.

By early afternoon the day had grown sweltering. Although all were sweaty, muddy, and exhausted, nobody stopped working. When the last of the wreckage had been removed, a cheer went up, but there was still more to do. Track had to be laid again, in reverse, and the dragline moved back to dry land.

Clouds had started rolling in and the wind had picked up by the time we finished, yet nobody hurried to get home. A spattering of fat raindrops suddenly fell and quickly passed. In the distance, scattered bands of clouds melded into a solid mass. Resting on tailgates and folding lawn chairs, people told stories and watched the sky darken. They'd swapped their bottles of water and Gatorade for cans of beer, or gin and juice, compliments of Duckies. Pop moved from person to person, thanking each of them.

"Ain't no need to thank us, Pop," the judge said. "It was your boat down there, but we all want our canal opened up. Mother Nature took it away. Now maybe she'll give it back."

"Right," Gertrude shouted, louder than normal. She'd dropped her hearing-aid battery into the marsh while attempting to change it and didn't have a spare. "Besides, Jaxie's the one ought to be thanked."

The declaration caught me by surprise. "I am?"

"Weren't for you, Avery wouldn't have found Devil's Tail or the *Aldora*!"

Gladys patted me on the back. "And if it weren't for you, we wouldn't know the truth about Lester Spear."

Councilman Rusty, one of Lester's biggest supporters, spoke up. "A person says he's interested in the welfare of this town and wants to be our leader, seems like he'd be here, pitching in. Or be with the chief at the movie house, helping out. But ain't nobody seen hide nor hair of the man."

"I'll bet Lester took off, like a scared jackrabbit," Gertrude yelled.

A consensus of agreement made me smile. Those who'd given Lester the benefit of the doubt, even after my disclosure at the council meeting, now snatched it back.

Justin found my dirty hand with his dirtier one and squeezed. The townspeople had accomplished something huge, and being a part of it felt great.

Strong wind gusts and another sudden spattering of rain announced Hailey's arrival, like a warmup band preparing an audience for the real show. It was time to head to our respective homes for a shower and a meal, the last hot water and cooked food we might have for a while. But before we did that, everyone joined hands and said a prayer.

23

Hailey made landfall late Sunday night, as it neared midnight. Gaining momentum, she traveled at an astounding forward speed of twenty-six knots, or almost thirty miles an hour. Justin had boarded up the remaining windows before rain began slamming against the house in sheets. Except for a few peepholes cut in the wood, we couldn't see outside at all. We filled gallon jugs with water to use for drinking and brushing our teeth, since the water supply might become contaminated. Then there was nothing to do but eat and drink and play cards. And hope we lived through it.

I lit a jar candle in the center of the table—so that we'd have some light when the power failed—and looked at the people around me. Our little group made a strange and wonderful family. Pop and Millie, who hadn't shared words in thirty years, but now gushed over each other like kids in love. Me and Justin, who'd worked together for years but never bothered to get to know each other. And two cats, one dog, and a raccoon. Were it not for the relentless frightening noises made by the ferocious wind, rain, and lightning, it would have been an enjoyable evening, just spending time together. To take my mind off the storm, I studied the faint shadows flickering across Justin's unshaven face. He looked good in candlelight. He would look good in any light, I decided. Especially without the ugly glasses hiding his eyes.

He caught my glance and read my thoughts. "Lasik surgery next month. It's already scheduled. Since you're so fascinated with Emerald Eye, I promise not to cancel the appointment this time. Then you can have an unobstructed view of *my* green eye any time you wish."

Pop chuckled. "I'm pretty fascinated with Emerald Eye myself, lass. Oft' wondered what it would have been like to live a life on the sea."

Millie patted Pop's knee. "Everybody's fascinated by pirates. There's something so . . . romantic and dangerous and, well, downright *sexy* about them."

Pop sat up a little straighter. Fanning his poker hand in front of him, he might have flexed his biceps, but I couldn't tell for sure.

I had only a pair of three's and knew Justin held a full house. I'd sneaked a peek at his cards when he held them out for a better look. I laid my cards down to fold when it hit me. "Pirates! That's it," I said, floored by the obvious. "The avenue to revitalizing Rumton. The whole reason I was sent here to begin with!"

Following my train of thought, Justin smiled. He had a beautiful smile. Leaning over, I kissed him, not caring that Pop and Millie watched.

"Eh?" Pop said.

"People would come here if we put the word out that this was a pirate town! It's all about the marketing," I said, loudly, to be heard over Hailey's furor. "The potential is huge."

Bellows of thunder, deep enough to rattle the three-hundred-year-old house and vibrate our rib cages, rolled over us as the assault continued. One exploded directly overhead, and Millie jumped from the menacing sound. Rattled, she fluffed her hair and drank some wine. "First thing we ought to do is change the name back to Rum Towne. Way it used to be, back when pirates traded here."

Pop folded. Justin and Millie showed each other their cards. Justin won the hand. "That's a great idea, Jax. I'd bet we could find a distributor to bottle a line of private label rums just for Rum Towne."

A campaign of ideas erupted in my head. "Exactly! Light and dark rums. And a coconut rum and a spiced rum. We could even have an artist come up with a rendition of Emerald Eye to put on the label. He could be our town mascot."

Pop chuckled and his green eye shone.

"What?" I said.

"Was just thinking, lass. When you first came 'ere, you couldn't wait to get back to the city. You hated this place." He swallowed a hefty slug of bourbon on ice and, leaning back, let out a deep belly laugh. "Now you're calling it 'our town,' like you've been 'ere fore'er!"

Everyone slid quarters in to ante up, and Justin dealt another round. "Jaxie's coming around nicely."

Millie slapped the table. "I could make rum cakes to sell! And rum candy and cookies, too. Got some prized recipes that were my great-grandmother's. I'll open me up a little bakery, right next to Pop's B and B."

We thought about that while the house made terrifying sounds, as if pieces of it might fly apart at any minute. I downed my wine, and Justin refilled the empty glass. The cats got so freaked out that Millie had to sedate them. She left them locked in one of the spare bedrooms, yowling. Flush and Bandit were jittery but content to stay with us.

We watched the Weather Channel until wind ripped the satellite dish off the house, then listened to storm reports on the radio until the station went dead, and finally put on a jazz CD until the power went out and everything went dark. I lit more candles and Pop distributed flashlights. We continued to play cards and to brainstorm revitalization ideas to keep our heads occupied with something other than the fact that we were at the mercy of a deadly storm. An ensemble of unfamiliar noises filled the room: earsplitting pops as trees snapped, violent blasts of winds thrashing the house at race-car speeds, and walls of rain pounding boarded windows. I completely lost track of time. When I looked at my wrist, I remembered Bandit had swiped my watch from my nightstand the night I'd had the dream and found Aldora's letter.

"If we make it through this thing, I'm going to strangle that raccoon!" I said. "She stole my watch."

Pop patted Bandit on the top of her head. "She just likes shiny things is all, lass. Check the spittoon, where she hid your car keys."

Using a flashlight, I moved slowly into the den and located the spittoon. Right on top, my watch flashed in the beam of light. I grabbed it, and noticed a small key fob lying beneath it. It was a mass storage device with a USB plug beneath a removable cap and a clasp at the other end. At the agency, we often gave Shine logo fobs to clients. It was a much classier way to present them with a digital copy of their ad campaign than to hand over a Zip disk or CD.

Curious as to where it had come from since Pop didn't own a computer and would have no need for a storage device, I brought it back to the table with me. "Any idea where this came from? I found it in Bandit's stash."

Pop turned on a battery-operated lantern and aimed it so the light shone on the key fob. "What is it?"

"A portable storage device for digital files. Some people call them flash drives, but they're also called key fobs because some people use them as key chains. See this clasp? You just hook it right on and carry it with your car keys."

"What does it do?" Pop said.

"Stores data, kind of like a compact disc. It plugs into a port on your computer." I read the lettering on its cap. "This one is a two gig."

A wrinkle formed between Pop's eyes. "Eh?"

Justin laughed. "A two gigabyte. That means it will hold a lot of data."

Millie cocked her head. "In that tiny little thing?"

I started to nod but jumped instead when an earsplitting crack of thunder exploded, seemingly inside the room with us.

"Huh," Pop said. "Can't imagine who Bandit swiped that from. I don't know anybody with a computer. Except Billy. And he hasn't been to the house in a long time."

I found my laptop on the kitchen counter and was glad I'd charged the battery before Hailey hit. Justin and I leaned in to look at the illuminated screen, and I plugged in the fob. It held three files. I opened the first with Acrobat Reader. A blueprint for a proposed retirement community, the file consisted of several detailed drawings. Flipping through the electronic pages, we saw plans for single-family homes and condos, as well as a golf course, clubhouse, exercise facility, and shopping center.

"Lester," I whispered. "The key fob is Lester's. He owns a development company that specializes in master-planned communities, remember? This must be what he planned for Rumton."

I passed the computer around for Pop and Millie to see.

Justin shook his head. "It looks like one of those giant Sun City communities in Florida, but it doesn't make sense. We've already established that large-scale residential development isn't feasible here. People don't want to retire to a coastal area that's landlocked."

Intrigued, I blocked out the raging storm and concentrated on the second file. A text document, it was some sort of an amendment or proposed legislation for the federal government to officially recognize extinct Native American Indian tribes. The proposal went on to say that sufficient written documentation must be in place to prove the existence of the tribes, including towns in which they had lived. It went on to talk about goodwill, and the reasoning statement was loaded with a bunch of warm and fuzzy crap. Fluff, I called it. I knew because I'd written my share of it for Shine Advertising and PR.

Beneath the proposal, a list of extinct tribes organized by state caught our attention. Those beneath South Carolina were marked with an asterisk. Pop and Millie waited while Justin and I read the rest of the proposed legislation, cheek-to-cheek. He pointed to the screen. "Open the other file, Jax."

I did. The last one was a set of plans for a gambling casino. It looked like something from Las Vegas, with row after row of slot machines and clusters of game tables.

Millie screamed when a crack of lightning hit something, which exploded with the sound of a cannon.

"Probably a tree," Pop said, and patted Millie's back to comfort her. "Hope it wasn't my big oak. I'd hate to lose that one."

I looked at my watch. Hailey had battered us for four and a half hours and showed no sign of letting up. Trying to ignore the sound and feel of destruction around us, we wondered why Lester would carry blueprints for both a master-planned retirement community *and* a casino. None of it made sense.

Justin stood suddenly. "My God, it's brilliant. A wicked scheme but brilliant."

From the beginning, Justin surmised, Lester's intent had been to erect a casino. He wanted to turn Rumton into a gambling destination similar to the one in Cherokee, North Carolina. Pop said that gambling was illegal in South Carolina, but a federally recognized Native American Indian tribe could operate a gaming facility if it was on tribal property and if the tribe was native to the area.

Pop stood, too, as the picture came together in his head. "And the only federally recognized Native American Indians in South Carolina are the Catawbas."

"Right. Several tribes are recognized by the state, but they've been unable to obtain federal recognition." Deep in analytical thought, Justin rubbed his temple. "According to your investigator, Lester is in bed with Senator Wands, who is also on the Indian Affairs committee. There's legislation that would give federal recognition to Indian tribes, postmortem. For goodwill, and all that. But once passed, it will come back to bite them in the ass because Lester will somehow produce a real live Native American Indian who supposedly belongs to one of the South Carolina tribes thought to be extinct."

"Meanwhile," I said, "he's buying up land to put the casino on, maybe in the name of his company, which is really owned by the supposed tribe. But he won't apply for a gambling permit until *after* the extinct tribes are recognized. He's going to resurrect a tribe!"

"Why, that scoundrel!" Millie piped up. "All that stuff about a high-tech think tank was pure hooey."

Pop brought a plate of her cookies to the table and refilled his bourbon, adding only a splash of water. I refilled my wineglass and Millie's, then gave Flush and Bandit a few treats. Justin nursed a beer. We munched cookies, wondering how many others were involved in Lester's plan, and again thought of Aaron's warning that we were in danger. Earlier, we'd called the hospital to check on him and try to learn more, but the nurse said that Aaron was in no condition to speak to anyone.

"It's simple, Jaxie," Justin said in a low serious voice. He pointed to the computer. "Not only did you stop the land vote at the council meeting, but, more important, you've got Lester's flash drive."

Pop bit into a cookie and slowly chewed. "He came 'ere on the way to Riley's funeral. Played with Bandit and fed her pretzels. That must be when she snatched the computer gizmo. Probably unhooked it and took it right off his key chain."

Another piece of the puzzle dropped into place. "That's why somebody broke in, Pop. It was Lester or one of his cronies, searching for the key fob."

As though she knew she'd broken Lester's plot wide open, Bandit hopped on the table and took a bow. Or she may have been just been after a snack, but it looked like a bow. She snatched a cookie from the plate, broke a piece off, dunked it in Pop's bourbon, and chewed with delight.

The danger surrounding us instantly became that much more real. Hailey wasn't the only threat: Somebody wanted Lester's casino blueprints back. Next time they might do worse than just break in and rummage through Pop's belongings.

Figuring we should tell somebody, Pop felt his way to the kitchen wall and found the telephone, the old-style one that was attached to a landline and didn't require power to operate. Miraculously, he heard a faint dial tone. Even though many of the poles that held the telephone lines surely had to be down, a signal was getting through nevertheless. He tried the police chief at the movie house but didn't get a ring. Next he dialed the Chat 'N Chew, since it was the town's gathering place and the quickest way to spread the word about something. Amazingly, Bull answered.

"Your place still standing, Bull?"

"Barely!" we heard Bull shout through the receiver before her voice was drowned out by a long screeching wind gust. Shouting back so he'd be heard over the static, Pop told Bull what we'd learned about Lester and asked her to tell the police chief if she saw him before we did. Assuring Pop that she would, Bull told him she planned to open her doors as soon as it was safe. He disconnected and started to make another call, but the line went dead. Another pole must have fallen and completely severed the already weak signal.

With the monster swirling over us and the fear swirling inside us, we were physically and emotionally drained.

"Nothing we can do but wait," Pop said. He and Millie decided to try to sleep. Bandit clung to him, and the three of them went to bed, Pop carrying the shotgun and Millie leading the way with a flashlight.

Justin blew out the candles. Armed with flashlights, we moved to the sofa. I lit a small jar candle on the coffee table in front of us so that the room wouldn't be pitch-black. Flush jumped up and burrowed his way between us. The three of us settled in to wait out the rest of the storm.

24

When the back door crashed open, we figured the storm had done it until two figures appeared in the kitchen. Justin reached for the .45 but immediately realized he'd left it on the kitchen table, where we'd played cards. Thankfully, the blackout would prevent the intruders from spotting the gun, as long as they didn't aim a flashlight at the tabletop. On the other hand, they'd probably come armed anyway. Whipping wind slammed the open door back and forth against the wall.

I aimed a flashlight just in time to see Lester throw his weight against the door. Struggling against the wind, he managed to force it to close. The other man, short and stocky and wearing a heavy parka and boots, wedged an ax against what was left of the door handle to secure it. When he turned, I recognized Marty, the supposed accountant Aaron had brought with him on his last visit to Rumton. The man gripped a menacing gun that looked as if it was equipped with a silencer. Drenched, both of them came into the living room, where we were, just as Flush trotted off to guard his master.

"Nasty little windstorm you got yourselves, here," Marty said. He pointed the gun at me. "Bring me a towel."

"Guess you're not here to examine financial statements this time," I mumbled, making my way past them to the kitchen. When I reached the table, I purposely stumbled against it, grabbing the gun we'd left there. I stuck it in the waistband of my jeans, at the small of my back. As I straightened up, a flashlight beam immediately found me.

I threw my hands up, like a criminal in front of a cop. "Sorry, I slipped. The floor is soaking wet."

I slowly backed my way to the counter, where I found a dish towel. I thought about shooting the guy instead of handing him the towel, but something told me he was much quicker than I was. Marty had to be a pro; trying to pull a gun on him would be suicide. I handed over the dish towel, wondering how my boss could ever have hooked up with such a guy.

Keeping the gun loosely pointed at both me and Justin, Marty wiped down his face and head. He pulled a tree branch out of his parka hood and dabbed at a jagged cut on his face, which left a thick trail of blood down his neck.

No longer playing the role of smooth politician, a bedraggled Lester pointed a shaking finger at me. "The bitch is here, Marty, just like I said she would be. She's more annoying than the mayor was. It will be a pleasure to kill her."

Justin spoke in a surprisingly calm voice. "*You* murdered Riley? I'm surprised you don't have people to do that kind of dirty work for you."

Lester spit on the floor and wiped a hand across his face to clear dripping water from his eyes. "Wasn't time to get somebody else. Besides, poison's easy. I doctored a beer, knowing Riley wouldn't turn down a free beer." He spit again, studying Justin in the dim light. "Who the hell are you?"

"Just a friend. What did Riley do to warrant murder?"

"He was in on the land buys. As mayor, he was our social lubrication. Help push everything through, and he'd get a little cut of each option. But he started asking too many questions."

Marty scowled. "Your mayor took advantage of a situation to

put a little cash in his pocket. Then he developed a conscience. Can't have it both ways."

I tried not to think of Riley's dead body staring up at me from the marsh. Hailey still roared loudly against a creaking, groaning house, but the force was not nearly as bad as it had been. We might have just survived the worst hurricane in history, only to be shot dead by a maniac.

"Where's the old man? He's got something we want back," Marty said.

"Pop is sleeping," Justin answered.

"Somebody's sleeping through this shit?" Marty said. "You Southerners are freakin' crazy."

Producing a gun of his own, Lester headed toward the bedrooms. A revolver, it was smaller than Marty's but just as deadly if it hit its target. A bullet was a bullet. Justin and I looked at each other, realizing that these two men had no intention of leaving any of us alive because we all knew too much. Lester and Marty were the danger Aaron had called to warn us about. If we didn't do something, Pop and Millie would be shot dead in their sleep. Spurred by adrenaline, I pulled the .45 from my waistband and fired three times in Lester's direction. The explosive cracks stung my eardrums, and their echo reverberated for several frozen seconds. When Lester twisted to look at me with a disbelieving expression, I wondered if I'd missed. Finally, he slumped to the floor and dropped his gun. Justin moved to grab it.

"Hold it!" Marty commanded, and Justin froze.

I'd turned my gun on Marty only to find his already pointed at me. It was a standoff, but his grip held perfectly still while my hands shook visibly.

"Stay where you are or I shoot her," Marty told Justin. "Be a shame, such a pretty thing." Keeping the gun on me and an eye on Justin, he sidestepped his way to Lester and squatted down.

Blindly feeling the floor, he found the revolver and pocketed it. And before I had a chance to react, he stood, spun me into the wall, and took my gun away from me.

"Let her go," Pop shouted from the hallway. Dimly outlined by candlelight, his silhouette showed a shotgun held in a tight mount against his shoulder, its long double barrel aimed at the man. Flush stood at attention by his side.

Marty shook his head in disgust. "Christ. Is everybody in this house carrying a piece?"

Lester moaned. A lot of blood oozed from his shoulder and mingled with soaking wet clothes. "The bitch shot me, Marty."

Keeping his gun leveled at me, eyes darting between Justin and Pop, the mobster walked to where Lester sat on the floor. "The name isn't Marty. You think I'd give out a real name, you're dumber than you look." The man jabbed Lester's throat with the toe of a boot. Lester clutched his neck and went quiet.

Pop kept the shotgun on the intruder. Outside, blowing rain and rumbling thunder continued, but Hailey's furor had diminished to intermittent slaps of wind instead of a steady onslaught. I'd be damned if I was going to die at the hand of some stranger after living through a brutal deadly storm.

"What is it you want?" I asked, rubbing my shoulder. It felt as if it had been pulled from its socket, and my hand throbbed, too. He'd twisted my fingers around one another when he disarmed me.

Rubbing sleep from her eyes, Millie stumbled into the kitchen, her flashlight beam pointed directly in front of slippered feet. "What's everybody doing? Is the storm over?" When she got a better look at us, she aimed her flashlight into the stranger's face. "Who are you?"

"Just visiting, ma'am," he said pleasantly. "You packing heat, too?"

"Heat?" Millie said, puzzled.

Deciding she was harmless, Marty instructed her to sit down. Seeing the drawn guns, Millie realized something was amiss and sat. The wind died down to an occasional angry gust.

"Lester lost something here," the man said after a minute. "It looks like a key chain. I need it back."

"No problem." I got my laptop from the baker's rack where I'd left it and put it on the kitchen table. The flash drive was still plugged into it. "It's right here. But the casino isn't going to happen. I've already e-mailed my contacts in Atlanta about what's going on," I bluffed.

The man's black eyes drew together, boring into me.

"The proposed legislation to give federal recognition to extinct Indian tribes is a brilliant idea," Justin added. "Unfortunately, the feds are keeping an eye on Senator Wands. Whether he ends up in jail is anybody's guess. But he's certainly too hot to push through any legislation right now."

Marty frowned, making the gash in his face start bleeding again. "I come all this way just to hear that bad news and get tossed around by a damn windstorm."

"Look, we don't know who you are and have no interest in your business," Justin said. "We just want to preserve the integrity of Rumton, and a casino doesn't mesh with that goal. Were you going to build a retirement community, too?"

"Nah, those blueprints were just to show the mayor and Aaron Ackworth to make them think that's what Lester planned to build."

"So who came up with the casino scheme?" Justin said.

"Lester and his buddy, the senator. Ackworth turned them on to Rumton, which would have made an ideal location. My people were just supposed to provide the backing to make it all happen." Sighing, Marty pulled the flash drive out of my laptop and pocketed it. "We got to start being more careful about who we do business with."

I shivered, wishing Aaron had never crossed paths with Lester. "Well, the casino isn't going to happen, but you've got your key fob back."

Marty shrugged, deciding to cut his losses. "I'm out of here."

Lester spoke up, weakly. "You leaving me to die, Marty?"

"Got no use for you and the old Indian man anymore."

Pop's shotgun remained on Marty. "Old Indian man?"

"Lester has documentation to prove his father is from a tribe thought to be extinct. We just had to wait for the legislation to go through, which would give the tribe federal recognition. Then we could put the plan into action, and we'd already have the tribal-owned land on which to build the casino."

Disgusted, Pop shook his head.

"You people never seen me. And I never seen you. Far as Lester goes, *nobody's* going to see him again." He aimed the gun to kill Lester, but Lester was gone. A trail of blood led to the front door.

Cursing, the mobster ran to the back door in the kitchen and kicked the ax out of place. The door swung open, and beautiful early-morning dawn filtered in as he slipped out and headed for the driveway. We caught a glimpse of a jacked-up jet-black Hummer leaving, bouncing over fallen pine trees.

It neared seven in the morning, and I thought with joy that we were all going to live. The bad guy hadn't shot anyone. We'd made it through Hailey. The house hadn't come apart, and the surge hadn't flooded us out. Even though Lester was still out there somewhere, he was injured and being chased by a pissed-off mobster.

Breathing a collective sigh of relief, we slowly went outside. Lakes of standing water surrounded the house, and it looked like a war zone. Downed trees lay broken and twisted everywhere. A wooden fence post had pierced the wall of a storage shed and stuck halfway into it, like a toothpick in a chunk of cheese.

Justin's car rested on its roof a few hundred yards from where he'd parked it. Somebody's johnboat hung from the branches of an oak tree, and a section of Pop's roof had blown off a corner of his attic and ended up in a heap at the end of the driveway.

But I looked up and saw heaven. A clear blue sky, lightening with the sunrise. A stillness so perfectly quiet that I heard only the blood pumping through my body and the sound of air moving in and out of my lungs. An immense and overwhelming sense of relief washed through me. Almost giddy, I felt more *alive* than ever before in my thirty-one years. I reached for Justin's hand and, intertwining my fingers with his, realized I wanted to spend time with him. Much, much, much more time.

"Let's get inside," Pop said, and whistled for Flush and Bandit. "Won't be long now before the rest of her moves over."

"What?" I said, frozen in place.

He looked up. "We're in the eye of the storm, lass. Hailey hit us dead center on. Another fifteen or twenty minutes, the other half of her will move o'er us."

Justin pointed to the horizon. In the distance, a vertical wall of solid grayish black cloud advanced steadily toward us. Lightning flashed deep within its guts, and mini funnels spun out of it like spokes on a moving wheel.

I wanted to scream or cry but was too flabbergasted to do anything other than stand there, unmoving.

Millie went back in the dark house first, and on either side of me, Pop and Justin put an arm around my shoulders to lead me in.

"No worries," Pop said. "House took the first 'alf of her without too much damage. We'll get through the rest of her okay."

"Have a piece of cake and you'll feel better," Millie said. "I made it with a pineapple and cream cheese filling."

25

As Pop predicted, we did make it through the second half of Hailey, and surprising myself, I actually slept through most of it. When she'd finished blasting Rumton and we ventured outside, the damage looked the same as it had during the eye of the storm. Only there was a lot more of it.

It was Monday afternoon, and the cloud cover rapidly dissipated to reveal a gorgeous sky. Birds returned to explore their new habitat, and a few animals, such as squirrels and rabbits, cautiously came out of hiding to investigate. We didn't have electric or telephone, but I was thrilled to find that my satellite Internet service worked fine. I went online and sent Sheila a short e-mail to let her know we were okay and that I'd call as soon as I found a working phone. Justin fired off a few e-mails of his own—to Avery and to the office—before removing boards from the windows so we could see without using flashlights. We showered in cold water, used jug water to brush our teeth, dressed, and headed out to see who needed help. Justin loaded a chain saw, gas can, and ropes into the back of my Range Rover, and everyone, including the animals, piled in.

Destruction lay scattered everywhere. A blanket of huge uprooted trees and thick broken foliage covered the ground, along with building debris and household items like broken furniture.

It was slow going because we had to make several stops to

clear fallen trees from the roads, at least enough for a vehicle to pass through, and I quickly realized why Justin had brought the chain saw. Residents milled about, assessing damage and checking on one another. When they found something of value, they staged it in a central location, sort of like a lost and found, where people could claim what Hailey took. Elwood's carvings had turned up everywhere and stood in a line on somebody's front lawn, a wooden army of animated characters. The cleanup effort was already under way.

When we stopped in front of Millie's house, everyone fell silent. It had no roof at all, and most of the walls had ripped away from their foundation. We saw all the way through the house to her back porch, where, oddly, an unharmed wooden swing hung defiantly. Everything between us and the swing had been drenched and tossed around, like contents of a giant blender.

We walked through the destruction to take a better look. In shock, Millie cried silently as the realization that her house had been demolished sunk in. Sniffing, she suddenly straightened up, blew her nose loudly, and stomped straight through the standing water and debris to her back porch.

"I love this swing," she declared, and sat down to swing. Putting an arm around her, Pop sat, too. I kept my fingers crossed that the bit of framework holding it up by chains didn't come crashing down on them.

"Well, Maddie," Pop said after a while, "you can live with me. I've got plenty of room. And my place needs a woman's touch."

Wiping away a stray tear, she nodded. "Darn right it does! I could do a lot with that old house."

"Maybe we'll decide to open that bed-and-breakfast after all, if you want to cook for the people."

Millie's face brightened. "Really?"

When he patted her back and she kissed his face, I was the

one who wanted to cry. Pop and Justin unhooked the porch swing and loaded it into the Range Rover, securing the hatchback with rope. With Justin at the wheel and Flush in the backseat between me and Millie, we continued downtown.

The storm had flattened a string of buildings, and their cinder-block footprints were all that remained. But luckily, they were old retail shops, vacant for years. We were relieved to find the brick movie theater standing proudly, untouched. Already at her post inside the ticket window, Amy handed out free cases of bottled water. Volunteer firefighters compiled lists of which residents needed help covering broken windows or roofs, or clearing fallen trees from their driveways and roads. Or, in some cases, needed a place to live. But, miraculously, they told us, not a single person had been seriously injured or lost his life to Hailey. The police chief and a crew of volunteers were out making the rounds and reported in on battery-operated two-way radios. It seemed that Rumton had been very fortunate.

We made it to Chat 'N Chew to find a crowd gathered around something on the sidewalk. I thought it might be an injured animal, the old black and tan basset hound perhaps, and ran up to take a look. Mumbling incoherently, Lester sat propped against the brick wall, tied up with what looked like a pair of trousers and a tablecloth. I wasn't even going to ask whose pants they were.

"Hiya, hon!" Bull shouted. "Everybody okay at Pop's?"

"Aye," Pop said, walking up with Millie, the two of them holding hands. "What 'appened 'ere?"

"Lester got caught up in Hailey's backside, and ended up here, lookin' like a drowned beat-up possum."

"Bull tackled him!" someone said.

Bull hooted. "Yep, I sure did. Took him down, just like I did with Bucky Junior that time he got all liquored up at his mama's party. After what Pop told me on the phone, I wasn't letting this shyster get away!"

"Somebody shot him in the shoulder," Gertrude yelled. "Bleeding's done stopped, though."

Bull nodded. "Wonder if it was his friend who shot him?"

"Friend?" Justin said.

"Short fellow in a parka. He come bustin' in here with a gun drawn and said he was looking for his friend Lester to settle up on something. But when the guy saw Lester, he put his gun away and doubled over, laughing like crazy. Said something about the wrath of the people in this town bein' a fate worse than death. Whatcha suppose he meant by that?"

Since the electric had gone out, and her generator powered the walk-in cooler, Bull enlisted some help and fired up a giant grill outside to cook the contents of her freezer. Anybody who cared to stop by was given a free meal or a plate to go. Our crowd gratefully accepted hot dogs, including Flush and Bandit. As soon as we ate, we headed for Devil's Tail, collectively holding our breath.

Even with the four-wheel-drive SUV and chain saw, it was rough going. We had trouble locating the original dirt road, but Pop navigated and Justin maneuvered us in the direction of the shipwreck site. The jagged bottom halves of snapped pine trees stuck out of the ground everywhere, and the dense foliage surrounding them had disappeared to reveal bare limbs. We drove through mud and water until it became unsafe to do so, then found a patch of high ground to park on.

When we came to a stop, Flush and Bandit jumped out and took off to investigate. I heard barking and then a belly-flop splash. We got out to spot a narrow creek of flowing water about fifteen or twenty feet wide. Dog-paddling right down the center of it, Flush chased a floating stick. It moved faster than he did, though, and spiraled in a mini eddy when it hit a wall of oncoming salt water. Like a giant funnel, the creek opened into a wide winding channel that churned muddy water through it.

"Lord God Almighty," Pop said. "It worked."

"It's open! Devil's Tail is open!" I jumped up, slipped, and fell, not caring a bit about the mud. "I can't believe it worked," I said, grabbing Justin's hand to let him pull me up.

Laughing, he wiped a glop of mud from my chin. "That's Skirr Creek flowing from the waterway. Only before, it was a trickle. Now it's wide and deep enough to feed the canal." He shook his head, looking very much like Pop. "I'll be damned."

"So the canal winds eastward to the ocean, right?" I said. "And it's big enough for boats, right?"

"Aye," Pop said, wiping an eye with the backside of his hand. " 'Bout a mile of winding, I'd imagine. And plenty big enough for fishing boats."

"Then this is where our marina should go," Millie said.

Pop nodded, agreeing.

In awe, we stood and stared and dreamed of Rumton's marina. But then we looked around and realized that all the wreckage we'd piled into a giant heap was no longer there. The remains of the *Aldora* had vanished.

Pop smiled, stretched out his arms, as though hugging Mother Nature. "Ocean took 'er back."

Dripping wet, Flush bounded up to us and shook his entire body, starting with his head, to spray a wide arc of muddy water. Following Flush, Bandit appeared and scampered up Pop's body to sit on his shoulder. Chirping happily, she clutched something between her front paws. Justin took the shiny object and, grinning, handed it to Pop.

"What is it?" Millie and I said together.

Green eye sparkling, Pop flipped the item high into the air and caught it. "Gold coin of some sort."

26

Hailey made headlines worldwide and journalists couldn't stop talking about her. Millie flipped off the television. The day was cooler than usual but pleasant, and we'd decided to walk to the town meeting. As we headed out, Pop told Flush to stay. Content to lie in the yard, he barked once at the cats but didn't bother to chase them. Pop had talked Millie into letting her cats outdoors, which she reluctantly did. They loved it. They weren't declawed, and their favorite place to hang out was the sprawling live oak in front of Pop's house. Millie's swing hung from the same tree; she'd sit and read while Bandit and the cats frolicked above her.

It was Wednesday and I had another glorious two weeks in town, after which I would travel on an as-needed basis. In light of new information and a recommendation from Justin, Shine partners approved reinstating the Rumton revitalization project and agreed to have Justin remain as well. If we played our hand right, it could mean national headlines for the agency, which translated to a good dose of prestige and almost guaranteed new business. Although distraught about Aaron's resignation from the firm, the partners were very happy with me.

The Rumton town meeting had been called on a day's notice, and I kept my fingers crossed for a good turnout at the movie house. We were officially announcing the reinstatement of the revitalization project, even though everybody already knew everything. They knew Millie had moved in with Pop and wanted to open a bed-and-breakfast; they knew water flowed through Devil's Tail; they knew about Lester and his foiled plan; and they knew the whole Emerald Eye story. As I'd learned, Rumton didn't do secrets very well. The only thing they weren't aware of was the possibility that Flush's food bowls might be valuable Ding ware, and that if they were, Pop planned to put all the money into the revitalization effort in the form of a charitable foundation.

A string of cars, trucks, one riding lawn mower, and two horses greeted us when we turned the corner. It looked as if the entire population had come, and my heart pounded from nerves. I'd wanted a good turnout, but a crowd this big meant one of two things: Either the people were fully behind me or they were ready to chase me out of town. There would be no middle ground. A fleet of generators sat side by side near the front doors, and we were careful to step over the tangle of cords.

"There she is now," Gertrude yelled when we went inside. "With Justin, her new beau! I told you it had to be somebody from 'round here!"

"He's from *Atlanta*, Gertrude," somebody countered. "They work together at that agency."

"Well, sure, he hangs with them prissy city boys," Gertrude admitted. "But he's a Rumton man. Heck, him and Avery practically grew up here."

We made rounds in the lobby, circulating and shaking hands, while Pop introduced me to people I'd not yet met. The volunteer squad hustled to serve drinks and generator-powered popcorn. One of the squad told me they hadn't been so busy in years. The big rubber boot was already half full, and the meeting had not yet begun.

Fifteen minutes later, Councilwoman Delores called the unofficial gathering to order and thanked everyone for coming. The first thing she did was ask the police chief for an update on Lester. Acting as though he'd singlehandedly broken the case wide open, he explained what I'd suspected all along: Lester Spear Smoak was a con artist and a criminal. He'd been arrested on several charges, but the first-degree murder of Riley topped the list. Currently incarcerated at the Broad River Correctional Institution in Columbia, he remained in its hospital. The chief went on to say that the feds were interested in Lester, as was the state of Texas.

"Be fine with me if the rat ends up in a Texas jailhouse," Millie said from her theater seat. "Those Texans don't mind executin' a prisoner!"

The chief finished by recognizing Bull for restraining Lester at the Chat 'N Chew until county law enforcement arrived to haul him away. Cheers and whistles followed, and Bull stood up to take a bow.

Then it was time for Justin and me to talk. He started by tossing out a few statistics on other small towns that had turned around their economic situations by implementing a revitalization plan. Then he turned the podium over to me, and I looked into the faces of some two hundred people.

"I've learned so much since coming to Rumton last month," I began, "and I can't even put into words how thankful I am to have had this opportunity. But what we need to discuss today is whether you like the idea of turning Rumton into a themed town to attract visitors. No big developments, no high-rises, no shopping malls . . . but rather small quaint shops and attractions that will bring in families who want a friendly, unique experience. Families who will spend a night or two and spend some discretionary dollars." I took a deep breath and told them about several small towns that catered to tourists in unique ways. If we capitalized on the pirate theme, I told them, we'd be enhancing and actually *preserving* the town's identity by resurrecting its roots.

"You ain't got to sell us on the idea, Jaxie," Councilman Rusty said, "we're all ready to go. We just want to know about the bowls! What's up with Pop's bowls?"

I couldn't stop myself from laughing. I should have known they'd already heard about the bowls. "As you all *apparently* already know, Pop has some old bowls from China, which might be very valuable to a collector. We're waiting for someone to contact us, but we should know in the next few days what they're worth or if they're worth anything at all. If they are, Pop wants to donate the money from selling them to the revitalization effort."

A collective cheer went up as people clapped and yelled their thanks to Pop. He stood and, visibly moved, cleared his throat a few times. "Those bowls were a gift from Emerald Eye to his sweetheart, Aldora. And I can't think of any better way to put them to good use."

I didn't want to dampen their spirit, but when the applause died down, I spoke up. "Keep in mind we don't know if they're authentic or even how much money they'll bring if they are. But, look, we can implement a plan with or without a cash reserve. We might get a grant to build a museum, and Shine is here to do your marketing plan. With participation in opening bed-and-breakfasts and shops and such, it'll work!"

"Oh, we're all ready to participate, we're all ready," Billy informed me. "Sure would be easier to do *with* the cash reserve, though! I mean, I'm a descendant of pirates, too. And us pirates, we typically aren't all that patient."

"You're a pirate, too? How do you know that?"

"Oh, I've got an old cutlass been in the family forever. *Forever.* Got some initials carved in it. My daddy told me a story, from his great-great-granddaddy about his granddaddy, who settled here after they tried to hang him, but he got away. He was a pirate."

I couldn't believe it. "What's a cutlass?"

"A little short sword. Got a wide blade. Buccaneers liked to fight with them because they didn't get caught in the riggin'."

"Well, why didn't you tell me this when I searched for information on Rumton's past? I even put an ad in *your* newsletter!"

He shrugged. "Didn't much like you then."

It was a good thing I had thick skin. In the PR business, you had to or you didn't survive.

"Don't worry, sugar," Gertrude shouted. "We all love you now!"

Amazed and enlightened, I made notes of everyone's ideas as they came pouring from the audience. There were quite a few pirates in the crowd, it seemed, and they were right proud of it.

"Heck," somebody said, "we're all pirates in spirit!"

Justin suggested forming a revitalization committee that would oversee the entire effort, handle funds, work directly with Shine, and report to the council. Within minutes, people were nominated and voted in by a show of hands. Eleven people made up the committee, including Pop, Billy, Gladys, a retired banker, and a retired attorney. The sleepy uneventful town of Rumton had simply come alive, and people who were previously content with their status quo were now ready to make things happen!

When the meeting concluded, my list of notes was long and I couldn't stop smiling. Elwood had decided to open a shop and sell his carvings. Bull planned to change the name of Chat 'N Chew to Booty's, and figured it was time to go ahead and print up a menu with entrees like First Mate's Meatloaf, Cannonball Chicken, and Galley Greens. Getting in the spirit, Walter announced that Duckies was now called the Captain's Quarters, or it would be as soon as he had a chance to paint over the sign. In addition to Millie and Pop, three other people planned to open bed-and-breakfasts. Gladys proudly announced that her granddaughter had just graduated from medical school and would follow in her footsteps by opening a family practice in Rumton. Millie decided to call her bakery Rum Runners, and everything she made would have a splash of rum in it. Startling everyone, the judge announced that he had decided to open up a little chapel to perform weddings. People could get married just as they did in Vegas, he said. Only his chapel would be done pirate-style and he'd wear a ship captain's attire rather than a robe. Before the meeting adjourned, the people unanimously decided to change the name of their town back to Rum Towne.

Epilogue

Not only were the bowls genuine Ding ware, but they had an intriguing provenance, which I learned meant the story behind them. When the anonymous art collector's representative saw the original poem written by Emerald Eye to his love, Aldora, he'd licked his lips as though the background information made the bowls that much more appealing. Remembering how he'd originally offered an even $1 million for the pair, I smiled. As Pop had contemplated the offer, I caught his green eye and reminded him that Flush was really going to miss eating out of his Ding ware. Agreeing with me, Pop held out until the man upped his offer to $1.8 million. After buying Flush a new set of elevated, personalized food bowls, we celebrated at Duckies and toasted the dog, who had his own chair at our table and drank a Coors Light. The next day nobody was surprised to see that Flush was perfectly content to eat from his ten-dollar bowls.

It had been exactly nine months since I'd first set foot in Rum Towne. With the help of Pop's bowl money and the unrelenting spirit of the townspeople, Shine Advertising and PR had accomplished a feat that changed lives forever.

Propped on a swiveling captain's chair at the bar of Captain's Quarters, I drank a spiced rum and orange juice while I read *The Wall Street Journal*. In the marketing section, an article on Rum Towne included a rendition of Emerald Eye, along with a photo of Bandit perched on Pop's shoulder. Even better, it referenced Shine Advertising and Public Relations three times.

Keeping an eye out for Justin and watching visitors stroll in and out of Rum Runner's Bakery across the street, I read the story a third and a fourth time. The staff writer played up the fact that the entire population lived in character, and tourists ate it up. The bed-and-breakfasts stayed booked, and the judge had already married twenty-one couples, or, as we called it in Rum Towne, made them "walk the plank." The downtown district had come back to life with five retail shops and the promise of more; a medical practice opened by Gladys and Elwood's granddaughter; a bank; a pirate's tavern; and the much-anticipated museum, currently under construction. Surprisingly, the writer noted, one of the most popular activities in Rum Towne was watching the judge hold court at the movie house. The water tower–decorating festivals, which took place the first weekend of each month, were a close second. If there wasn't a scheduled holiday that month, Rum Towne made one up. After all, he noted, pirates never needed an excuse to celebrate. He also interviewed both the new town doctor and the first young couple to move to town in more than thirty years, which I thought was a nice touch. A councilman's granddaughter was pregnant with her first child, and the family decided Rum Towne would be a perfect place to raise children. Her husband was a boat captain and planned to offer sightseeing tours along the waterway on a pontoon boat, in addition to chartered deep-sea excursions on his fishing boat. The baby would have no shortage of doting godparents, the journalist wrote, because every resident in town had tracked the girl's pregnancy with genuine excitement. She'd already received enough baby gifts to accommodate ten children.

Thinking of the carefully orchestrated marketing campaign, I had to wonder if the successful revitalization was due to our PR efforts or the fact that the town held magic. Everyone who visited promised to return and, more important, to tell their friends.

"How many times are you going to read that thing?" Justin asked, sliding into a captain's chair barstool beside me.

I kissed him full on the mouth in greeting, but kept my eyes open. I couldn't get enough of his green eye. I just loved looking at it, especially since it was no longer obscured by ugly glasses. "I don't have a photographic memory like you do."

We'd come to town to watch the ribbon-cutting ceremony for the small marina and, as always, stayed at Pop's house. I still enjoyed working in the city, but I'd come to feel as though Rum Towne was home.

Looking through the window, I saw Pop and Millie emerge from her bakery, holding hands and laughing. They walked over to meet us for lunch, and the four of us settled in at a table. We ordered a Privateer's Pizza to share, and a pitcher of sweet grog, which was half tea and half Pepsi, served over ice.

"Me and the mayor are getting hitched," Millie announced without preamble, waving her ring finger in our direction. It held a huge diamond. "Gonna let the judge do it at the Caribbean Chapel."

Although Pop was living in sin with his girlfriend, the town had unanimously elected him as their new mayor. Everyone wrote him in on their ballots. Afterward, they had to persuade him to take the position, but once Pop thought about it, he figured he might enjoy leading the town. Especially since the entire community had taken an active interest in revitalizing it. And now Rum Towne would have an official first lady. It was exciting news.

"Congratulations, you two! When's the date?" I said.

"Tonight," Pop answered. "Can you make it?"

Justin took my hand. "Wouldn't miss it. In fact, it's perfect timing. We were going to give you this as a thank-you for all you've done, but we'll make it a wedding gift instead." He slid a small wooden box across the table.

Pop opened it. "Looks like the key to my Cape Dory."

I smiled. "It is."

"Only now she's docked in the very first slip to be purchased at the new marina," Justin said. "One with your name on it."

"Not only that," I added, "but she's got a brand-new motor, *and* her refrigerator is stocked with your favorite beer."

Pop's eyes showed real surprise, and he remained speechless for a minute. "Two of you are something else. I love you both."

"We love you, too, Pop," I said. "You're the best. By the way, where are you going for your honeymoon?"

"Got us a private jet rented for three weeks," Pop said, and my mouth fell open. "Fella bought the bowls called to ask if 'twas true that my dog ate out of them. Wanted to know if I had any more Ding ware lying around, perhaps in use as a kitty litter box or some such."

Nodding, Millie fluffed her hair. She positively glowed. "As it turned out, he owns a fleet of Lear jets. When you rent one, the pilot comes with it and you just tell him where you want to go." She waved a hand, as if she flew private jets every day. "Way better than flying commercial."

"Aye. We're going to island hop 'round the Caribbean. Relax at some fancy resorts along the way."

I shut my mouth to swallow and opened it again to speak. "*Island hopping* on a *private* jet?" Pop had given every dime of the $1.8 million dollars to the newly formed foundation to benefit the town. While he and Millie lived comfortably, he still wore the same old clothes and drove the same old truck and watched the same old television. *Where had they gotten the money for a Lear jet and a three-week honeymoon?*

He met my questioning look. "You didn't think the coin Bandit found at Devil's Tail was the only one out there, did you, lass?"